STORIES THAT MAKE YOUR HEART . . . GO BUMP IN THE NIGHT

"CLANCY'S BRIDE"
by Terry Bacon

Only the town's drunkard knows the truth, but Clancy's pretty young bride has committed a sin that will chill the blood . . . and may send Clancy to the hangman.

"THIS IS DEATH"
by Donald E. Westlake

Nothing is scarier than a horror that is convincingly real, and when an unhappy husband decides to end it all, he finds out too late exactly what he's just begun.

"THE THEFT OF THE HALLOWEEN PUMPKIN"
by Edward D. Hoch

Nick Velvet steals for a living, and his client has a simple little theft in mind: to snatch a plastic pumpkin from a rich man's porch . . . a prank that is a prelude to murder.

AND THIRTEEN MORE CAREFULLY SELECTED HALLOWEEN STORIES
exclusively from the pages of
Alfred Hitchcock's Mystery Magazine
and *Ellery Queen's Mystery Magazine*

HALLOWEEN MYSTERIES

Stories from
Ellery Queen's Mystery Magazine
and *Alfred Hitchcock's Mystery Magazine*

Edited by Cynthia Manson

SIGNET
Published by the Penguin Group
Penguin Books USA Inc., 375 Hudson Street,
New York, New York 10014, U.S.A.
Penguin Books Ltd, 27 Wrights Lane,
London W8 5TZ, England
Penguin Books Australia Ltd, Ringwood,
Victoria, Australia
Penguin Books Canada Ltd, 10 Alcorn Avenue,
Toronto, Ontario, Canada M4V 3B2
Penguin Books (N.Z.) Ltd, 182–190 Wairau Road,
Auckland 10, New Zealand

Penguin Books Ltd, Registered Offices:
Harmondsworth, Middlesex, England

First published by Signet, an imprint of New American Library,
a division of Penguin Books USA Inc.

First Signet Printing, October, 1991
10 9 8 7 6 5 4 3 2 1

Grateful acknowledgment is made to the following for permission to reprint their copyrighted material:

Clancy's Bride by Terry Bacon, Copyright © 1982 by Davis Publications, Inc. Reprinted by permission of the author; *The Night Watchman* by David Braly, Copyright © 1983 by Davis Publications, Inc. Reprinted by permission of the author; *Fun and Games at the Whacks Museum* by Elliot Capon, Copyright © 1990 by Davis Publications, Inc. Reprinted by permission of the author; *Tony Libra and the Killer's Calendar.* by Richard Ciciarelli, Copyright © 1982 by Davis Publications, Inc. Reprinted by permission of the author; *Sitter* by Theodore H. Hoffman, Copyright © 1988 by Davis Publications, Inc. Reprinted by permission of the author; *The Ghost of Monday* by Andrew Klavan, Copyright © 1987 by Davis Publications, Inc. Reprinted by permission of the author; *Behold, Kra K'L!* by Richard F. McGonegal, Copyright © 1989 by Davis Publications, Inc. Reprinted by permission of the author; *House by the Road* by Janet O'Daniel, Copyright © 1987 by Davis Publications, Inc. Reprinted by permission of the author; *Kiss The Vampire Goodbye* by Alan Ryan, Copyright © 1985 by Alan Ryan, Reprinted by permission of the author; *The Dog* by Pauline C. Smith, Copyright © 1986 by Davis Publications, Inc. Reprinted by permission of the author; *The Black Cat* by Lee Somerville, Copyright © 1990 by Davis Publications, Inc. Reprinted by permission of the author; all stories previously appeared in ALFRED HITCHCOCK'S MYSTERY MAGAZINE, published by Davis Publications, Inc.

Ghost in the House by George Sumner Albee, Copyright © 1962 by Davis Publications, Inc. Reprinted by permission of the author; *The Theft of the Halloween Pumpkin* by Edward D. Hoch, Copyright © 1983 by Edward D. Hoch. Reprinted by permission of the author; *In the Morgue* by Dashiell Hammett, Copyright © 1959 by Dashiell Hammett. Reprinted by permis-

REGISTERED TRADEMARK—MARCA REGISTRADA

Printed in the United States of America

PUBLISHER'S NOTE

These stories are works of fiction. Names, characters, places, and incidents either are the product of the authors' imaginations or are used fictitiously, and any resemblance to actual persons, living or dead, events, or locales is entirely coincidental.

Contents

Halloween is that time of year when witches, ghosts, vampires, and other unworldly spirits creep into our imaginings and prey on our darkest fears. The eerie stories in this collection come from *Alfred Hitchcock's Mystery Magazine* and *Ellery Queen's Mystery Magazine* and feature our favorite Halloween spooks. These chilling and ghoulish tales will haunt you for some time to come.

Among the treats (and tricks!) you will uncover arc sinister black cats, haunted portraits, demons, monsters, the living dead, and other Things That Go Bump In The Night. Their devilish doings will fill you with terror, so be warned: If you read this book on Halloween Eve, at the stroke of midnight, just before going to sleep, don't be surprised if you find yourself looking over your shoulder, checking under the bed, and making sure all your windows are locked tight. . . .

Pleasant reading, and pleasant dreams.

—*Cynthia Manson*

THE HAUNTED PORTRAIT

by Lawrence Treat

Sometimes I watch a guide bring his group into Gallery 18, in the East Wing of the museum. Usually they are a mixed group of sightseers, and they come to see this particular canvas. They stare at it and mutter to each other. Then the guide speaks.

"The picture you're looking at," he says, "is a portrait of Evelyn Anders, and it was painted shortly before her tragic death. The artist is Swithin St. John, and this is considered his masterpiece.

"I call your attention to the eyes. Please notice the way they follow you no matter where you go. You can't escape them. They watch everybody who comes into this room, and it's said that they're seeking out her killer and will accuse him when he comes into this room. If he is here now—"

The crowd giggles nervously. There *is* something about the eyes. They were painted with a mixture of oil and luminous paint, and the effect is eerie.

"It is also said," the guide continues, after the crowd has become quiet, "that she will actually speak. Others maintain that her hands will move. Please study the hands."

They are worth studying. They seem restless, as if they had something to do but were not sure what. They appear to have a life of their own.

"Employees of the museum were the first to hear the sounds. They usually occur towards late afternoon, shortly before the museum closes, but they have been heard at other times, too. Please listen."

The people in the group strain their ears. Hearing nothing, they look at each other sheepishly, as if they had been duped. But sometimes they catch the sound of a moan. It may be faint and far off, but it is unmistakable. The crowd gasps, scarcely able to believe. Occasionally a woman, oversuggestible, screams. The group stands there for a moment or so—the people are too stunned to move; then, as if released from a spell, one person after another starts to leave, to find his or her way to the main exit and to the fresh air outside.

Usually, however, there is silence, and after a few moments the guide continues: "It is believed, too," he says, "that Mrs. Anders wrote the name of her murderer, here on this canvas, and that some day the name will emerge in letters of blood. Or perhaps, as in the Bible, a hand will appear and write upon the wall: *Mene, mene, tekel, upharsin*. Does anyone see the words?"

The guide is laughing at his little joke. Then he turns and crosses the room. His shoes make sharp taps on the polished wooden floor.

I am Dr. Guy Nearing, curator of the museum, and at first I am delighted. A haunted portrait? Great—a happening! It should pull in the crowds, and it does. At one dollar a head.

But as time goes on I begin to dislike the crowds. They come to scoff, or else to stare at what they consider a freak. For me, however, it is something quite different. I find myself engrossed by it—whatever *it* is. Late afternoons or early evenings, after the museum has been closed to the public, I wander over to Gallery 18, and I look. I think of the few bits and pieces of the story that I know from having read the newspapers, and I am disturbed.

One night last March, Mrs. Ewald Anders, wife of a wealthy real-estate man reputed to be a front for the Syndicate, was stabbed to death while lying in bed. Her husband was away at the time. An undetermined amount of cash and about $20,000 worth of jewelry were taken, and the original assumption was that a cat burglar had climbed up to Mrs. Anders' bedroom on the second floor, and when she woke up and saw him, he knifed her in panic and fled. But the autopsy showed that she had taken several sleeping pills and that it was almost impossible for her to have awakened. It followed that the robbery therefore was a blind, and that the crime was deliberate murder. The police leaned to the theory of a hired killer. Still—why?

Swithin St. John, who painted the portrait, is Ewald Anders' half brother. They had the same mother—witness her fondness for the two stilted, exotic names. Swithin, Ewald—what a pair! At any rate, Anders gave Swithin the portrait commission. Over the years Anders had supported his half brother and even arranged for a couple of one-man shows which, for some reason, had been flops. Thus the name of Swithin St. John was hardly known until he did the portrait of Evelyn . . .

I stare at it in the dim light of the closed gallery. The eyes, gleaming, iridescent, gaze back at me. I want to leave, but I cannot. The painting has a strange obsessive quality, a latent sexuality that somehow the artist's brush has brought out. I realize that over and above the legend and the publicity that have made the painting notorious it is unquestionably a masterpiece.

I keep asking myself why. What precise quality, what shade or flush of emotion has lifted this portrait out of the ruck and made it so magnetic, so outstanding? For, as surely as I stand here in the empty museum, St. John has communicated something deeply human in Evelyn Anders.

It bothers me. It keeps bothering me. I can't let it go. I come here at night, not because I believe a painting can tell me anything about a murderer, but because I am haunted by it, by the subject. I stand here and I think of her as if she were still alive. I begin to wish that some harm would come to her—she seems almost to be asking for it—and I have an impulse to lash out and end forever this unnatural spell.

But I do not move away. Instead I turn on my flashlight and slide the beam slowly along the length of her arms. I feel as if I were caressing her, and the thought horrifies me. I focus the light on her painted eyes. They are silvery and lustrous, but they are also tragically sad—as if they had glimpsed her ultimate fate.

Finally I turn away, shaken, for I have learned something I wasn't supposed to know. But what? What dark secret? Whatever it is, it remains in some lower segment of my brain, pressing in, torturing me, but never coming to the surface.

Back in my office I sit down shivering. I take a drink, but it does no good. I leave the building. Dewey, one of the night watchmen, says good night to me, which is my first normal experience of the evening. It does not help. I go out to my car. Although the night is warm I feel so cold that I turn on the heater as I drive home.

I think of her the next day and I decide I must find out who killed her. Absurd? Of course. I admit it. Nevertheless I ask questions and I set about finding out all I can about her, about her husband and about St. John. The next day I manage to bring St. John to my office and lead the conversation around to Evelyn Anders.

He talks freely. He says she was obsessed with death, that she had little to live for. She had no children to occupy her thoughts and time, and her husband's extra-marital affairs were too flagrant for her to ignore them. Yet she was dominated by him and felt emotionally suffocated.

St. John breaks off abruptly and taps his fingers nervously on the arm of his chair. He is trying to tell me something that he fears to utter. He wants to blacken Ewald, wants to implicate him in a murder, but dares not. He is secretive, cryptic, oblique.

St. John's hate is obviously bitter and venomous, but he tries to control it. When he praises Ewald, the words stick in his throat. He manages to say that Ewald has charm, that women fall for him—beautiful women like Marguerita, the Spanish dancer known as La Flama, whose troupe is performing here this season. But in the middle of reciting Ewald's charm St. John blurts out that La Flama is more in love with Ewald's money than with Ewald himself.

St. John, I feel, is being pulled in opposite directions. He longs to accuse Ewald, but is afraid to, for Ewald supports him and St. John needs that monthly stipend. Besides, he can't forget that Evelyn was murdered by a killer who scaled a high wall and climbed a drainpipe in order to reach her room. St. John himself would never be safe. Not if he accused his half brother of murder. But what if the painting itself makes the accusation—is that St. John's subtle, devious method?

We talk of the portrait. I admire it, I praise its technique, and I say that only a painter who was in love with his subject could have achieved such a masterpiece.

St. John grows livid. "In love with Evelyn? Me?" But the very intensity of his denial convinces me that he was.

He gets up in a fury. He can no longer restrain himself and he spews out his hate. He says Ewald was always sly, shrewd, dishonest. All he ever thought of was money and how to get the better of people. Ever since he and Ewald were children, Ewald managed to put the blame on St. John and take the credit for himself. Ewald lies, steals, kills. Even when Ewald finances exhibitions for St. John, Ewald managed to sabotage them at the same time. He ordered the gallery to cancel its advertising, and he arranged for devastatingly bad reviews.

After a while St. John calms down. He is aware that he has told me either too much or not enough, and he is still fuming when he leaves. I realize he's playing some kind of deep game, which leaves me in confusion. I decide that Ewald, with his underworld connections, would just as soon have had his wife killed as bother to divorce her. But I'm convinced that St. John had an affair with Evelyn and couldn't trust her with the secret. And if Ewald found out it would mean the end of St. John's allowance, if not of his life.

So—did St. John kill her, or did Ewald Anders? And what does La Flama know about it?

I decide I have to see her, so I buy a ticket for her next performance. It is in one of the smaller theaters, and I watch her in fascination. She is wearing black tights. She seems weightless. She whirls across the stage like a living flame, she seems to soar, to float, and she finishes in an amorous swoon. She is beautiful, and at the end of the evening I go to the stage entrance. I send my card in, my official one as curator of the museum, and I'm told that La Flama will see me.

I go into her dressing room. She is sitting in front of her mirror, and she turns around to greet me. I can sense some of the passion and excitement that she conveyed while she was performing onstage, but now it is muted. To my surprise she speaks English with no accent, and I compliment her on it.

"Ewald has had me take lessons," she says. "He does not like a—" She bites her lip and turns away. She has almost said *wife*, and is angry at herself for the near slip. "He does not like a friend to have a foreign accent," she says.

"You have a good ear," I say. "Even with lessons very few people can wholly overcome an accent."

"Very few people are like me," she says imperiously. "I was born a peasant and could neither read nor write until a few years ago. Now—why did you wish to see me?"

"I wondered if you could tell me anything about the portrait that St. John did of Evelyn," I say. "There are—"

She interrupts. "What would I know of that?" she says. "I do not like this conversation. The subject is unpleasant."

"Exactly," I say. "And that's why—"

She interrupts again. "I have no more time," she says. "Ewald is waiting for me. Please go."

I leave. I realize I should not have spoken to La Flama. My interest in the portrait is something I should have kept to myself. Evil surrounds that painting, permeates it. I ought not to subject other people to the spell.

I recall the circumstances under which Ewald donated the painting. I knew who he was, because part of my job is to obtain gifts and loans for the museum, and to accomplish that I have to know about every wealthy collector in the country. And Ewald Anders, with his fifty millions or more and a valuable art collection, was a name I knew well.

"Dr. Nearing," he said to me over the phone some four months ago, "I'm Ewald Anders. I want to donate some paintings to the museum."

"We'd be most grateful," I said, and we made an appointment.

Ewald's reputation was unsavory, and I was of course aware of it. He placed rackets money, mostly in real estate, and people were afraid to bid against him.

I expected a tough overbearing man, but Ewald was small-boned and delicate. Nevertheless he had a quality that made me keep agreeing with him. And I'm not a yes-man.

"You're wondering what I'm going to offer you, and why," he said. "But I guess you know something about my collection."

I nodded.

"I want you to exhibit a portrait of my deceased wife. My half brother, Swithin St. John, painted it."

"If I may see it—"

"You don't have to see it," he says. "Two hundred thousand dollars' worth of other paintings go with it. Take it or leave it—which?"

"I'll take it."

"Naturally. I'm sure you know how my wife was killed. Everybody does. Well, Swithin painted her portrait just before her death. I didn't get it until afterwards—he claimed he had to put in some finishing touches. Well, I want it out of the house."

I nodded again.

"Let me tell you something. My wife was the kind of woman who practically begged to be hurt. You'll find out what I mean when you see the painting. Well, there's a story going around that I had something to do with her death, but when people see her face they'll realize why she was killed. She begged for it. Whoever went into her room and took her jewels saw her lying there and stabbed her. He couldn't help himself."

"I'm anxious to see that picture," I said.

Anders' eyes bore into me. "You'll hate it," he said . . .

The legend that Evelyn Anders would identify her murderer began shortly after the portrait was first exhibited. A clever publicity agent can plant stories like that and, once planted, they flourish. But when I heard reports of sounds, of the moaning of a spirit in agony, I had my doubts and I decided to investigate.

One night I take a flashlight and go through the dimly lit halls to Gallery 18. The low-watt ceiling bulb catches the painted eyes and makes me uncomfortable. Resolutely I take down the painting. Its gilt frame is heavy and it thuds to the floor. Dewey, the night watchman, hears it. He comes thumping through the galleries and arrives out of breath.

"Oh—Dr. Nearing," he says.

I have my flashlight trained on the back of the picture, and I motion to him. "Come here," I say, "and look at this." He does so, and I glance at him. "Well?" I prompt. "What do you think it is?"

"It's some kind of a mechanism," he says. "A spring. You can wind it up, and that thing—" he points to a small rasplike piece—"it rubs along the canvas and makes a noise. I guess that there diaphragm picks it up and magnifies it. That's how the groans are produced."

"Talking dolls use more or less the same mechanism," I say.

Dewey makes no comment, but I realize he's

been much too clever in figuring out how this works. I decide to accuse him directly.

"Who pays you to wind this up?" I ask.

Dewey doesn't answer. "I could fire you for this," I remind him, "but if you tell me who it is, you can stay on."

Dewey isn't sure he can trust me, but he has no choice. "Mr. St. John," he mumbles.

I am not surprised. St. John has a good thing here. He constructed the groaning mechanism and he'd probably been responsible for the story of the portrait concealing a secret. The legend has made him famous.

I tell Dewey to hang the picture again. "No point in talking about this," I say. "Let's leave things as they are. Okay?"

"Yes, sir," he says, and I return to my office . . .

A month goes by. The moans continue, although less often. I am told that La Flama has visited the museum several times, as have both St. John and Anders. All three come alone and study the portrait, but I neither see nor speak to any of them.

The crowds are beginning to thin out. I'm worried about the drop in attendance, and now that nothing has happened, people are losing interest in the portrait. But I am more fascinated than ever, and I try to avoid looking at the painting. But I cannot.

I visit it regularly, after hours, and one night I make a discovery that disturbs me. I have a flashlight with me, and in its oblique light I discern something pushing through the bluish background. A message? But it is still too vague.

I go there the next night, and the night after that, and gradually I can distinguish that yellowish letters are emerging, and that the second one is a W. There are three or four more letters, but whether the name will turn out to be Swithin or Ewald, only time will tell. And, while up to now no one else has noticed the emerging word, it will soon be all too obvious.

The museum has a photograph of the painting, which is routine with all exhibits, but I take a series of color films with my own camera. I hope that when I develop the roll I'll be able to trace the day-by-day emergence of the writing.

I come home one night around midnight. A cop is waiting for me and he tells me they want me back at the museum.

"What for?" I ask.

"They'll tell you when you get there."

"Look," I say. "I'm not going unless you tell me why. I don't have to go, do I?"

"Mister," he says, "aren't you a little curious?"

I am, so I go with him.

There are a half dozen patrol cars in front of the museum and a couple of emergency vehicles. The cop I'm with takes me inside. There are more police in the lobby, and they ask me to wait for Inspector Rogers.

He is a dapper little man and he is strictly business. His voice crackles and his words bite, and the way he pronounces my name rubs me all wrong.

"Dr. Nearing?" he says. "Somebody hacked up the painting of the Anders woman, and we want to know who did it and why. So tell us."

"Hacked it?"

"That's what I said. Into ribbons. With a knife."

I need time to think this out. I know why it was mutilated, but I'm not ready to talk about it. "May I go see the painting?" I ask.

"No."

"Why not?"

"Dr. Nearing, I'm running this and I ask the

questions. So who would do a thing like that, and why?"

"What else happened?" I ask. "All these police, the cars outside—you're not that interested in vandalism, are you?"

"A watchman got killed," he says. "Knifed. Name of Dewey."

Murder. That changes everything, and I withhold nothing. I tell Rogers about the groaning mechanism in the back of the picture and about the yellowish letters beginning to appear.

"I'll send the pieces up to the lab," he says. "They'll put them together, and then they can bring out the full name. Just a matter of chemistry."

"And then what?" I say. "St. John and Anders hate each other and each of them would love to see a murder charge brought against the other. The name you find will merely prove the existence of the grudge. So where will you get with your chemistry?"

"Just leave that to us," Rogers says.

I glare at him but he merely nods, thanks me, and trots off. Interview over. I stand there and think of what the loss of the painting means. Dwindling crowds, dwindling revenue. If only—

I get a brainstorm, and the idea is so good I don't want to lose another minute. I go to my office and I call Jacobus.

Jacobus is a Dutch artist who does work for us. He was trained in the best European tradition. He knows paints and techniques. He can imitate a Rembrandt or a Velasquez or a Cezanne, and we use him to restore and touch up. He can duplicate a glaze or a varnish that was used 200 years ago, and do it in such a way that it will age at the same rate as the rest of the picture. So why can't Jacobus reproduce the portrait of Evelyn Anders?

Over the phone at this hour of the night it

takes him a minute or so to wake up. When I explain what I want he asks me if I have a color photograph. I say I have one that I took yesterday, but the film is still in my camera.

That's fine with him. His hobby is photography. He tells me to bring the camera, he'll develop the film, and he'll have the duplicate portrait ready within a day or two. I bring him the camera, then go home to bed.

I wake up early and prepare my publicity release. I state that the painting was miraculously saved, that it will be on display later this week. I say that personally I don't believe any name will appear, that I don't think the secret of who killed Evelyn Anders is actually in the painting, but that nevertheless we, the museum officials, are watching the portrait closely.

I figure that my announcement will pull in crowds, and I arrange for extra guards to handle the expected mob. But what I don't foresee is that Rogers will come down on my neck.

He doesn't call me personally and doesn't ask when I'll be in my office. Instead, a police sergeant phones and informs me that Rogers is on his way and I'm to stay put.

He doesn't bother even to say hello. As he walks through my doorway he's asking me what the hell the idea is. I tell him I'm running this museum and I don't have to explain anything to him.

"You're trying to use a homicide to attract a crowd," he says. "Suppose I call a press conference this afternoon and expose your publicity stunt and say we have the painting in the lab right now, and that you're a fraud."

I give in and tell him about Jacobus, and Rogers does a complete about-face. "I'd like to work with you on that idea," he says. "But first, I'd better bring you up to date on where the investigation stands."

According to Rogers, the killer managed to hide somewhere, perhaps in a closet, when the museum was cleared for the night. He waited until about seven o'clock before he went to Gallery 18. Then he took down the painting and began methodically to cut it up. He was doing a good job of shredding it when he heard Dewey approach. The killer probably stepped to one side of the doorway to Gallery 18. When Dewey came through, the killer knifed him without warning. No sign of a struggle. And when Dewey failed to report in at the conclusion of his regular round, the alarm was sounded, but by that time the killer had escaped. Unseen and unheard.

The police had taken the shambles of the painting and laboriously pasted the pieces on a new canvas. The area with the emerging letters was in ribbons, and it was impossible to develop the individual letters. Nevertheless, the laboratory men analyzed the paint scrapings. They are experienced at this—they are constantly analyzing scraps of paint collected from automobile accidents. They did it spectrographically and have discovered that, although the main background of the portrait was a Prussian-blue oil, the area where the letters were beginning to appear was a phthalocyanine blue, which has a tendency to oxidize after a few months of exposure to air. Furthermore, the phthalocyanine letters were painted directly onto the finished canvas, and not over-painted at any later time.

"Then you have St. John cold," I say. "You've spoken to him, haven't you?"

Rogers shakes his head. "Not yet. He left town this morning, but I'm having him brought back. I expect to talk to him later on today."

"Well," I remark, "he's the only one who could

have painted in the name, so it has to be Ewald's. Right? He wouldn't paint in his own."

Again Rogers doesn't answer. Instead, he asks a question of his own.

"Where is that reproduction of Jacobus'?" he says. "I'd like to see it."

"It hasn't come in yet," I say. "When it does it will have to hang a few days. I can't exhibit it until the smell of fresh paint goes away. And as for the name, all Jacobus can do is copy the blur that was there yesterday. And believe me, except for that one clear letter, W—it was just a blur."

Rogers gets up and leaves. I have some outside appointments, so I leave, too, but I can't get my mind off the Jacobus copy. Suddenly I wonder exactly what that photograph of mine revealed—the one I gave to Jacobus. For camera lenses sometimes bring out what the eye can't see, and Jacobus undoubtedly reproduced whatever the camera revealed.

I phone my office. Jacobus has delivered the painting and it's hanging where the old one used to. For some reason that information sets off a train of thought and now, perhaps for the first time, I think the case through, carefully and logically, and I conclude that there is only one person who could have engineered the murders of both Evelyn Anders and Dewey. But how to prove it?

I'm nervous. I think of Dewey last night. I wonder if it can happen again. The killer must have read that the picture will be shown soon. Does the killer believe that the original has been reconstructed, or does the killer suspect a hoax?

I phone my secretary and I order four of the guards to stay on after the museum has closed. I leave instructions for them to patrol in pairs and to be armed. My secretary suggests that we keep the lights on all night, but I veto the suggestion.

I return to the museum about 7:00 p.m. and immediately take a flashlight and head for Gallery 18. I don't want the guards to know what I'm doing, so I take off my shoes and walk silently. As I go through the deserted rooms I realize that the guards are not too fond of patrolling. I see no one. I have an eerie feeling—the museum has never seemed so deserted, so utterly quiet.

I make the turn into Gallery 18. I see a figure in front of the Anders portrait. An arm is raised, a knife slashes down and glints in the dim light.

Perhaps I make a noise. More likely some sixth sense warns that figure in black. It turns, sees me. For a fraction of a second it hesitates. Then the figure launches itself at me. It leaps like a panther, silent and deadly. I yell, switch on my flashlight, and jump aside. The beam of the light is blinding. I throw the flashlight at the knife and start to run.

My yell has been heard. Somebody turns on the main lights, and the small lithe figure of a woman comes into view. She swerves, she is no longer bent on killing me. She has to escape, but the maze of galleries confuses her; she dashes to the left and finds herself at a dead end.

She whirls and speeds off like a projectile. Three guards are waiting for her. She leaps high—on the stage she seemed to have soared ten, fifteen feet, but it was an illusion. She hurls herself and lands squarely on a burly guard. The knife clatters, and three men grab La Flama and hold her down. She screams at them in Spanish. I turn around, head for my office, and call the police.

Later on I speak to Rogers. "I guessed it was La Flama," I say, "because of the Dewey murder.

He was old and slow, so why kill him when anybody could have easily escaped in the semidarkness knowing that Dewey's identification would be shaky at best? But there was enough light for him to tell the difference between a man and a woman, and if Dewey had been left alive to identify the vandal as a woman, La Flama was lost. So she had to kill him.

"As for the murder of Evelyn Anders, here was La Flama with fifty million dollars at stake, and Evelyn in the way. La Flama could climb like a monkey. So—kill Evelyn, and Anders would be free to marry."

Rogers agreed. "We've been looking for La Flama ever since this afternoon, when I spoke to St. John. He told me that Anders had refused to divorce his wife. *She* wanted a divorce, she wanted to be free of his domination, but he refused because she was his protection against designing women who wanted to marry him for his money. And La Flama was shrewd, designing, and ruthless.

"St. John had a strong suspicion that La Flama had killed Evelyn, but he had no evidence, no proof. So after the murder and before he delivered the painting, he painted in her name, hoping that between her guilt and her deeply ingrained peasant's superstition she'd eventually get scared and give herself away."

"But he didn't paint her name in," I say. "The letter was a W—remember?"

"A W is an M," Rogers says, "when it's upside down. And that's how St. John painted it—upside down. Because everything he ever did was evasive and roundabout. He was afraid to accuse La Flama openly—he could only bring himself to do it indirectly, upside down."

"M? Of course! La Flama's real name—Marguerita."

And I make a notation on my pad to instruct Jacobus to paint in an M so that people can read it clearly. And when the meaning of the initial is revealed, won't that increase our attendance!

CLANCY'S BRIDE

by Terry Bacon

Take it from me, John Clancy was not hasty, as so many have claimed. If anything, he wanted too much proof. And who should know but meself? Wasn't I there?

They'll likely hang him, though. That's always the way o' it. You don't kill a wife in Kildorrery without collectin' a few frowns. Not that any one o' us cared a mite for her, the witch, comin' into town the way she did. For lack o' somethin' better, I was there at the station the day she stepped off the train. I managed a few pennies before old Sullivan ran me off, but still I got a good look at her, standin' there on the porter's stool, lookin' us over like a lioness surveyin' a herd o' cattle. She tossed back her hair, then stepped to the platform, her skirts billowin' up over fine, pearly legs. If there's been a prettier woman in County Cork, I've not seen her. Oh-h-h, but what lay below that fine flush o' cheek! There's dreams, lads—and dream she was—and there's nightmares.

But to look at her, lads, not knowin' what would come, it gave yourself a turn, it did. I thought one so grand as this good for a pound at least. But, Dinky, you were there. You saw what she did.

You don't mind, do you, Murph? Just a wee bit, a little to top her off. Haven't I always said there wasn't a better man in the county entire? There's a lad.

Where was I then? Clancy's bride. "Miss," I says, "could you spare a few pounds for a man who lost his only home in the fires?" Oh-h-h-h, the look. The look. It chills me to the quick thinkin' on it even now. I never did see such eyes, such wicked, slippery eyes, searchin' for what, only the Lord knows, then lightin' on this or that like a cat on its prey. She took the warmth right out o' you, she did. Dinky, you saw it. Had I not known better, I'da swore it was the Medusa herself, there in the flesh, turnin' me to stone. You don't dare the divil to spit in your other eye, I says to meself, and turned away while I could, crossin' meself three times for luck and grace.

Poor Clance, he couldn't 'ave kept that farm up without a woman's help. And he wasn't fixed for nothin' else. You don't know this, o' course, but he always planned on that lass o' Duf O'Donnell's, Mary Ellen. Lord as my witness. Mary Ellen O'Donnell. She was a bright one. A looker too, in her own way. If John could've brought himself to it, might none o' this . . . Pardon me. Well, now I think on it, *she* would've come anyway. Still, you all know how John was so much to himself. Before he could gather the courage, Mary Ellen had wedded one o' them O'Reillys, Dugan, I believe it was, from Drumcollogher. Like to broke John, it did. 'Course he wouldn't 'ave showed it.

Lordy, you wait for so long for somethin' and it's snatched right away from you like you hadn't a right to wish it a t'all. Makes a man dry just thinkin' on such forlornliness and despair. As my witness, it does. By now, John's folks were gone. Both at once and too soon for anyone's comfort, least o' all John's.

Aye, but you've done your mother proud, Murph. I'd stake meself on it, I would.

We were there to see the wreck. Me and Holly McCarthy. And Michael Scanlon. Believe we were off to Cork. Did I tell you? . . . Anyway, John's folks. *There* was a story. Damn near kilt the horse as well, and wasn't enough left o' the wagon to build a decent fire. Jez got away, though. That's their dog. Jezzer. Well, that whole suit o' clothes brought John to the brink, you can imagine. Me and him shared some pints the days after. You might say we got real close, though I'm not the farmer. Jus' never had the hands for it. But we spent some time, me and Clance.

Which was how he came to be in town the day she arrived. I happened over, tellin' everyone about this fancy dress who'd traded her eyes for meanness and hadn't the mercy o' a stepped-on snake. Clance got naturally curious, what with my tellin' o' it, and went off to see it for himself.

Now *that* part you might say was hasty. It wasn't but a matter o' weeks before they were everywhere together. Everywhere but here. I tried talkin' him some sense, but, hell, you can't talk nothin', let alone sense, to a man with so many wants in the company o' her with so many provides.

The part none could figure, the strangest part, was why a woman such as her would settle for the likes o' him, her so used to finery and what. I s'pose it was jus' that ole Clancy was first in line. He was the hungriest o' us, and she had a good eye for hungry. I'll tell you, she did. Still, you don't put a racehorse before a plow. Clance should o' known that. He had the fever—and he wasn't there with me to see those eyes. But he should've asked himself, where did she come from? Where're her relations? The lot o' us were taken up with that business about George Collins' son, sure, but most o' us found time to wonder, where in God's earth did this woman belong? Take it from me, you get off a train, it's sure you got on it someplace. Yet here's this woman callin' no place home, havin' no life before, no relations, no history a t'all. And if that doesn't strike you strange it's 'cause you're sleepin' with banshees.

I asked meself, lads—you ask yourselves now—what comes from nowhere? Eh? What comes from nowhere?

Aye, no good, all right. That's what she was. Clance should o' seen it himself. . . . Lord, Murph, talkin' 'bout that woman has cut me tongue. 'Ave you got some antiskeptic tucked away, me boy? Aye. That'll do.

Now, you know, all this come about durin' the troubles with that Collins boy, Stephen. There's one was never right. Crazy Collins. Always after the young ladies, he was, grabbin' 'em here and there. Stealin' his pinches, and takin' licks for it, which made him the madder. Not yet a year ago now, he burnt Pat Maloney's shed down after old Pat thrashed him for bein' under Colleen's skirts uninvited. If that was all o' it, the boy might o' got away with his lumps, but he was a nasty one, too. A thief as well. Farmer would miss a hen, and it doesn't take a dog to tell you foxes don't roast chicken on a spit. They don't kill sheep neither—then stake 'em up to look like they were breathin' God's own air. That boy was a looney, all right.

George—that's his dad—stood by the boy long as he could. He helped Maloney build back the shed, you know. And he made good a few hens the boy had for dinner. Finally, George says, "You never seen him. Did you now? What makes you think it was my boy done it? I'll not pay for pranks done by ever' roughneck in the county, I won't." I was there when the sheriff came to the Collinses' to put a stop to it. "Come right on in," George says to him. "He's not here, I swear it. Dunno where he's off to, but he'll not step foot in this house again. What? My word's no good, is that it? Come have some tea, then. You'll see it for yourself." He was gone, like George said, gone into the forest, makin' his meals from other people's livelihood. Never did find the boy. You could tell where he'd been, though, by followin' the trail o' missin' chickens.

Middle o' all this, Clance took himself the new wife. 'Twas a big weddin', what with everyone so curious 'bout the new missus. You never saw anyone so proud as Clance. For her part, well, she sailed through the proceedin's with a sharp-toothed grin if ever I saw one. Whether from the plain joy o' it or from mischief, I dunno, but she put on the face.

In the months to follow, Clance had me out to help, now his dad was gone. His wasn't a big place, and Clance, he wanted more o' it, havin' a new bride. He would not say as much, but plans escaped him now and again. Rebuild a coop, say, and, "Might as well make it a little bigger, don't you think, Kelly," he'd ask me. She'd be there, watchin', and wasn't *there* a change? Like she'd not seen me before. Just as cordial. She'd let out a hand to be shook, and smile. But she knew, all right. She remembered the day at the station.

One day as I'm leavin' for the pub she glides up and smiles. Then she reaches into her pocket and holds up a five-pound note. "I don't take charity, missus," I says to her. "Have to pay for what you've done," she says back. I'll not forget *that*, not if I live forever. "Have to pay for what you've done." Thank you, Murph. Anyway, I told her it was for a friend. I could not rightly ask a wage. Didn't she keep holdin' it up, though, flutterin' in the breeze? She knew.

Then there's the day Clance slaughtered a hog. I wisht I was here, havin' a drink like a gentleman, but there I was, helpin' him rake the guts. A right gruesome job, that. I turned to get some air, and there she was, hair fallin' down around her shoulders, starin' at that beast like she'd seen the divil himself. I thought, poor lass, she'll not 'ave pork again. Gone white she was, mouth hangin' open. Clance tole her she ought not to see this, but there she stood. S'pose she felt it a duty, now bein' a farm wife.

Clance told me later she'd started helpin' him herself. "Took right to it," he said. I didn't believe it, though. Not a woman like that. As I'm sittin' here, Clance shoulda seen it. That shoulda been enough. But not Clance. "I'll tell you, Kelly," he said to me, "I took the prize. I was right to bide me time and wait for the right one to come along." Then he leaned to me and said, "Pays to persevere." As my witness, his very words, like it was the wisdom o' Solomon himself. Solomon Clancy. Who counted on Mary Ellen O'Donnell.

By now, things were heatin' up with the Collins boy. He'd grown tired o' chickens and started in on goats and sheep. Chickens are one thing, sheep another entirely. Kevin McHenry and his younger brother, Tully, saw the lad makin' his way up Knocklong Road toward the mountains. They found a carcass nearby, all but the shanks, which Crazy Collins kept for his supper. The sheriff called every able man into the Galtees. "He's in here, lads," the sheriff said. "We'll comb these mountains till he's found." Off we went, then, the lot o' us, lookin' more like a Sunday picnic than a searchin' party. And nary a drink along the way for those with a thirst.

Could o' used a man like yourself, Murph, to put some life in it. Ah-h. See what I mean, lads?

'Course we didn't find him. Jus' collected a ration o' scratches. It went on like that. A goat missin' here, a lamb there. Searchin' party would no sooner get back than out it went again. One day I'm here in the pub and in comes Clance, lookin' drawn like I'd not seen him. He pops down for a pint, and I wander over. "Order another," says I, "and we'll share the sorrows." Full o' woe, he was, top to toe. "What's troubling you, Clance?" "It's me bride," he tells me.

Now I'm not one to raise the dead, but I says to him nevertheless, "Not as if I didn't say it, Clance, you heard it often enough. That one'll never make a farm her home. It wasn't meant to be."

"That's not it," he says. "She's nearly runnin' the place herself. I never saw a woman like it more, 'specially the stock." Well, *that* part was shock enough, but I never would 'ave figured the rest. "She's taken a lover," Clance moans, lookin' down his beer. Lord Amighty, thought I. You know right enough a body's wicked, but which direction the wickedness will take is a bushel o' surprises. It always is.

"Do you know who it is?" I inquire. "No," he says, "but I'll find it out soon enough. And when I do, I'll kill 'em both. I swear it." You don't need much o' a nose to smell *that* kind o' trouble. "Jus' throw the witch out, Clance," I tells him. "She's not worth hangin' for." But he wouldn't 'ave it. "You come with me, Kelly. You come to me place tonight."

Lord 'ave mercy, that's how it started. That's how I came to be there. She had not been sleepin' with him like a wife. Not for a month or more. "Every night she goes out," he told me. "To meet her lover. That's what it is. She comes back then, washin' herself, changin' her dress. I tell you, Kelly, she's lost her enthusiasm for me." Enthusiasm. As my witness, that's what he said. "I'll kill her before I have to live with it."

There was a man shamed one end to the other. So I did as he said. I walked out as the sun went down, and waited in the barn. I kept expectin' Jez to waltz in and gimme a lick, but she was nowhere around. Gone off, I s'posed, makin' her rounds o' the neighborhood. Well, it was a long walk, and me not used to such. Though havin' the nerves 'bout what we were to do, I fell fast asleep. How long I dunno, but I was waked by a black thing loomin' over me and nearly lost meself right then and there. It was only Clance, in the dark. "She's left," he whispered to me, and out we went, me still not happy with events. We went on and on through the night, Clance ahead 'cause he knew the land.

I kept thinkin', what'll I do when he finds 'em there together? Lord knows I cannot stop a man the size o' Clance. If he has a mind to kill 'em, he will. Presently, I heard a bird squawkin' and looked up to see the Galtees risin' on me right. We were on a road now, on Knocklong Road. Clance held me up with his hand and pulled us both down. "There," he said, pointin' to a hill before us. The road ran over it, and I could see her in the moonlight. Very dim, sure, nearly a shadow, but it was her, passin' over the hill.

Lord Almighty. It was a dark night, Murph. It was a cold night. Do you not feel the chill? What? I had not thought o' that, but you're right, o' course. That'll take the chill, sure.

Where was I then? The road. I did not see her again, not on the road, anyway. Clance, he must o' 'cause on he went. Then he stopped. "She's up there," he said, lookin' to a footpath that went up a little rise toward the forest. Atop the rise, jus' before a dark line o' trees, sat a house. For the moment, I lost me bearin's, then saw it was the old country rectory o' St. Mary's. You must know the one. It's been empty these seven years. I wondered, as I looked to it, if the land was still holy. Addin' sacrilege to adultery, there was a grave crime indeed.

Up we went then, toward the dark house. "Clance," I whispered, for I dared not say it loudly, "I see not a light inside. Are you sure you're not mistakin'?" "She's here," is all he would say. But, on me oath, the place looked deserted. No sign o' life a t'all. Then I smelt it, that foul, sweet odor that works its way into your clothing and your head and never comes out. Somethin' here was dead, though what, I could not say. But the stench, lads, it took your breath, it did. We had not gone twenty paces more till we saw the cause o' it—the gray remains o' a goat. It lay beside us in a clump o' bush.

Clance stared at it; a quarter hour no less, he stared at it, sure o' what it was but still not understandin'. "There's what we smelt," I told him. "Can we go, for the love o' God? Either on or back but in any case not stay here a minute more."

"Collins," was his answer. "She's layin' with Crazy Collins." My God! The truth o' it could not 'ave shook me more if I'd been struck by thunder. The sheriff had not gone north enough. All along, the Collins boy was hidin' in the rectory. And he'd got Clancy's bride for lover.

Oh-h-h, the foul spirits! I felt the bile rise in me as well. By the time I gathered meself, Clance was well ahead, nearin' the door. I ran to catch him, my mind workin' reasons why he should not take her life. I reached him jus' inside the door. We stood there, lookin' into the blackness o' the room, waitin', listenin' for them, hearin' not a sound but smellin' the foul sweetness ever stronger. In me head, I could see the place littered with leftovers o' Collins' meals. How a woman could lay with such a man, I did not know. The smell alone brought tears to your eyes.

When he knew they weren't in the room, Clance lighted candles he'd brought out o' his pockets. He gave one to me, and I saw it was a sittin' room. Collins wasn't a neat one, that's sure. The room was thick with dust, the furniture moldy gray, rottin' where it stood. Clance pointed to a scrap o' petticoat on the floor beside the hearth. It had not lain there long. Dust barely covered it. By a chair, a little slip o' scarf. Blue, it was, like one I'd seen her wear. Clance walked to the sofa and picked off a pair o' gloves someone had dropped. They'd been white, but now were spotted black. He ran them through his fingers, then shook them at me. These are hers, he was sayin', though he spoke not a word.

Beyond Clance was a door. God Almighty, Murph, give a man a drink. Beyond Clance was a door. He threw down the gloves and started for it, me jus' behind 'cause I dared not be left alone. Clance was through it first. He held up his candle—and stopped, pullin' in a quick breath as though he'd seen a ghost. Here they are, I thought, and came 'round behind him.

There was Collins, directly before us. Starin' at us with those sunken, glazed-over eyes, smilin' that awful smile. I said to meself, Lord, if you have any mercy a t'all you won't make me die here. I'll walk inta the sea, I will, but don't make me die here. Then I saw the rest. All on a shelf that ran in place o' cupboards. Closest to me was a goat's head, cut off at the neck, barin' its teeth over a long, white beard. Beside it, in a line down the shelf, was a row o' sheep's heads, and the head o' a lamb. The cow's head was oldest—jus' patches o' dark, leathery hide over white bones. It lay shriveled in the corner, next to Jezzer's. Musta been old Jez. Her head was beside Collins', and as I looked again at his, I saw he was tryin' to warn us. I could hear not a sound, but it was a warnin' jus' the same.

This cannot be, I thought. It's only his head. But, sure, if his lips weren't movin', even pulled back over his teeth. He ground his jaws, like a man with a mouth full o' food longin' to shout. Then somethin' escaped his lips. Rice, white rice, that lay on the shelf, wrigglin'. Holy Mary, Mother o' God, I says to meself, and she who did this terrible thing . . . My God! She who did it isn't here! "Where is she?" I screamed at Clance.

But he would not hear me. He jus' stared, as if nothin' were here, as if nothin' had ever been, but what lay before us on that shelf. The candle slipped from me hand, and I could not bring meself to stoop to pick it up. "Clance!" I yelled at him. "Where is she?"

He could not say it, but he knew. There wasn't anyplace else she could be. She was in the house. With us.

I turned back to the room we'd left, knowin' if I saw her comin' at me with the axe, I'd die o' fright before she swung it. There were only shadows, and that jus' made it worse. She was in here someplace, watchin', waitin' for her chance, but where, I didn't know. I could bear it no longer and pulled at Clance's sleeve. "Clance! Oh, God, oh, God. Take me out o' here! I cannot do it alone!" He looked at me like he forgot I was with him, then took me hand and pulled me through the bloody kitchen, past his bride's collection. We ran into the backyard and nearly fell into a pile o' headless corpses that lay in our way. Clance found himself by then and was screamin' loud as me. The two o' us, we ran from that place, wailin' and cryin' like a pair o' frighted banshees.

God bless you, Murph. Well, we ran. And ran. Till we had not the breath to go another foot. 'Twas a field where we stopped, and there we clinged to each other all the long night—Clancy rockin' us back and forth on the ground, and me so full o' fright I dare do nothin'. Jus' watch, for that witch to fly screamin' at us out o' the woods. Jus' watch and sit, rockin' in Clance's lap, thinkin' what to say to him. Not, "Take heart, Clance. Your wife is not an adulteress, only a butcher." That would not do, but I could think o' nothin' else.

When the sun began to light the sky, Clance stopped rockin' and said to me, "She took to it too well. The slaughterin', I mean." There's a masterpiece, I thought, but what I said was, "You might say that." I looked at him and, lads, there was the face o' shame itself. Shame and disgrace. For, whatever this woman had done before, wherever she had been, she now was Clancy's bride. No matter what became o' her, he would have the shame.

He stood up, takin' me with him, then set me on me feet. "You go back to town, Kelly." His disgrace had grown to anger. "You're comin' with me, Clance," I pleaded. "No," he says, "I'm goin' to find her." Lads, I begged him not to go. I did not want to take that journey meself, not with her loose, but back he went, and I would as soon have followed the divil as gone back to that house. So down I ran to Kildorrery. I found the sheriff quick as I could. "I know where's Crazy Collins," I told him, with what breath I had remainin'. He thought I was in me cups and would not listen till I told the tale. "That's too rich for you," he decided, and off we went, ten o' us this time.

When we got to the rectory, there we saw Clance lyin' still beside a tree in front o' the house. His shirt—oh, bejasus—the blood that was there! The sheriff, he went inside for to see Collins, and I cried to him then to watch careful, to watch for the she-divil there. He came back through the black door, his face washed with the sight o' it. "She'll be no trouble, Pat Kelly," he said. "No trouble a t'all."

Her head was there, too, see, next to Collins'. Clance had given her a dose o' her own. He was not himself dead, jus' passed out from the night o' it. The blood, it all was hers. They waked him, and presently the sheriff said, "Why did you do it, John Clancy?" Clance looked at him and said, "Suffer not a witch." He would say no more, but he now knew what she was. I saw it in his eyes.

He should o' seen it sooner, though. He should o' known. Comin' into town the way she did. The sheriff, he thinks Clance done it all. Kilt the animals, and Collins, as well as the bride. The whole business. I know it better. Wasn't I there? I saw her way o' settin' her eyes on you like a cat on its prey. Oh-h, lads, she was the heart o' darkness itself, comin' out o' nowhere and turnin' black your dreams.

Lord Amighty. It's a dark night. It's a cold night. Please, lads, don't leave jus' yet. Come share a pint. This is not a night to drink alone. As my witness, it's not.

KISS THE VAMPIRE GOODBYE

by Alan Ryan

I never believed in ghosts or vampires or zombies or anything like that. I always thought that stuff was silly, maybe good enough to entertain women and children with a harmless little scare, but there was nothing in it for a private investigator trying to make an honest living. That's what I try to do. I try to make an honest living—honest enough to let me sleep soundly at night and enough of a living to keep the rent paid on a cheap apartment in West L.A. and a two-room office downtown, with maybe a little left over for a drink at night to help me forget the kind of people I have to deal with during the day. So when Mary Cantrell showed up in my office one afternoon and told me her father had been killed by a vampire, I nearly told her to take a walk.

She looked like what used to be called "a pretty little thing," back in the days when you could describe a woman that way and not get your block knocked off. What I mean is, she wasn't one of your modern, super-liberated women, all hard bony edges and a chip on her shoulder—not Mary Cantrell. She was little enough, maybe five two, and she was pretty, nobody could argue with that. I pegged her at twenty-three. Black hair tied up on her head in some way that's a mystery to men, except you know that if she ever lets it down around her shoulders, you better hold onto your heart and start taking some very deep breaths. Skin like milk. And those eyes. Those eyes were so dark and deep that you wanted to crawl inside right through them and be safe and secure for the rest of your life. I thought I could see in those eyes and in the way she held her head a kind of diamond-like quality, a nerve, a kind of spunkiness, a hardness in the center. She was wearing a dark blue skirt and a plain white blouse, no jewelry. She didn't need jewelry. She had those eyes. I liked her.

"I need your help, Mr. Kendall," she said.

"Where did you hear about me?"

Her eyes didn't waver at the question. That's something I watch for.

"The phone book," she said. "The Yellow Pages."

People say that to me more often than you'd think. So I looked her over, nodded, and I let her talk.

While she told me her story, I sat at my desk moving papers around as if I had an overwhelming load of urgent cases. And the more I listened, the more I realized that Mary Cantrell's spunkiness was definitely riding in the backseat today. She was scared, badly scared. And when a spunky girl gets scared, I get interested.

When she was done, I didn't let any expression show in my face. I said, "Tell me again. Go more slowly this time. Tell it in order and tell me everything."

"Aren't you going to write anything down?" she asked. She was looking at the expanse of bare, scarred wood I had cleared on the desk in front of me. Despite her grief at her father's death, and despite the scare that had sent her looking for me in the first place, she was thinking clearly.

"Don't worry about it," I told her. "I have a memory like a banker." That wasn't a good thing to say because her father, recently deceased, had been a banker. I didn't know that until she started the story again.

She looked at me closely for a few seconds, studying my face, and then obviously reached a decision.

"All right," she said, in a very businesslike sort of way. Not only did I like this girl, I was already beginning to admire her. And even if her story sounded crazy, she might just be able to make me believe it.

"My name is Mary Cantrell," she began. "My father is . . . my father *was* Jonathan David Cantrell, the founder of California Trade Enterprises, with headquarters in Santa Barbara. Are you familiar with it?"

"They own the California Trade Bank?"

"Yes."

"Even as we speak, I owe CTB fourteen hundred ninety-two dollars, give or take some change. We share ownership of a car."

She didn't blink.

"My father was a multimillionaire."

She said it the way you might mention that your dad had always been pretty good at tying bows on Christmas packages.

"My mother died giving birth to me. I was always the light of my father's life, the living image of my mother, my father always said, and he raised me himself. With the help of our servants, of course."

"Of course," I said.

She heard the tone in my voice because I'd intended her to hear it. She hesitated for a fraction of a second, her eyes meeting mine, then decided to ignore it. That was good because, in the instant our eyes met, we both realized we'd been testing each other. We both passed the test.

"Despite the fact that my father never remarried, and I know he was very often lonely, ours was always a happy home. He and I were devoted to each other, and the servants have been with us for so many years that they're all like my own family."

"Any other family?"

"None," she answered at once. "Both my parents were only children. I'm the last in the line," she said, her voice wavering for the first time, "so the Cantrell name dies with me."

She suddenly looked as if she thought that might happen sometime soon.

"Go on," I told her. I sat back in my chair, trying not to make it squeak the way it usually does. I wanted to signal to her that I was satisfied she could tell the story straight, with all the good bits included, and I wouldn't interrupt again.

She got the message. She didn't fidget while she talked. She concentrated. Her eyes stayed fixed on that bare patch on my desk, as if the drama of her life was being re-enacted there in front of her and all she had to do was watch it and describe what happened.

"My father was always a very successful man, but he never sought any of the notoriety that often goes with success. He had no desire whatsoever to be in the public eye, no desire to show off his wealth, no political ambitions. I know that in his earlier years he turned down many opportunities, and people, business acquaintances, still sometimes came to him with offers while I was growing up, but he always refused. He was good at what he did. He was a genius at it, building companies and trading, and knowing that, seeing his enterprises grow and prosper, was satisfaction enough for him.

"He built Kirkdale for my mother forty years ago, up in the hills, and he kept it absolutely private. It was always our home and nothing else. I grew up there and I love it as much as I loved my father. No one was ever permitted to intrude at Kirkdale. The house itself is a work of art, the view of the hills and the ocean is magnificent, the sunsets take your breath away, and the gardens could win prizes anywhere in the world.

"But Kirkdale was ours and ours alone. He never brought work home with him. He never held meetings there, and no one from the office was even permitted to call him there. He always handled his business so carefully that no crisis could ever intrude on his private life. He even entertained elsewhere, so that strangers never even saw the estate. Only once, about seven years ago, he permitted a photographer from *Paris Match* to take pictures of the garden. It was a favor, really, to some French businessman, but my father always regretted it. We were besieged with requests after that. They were all refused.

"I'm telling you this as background, so you'll understand the context of what happened last night and this morning. Shall I go on?"

I slid a little lower in the chair. It squeaked but we both ignored it.

"There are nine servants at Kirkdale. Most of them have been with my father all of my life. The others were all screened more thoroughly than you'd think possible before they were hired. I'd trust any of them with my life. So did my father."

"Your father's dead," I said. When you have a suspicious mind, there are times when you can't keep your big mouth shut.

She pressed her lips together for a second. Ordinarily they were very pink. Now they turned white.

"Let me tell you the rest," she said. "This morning, my father didn't appear for breakfast. That happened rarely, but it did happen sometimes, so I didn't think much of it. He was getting on in years, and he was beginning to slow down a little. But when he hadn't come down by nine o'clock, I went up to his room. It was empty. The bed hadn't been slept in. I immediately had the servants search the house, and when he wasn't there, we searched all the grounds. The estate is very large and it took a while, about an hour, in fact, but we found him. He was in the rose garden. He . . . was dead, lying on the ground. At first I thought he'd had a stroke or a heart attack. I thought he must have gone out for some air and fallen right where he was, into a tangled plot of rosebushes. He was caught in the branches and tangled up in the thorns very badly."

She stopped for a moment and dropped her gaze onto the hands knotted in her lap. I waited. Then she sighed and raised her head again.

"What else was there to think? He must have just fallen there and gotten tangled. We were all very shaken, but we got him free and carried him inside to the house. I knew he had to die sooner or later, of course, but it was still terrible for me. All the worse, in fact, because his face and hands were badly scratched from the thorns. They're very long, nearly an inch and a half, and I was always warned, by my father and by the servants, to stay away from them when I was little. The bushes require a great deal of attention, too, but the flowers are particularly beautiful. They were my father's favorites in the whole garden, and of course I was struck at once by the irony, that it should be in that very place that he died.

"We laid my father's body on the sofa in the library. I sent the servants outside, so that I could be alone with him for a few minutes, for the very last time. There was no rush, after all, no family to notify, and the business would go on comfortably without him. He had always planned long ahead and seen to that. I just needed a moment to be alone with him.

"I used my handkerchief to clean a little of the mud from his face and hands. That's when I saw the marks on his throat."

I didn't move. You don't hear a story like this every day, not even in my business.

"There were two deep punctures. At first I thought they were from the thorns, but then I saw they looked different. They were deeper, bigger. The skin was slightly torn, and puffy all around, and a little discolored. I was terrified but I wiped the blood away. I didn't want to believe it, but I was looking right at the marks. There was no other possible explanation."

She was watching me for a reaction. She didn't get one.

"Do you believe me, Mr. Kendall?"

"Finish the story."

"There's not much more to tell. I tried to put that part of it out of my mind for a minute, as best I could. I said goodbye to my father, and then I left the room to give instructions to the staff."

End of story. I looked at her and waited, but that was it.

A vampire. Her father had been bitten and killed by a vampire. The most beautiful girl I have ever been privileged to gaze upon was sitting in front of me, telling me that, and she had come to my office to hire me to track down the vampire and bring him to justice. I have chosen,

I told myself for the ten-thousandth time, a very difficult line of work.

I sat up and folded my hands in front of me so they'd cover the worst scars on the desk. My hands have a few scars themselves, but the desk is a lot worse off.

"Who found your father in the rosebushes?" I asked her.

She looked startled, as if a glimmer of something had just appeared to her for the first time. "I did," she said.

"These roses were your father's favorites?"

"Yes."

"And none of the servants thought of looking there?"

"We looked everywhere."

"But the servants didn't look there. How many gardeners are on the staff?"

"Four, and the two outside men help them when necessary."

"That's six."

I thought things over for a while. I wasn't surprised to learn that I hated every bit of it.

"Who inherits?"

"I do."

"What about the servants?"

"They stay on with me, of course."

"Forever?"

"Yes, if they want to. Naturally, my father saw to it they'd be taken care of."

"Maybe *they* took care of *him*."

She shook her head. I liked the soft way her hair moved. "I couldn't believe a thing like that. You don't know them."

I tried a little smile. It didn't come out very well. "I don't know anything," I told her. "I'm just a blank page, soaking up information, impressions, ideas, waiting to see if any of them make sense. If you're lost in the Sahara and you come to what looks like a road, you figure it's got to go somewhere, right?"

I waited and made her say it. If we pursued this, we might have to go down some dark roads together. I wanted her eyes to be wide open.

"Right," she said, but she made me wait for it. I didn't mind a bit.

"Was your father dressed or wearing a bathrobe?"

"Just a bathrobe. Later, in his bedroom, I saw that the light was on and there was a book beside his chair. He must have gone out for some air after staying up reading."

"Did he do that often?"

"Not often, no, but sometimes."

"His hands and face were covered by scratches from the thorns?"

"Yes."

"And you wiped the blood from them with your handkerchief?"

"The only blood was on the puncture marks." Her eyes didn't waver, not even a little bit.

I was feeling very tired. There wouldn't be blood on the scratches from thorns if he got the scratches after he was dead.

"He was wearing only a bathrobe," I said. "No pajamas?"

"No."

"When he was carried inside, or when he was in the library, did you happen to notice the rest of his body? Maybe you looked for other scratches or marks, something like that."

"I did. There were a few scratches, but I didn't notice anything else."

"How was he lying when you found him?"

"He was facedown."

"When you found him, or when you brought him inside, did you see any discoloration, maybe in his face or his chest?"

"No. He was very white. Why? Would that mean something?"

"You don't want to know."

"I do."

She meant it. I kept my voice very even. "If he'd been dead for any length of time, which apparently he was, judging from the bathrobe, the bed, the book, and the light, the blood in his body would have settled to whatever part was lowest. It gets to look sort of purple."

"There was nothing like that," she said. "Nothing like that at all. He was very white. I never thought of anything like that. I didn't know that happened."

She didn't, either. I could see it in her face. And she could see what was in my face. If there had been blood in her father's body after he died, she would have seen the discoloration. No discoloration, therefore no blood. I didn't want to think about the next therefore.

"What about the police?"

She shook her head. "In the first place, they wouldn't believe me. In the second place, I feel obliged to preserve my father's privacy. It's the last thing I can do for him, Mr. Kendall."

"Call me Mike."

When I heard myself say that, I knew I was a goner. She nodded. She knew it too.

"I'll have to see the body."

That was what did it. She stared at me, those eyes almost making my head reel, and then I saw shiny tears welling up in them, threatening to spill out and drown both our hearts.

"You can't," she managed to say.

"Why not?"

'I told you I left him in the library to give instructions to the staff. When I went out, I saw Hawkins, my father's personal servant for more than forty years. I broke down then. I couldn't help it. Hawkins held me for a few minutes—he was always like an uncle to me—until I calmed down. We spoke briefly; then I asked him to call the other servants together and I went back into the library alone. My father's body was gone."

"And the library has at least three doors."

"Four," she said. She sounded about the same way I felt.

"A vampire," I said. I said it very quietly, very flat.

"Yes," she told me.

We looked at each other.

"Will you help me?"

We looked at each other some more.

Finally, she managed a pale and sad little smile, as if she regretted putting this burden on me, but there was strength and growing confidence in it, too. And there were those eyes.

I hadn't seen a pretty girl smile in six weeks, and that was in the movies. It made me want to fix things, shift the world around to where it belonged, so Mary Cantrell could smile like that all the time.

I told her: "I'm your man."

2

It's not every day you meet an albino Eskimo, and very few of the ones you do meet are named Danny Lavender. Nobody smiles when Danny tells them his name.

I met him a few years ago in a pedestrian underpass. He'd just been mugged and he needed a few bucks to get home. All I had was a ten, so I gave it to him. The next afternoon, around the time I usually start contemplating the big dramatic question of the day—beef pot pie or the Hungry Man turkey?—he walked into my office and put a nicely engraved picture of Alexander Hamilton on the desk in front of me.

I stared at the ten for a while, then I stared at him for a while.

"It's a big city," I said when the shock had worn off a little. "How'd you find me?"

He kept his hands folded neatly in his lap.

"I'm here," he said. He didn't say anything else.

"How'd you find me?" I said again. Dogged persistence is one of my long suits.

"I'm good at that sort of thing."

"What do you do for a living?"

"What do you need done?"

I looked him over. I'm no dwarf myself—six feet tall plus a couple more inches I carry with me for emergencies—but it took a while to see all of this guy. If you had to get to the other side of a river, you could walk across on his shoulders. I know a lot of people who don't have a head as big as one of his hands. He was wearing a suit that had forgotten it was ever new around the same time my own suit had lost its memory. He had a scarf around his neck, and he was holding gloves in one hand, a hat, maybe a fedora, in the other. A pair of sunglasses was sticking up from his breast pocket. No sunbathing for this beauty. His skin was as pink as a skinned rabbit's and his hair might have been previously owned by Caspar the Friendly Ghost.

"What's your name?" I said.

He told me. I didn't smile.

"How many guys did it take to mug you?"

"Five," he said. "Plus a couple of blunt instruments."

I made some eye contact with Alexander Hamilton, then I pocketed the ten and stood up.

"Let's go have dinner," I said. "I know a place where the burgers actually had a former association with beef."

We went to Joe's Place. I conduct a lot of my business there, mainly in the line of thinking things over by myself. It's bright, it's clean, the Formica is hardly chipped at all, and you can taste the syrup in the Cokes and the coffee in the coffee.

It's been known to get busy sometimes at lunch, but this was dinnertime. I led the way to my usual table near the wall. I've seen spies do that in the movies, and I figure I'm part of a great tradition. Joe came over himself.

"Hello, Mr. Kendall," he said.

He always calls me Mr. Kendall when I have somebody with me. He knows what I do for a living, and he figures it's a client and the formality makes dining in his establishment a little more elegant. I like Joe.

I ordered for both of us.

While we waited for the burgers, I asked Danny Lavender some questions. He used words as if you had to borrow them from the bank, but he got high marks for his answers.

He told me he was an Eskimo and that he was from the Klondike, which is so far up in Alaska that you don't need to know where it is. He told me he still had family there but he finally had to leave. Too much bright light for an albino.

"So you came to dark and storm-tossed California," I said.

"More buildings," he said. "More night work. I only work at night."

He was right enough about the night work. In a city like Los Angeles, everything, good or bad, top to bottom, depends on night work. Sometimes I think my whole life depends on night work.

I listened to him and I watched him. I liked the sound of his voice and the fact that he only used it as necessary. I liked the way he looked me right in the eye when he talked. I also liked the size of him and the easy way he moved it around. I liked the ten in my pocket and the way he'd found me to return it. I even had a feeling Alex Hamilton would have liked him, too.

I told him: "I might have night work sometimes for an associate."

He looked at me across the table. He wasn't going to ask. I admired that.

"Besides," I said, "I read in a book someplace that all private investigators have to wear hats. I hate wearing a hat."

"I've got a hat."

"You've got a job, too."

Just then, Joe brought the burgers to the table and set them down. "Joe," I said, "I want you to meet my new associate, Danny Lavender."

Danny stuck out one of his hams and Joe took hold of as much of it as he could grasp.

Within the next year, Danny Lavender saved my neck three times. I buy him a lot of burgers at Joe's Place.

My luck was running high and the car started on the first attempt. I followed Mary Cantrell out of the city and up to Kirkdale. The two cars going up the road like that must have looked like before and after.

I like driving. You can feel the ground beneath you, feel the wind in your face, feel yourself moving forward. It's easy to kid yourself that you're accomplishing something useful, when all you're really doing is driving a car. I didn't know what I was doing that day.

I thought about it and decided that I only believed two things just then. I believed there were no such things as vampires. And I believed Mary Cantrell when she said her father had been killed by one. So I thought about it some more, and decided that I really only believed one thing. I believed those eyes.

We left the coast highway and headed up into the hills. In a few minutes, we were on roads that don't deserve the name.

Then we got to Kirkdale.

It was surrounded by a fence, but the fence was discreetly hidden by trees and bushes. So was the gate. Mary Cantrell must have worked some widget in the car because when we got there a clump of trees very considerately and just as silently slid out of the way for us. When we'd passed through, they glided back into place and pretended they hadn't moved.

There are countries in the U.N. with less acreage than we passed on the driveway. I should have expected the house, but you never expect a house like that one.

Mary Cantrell had told me it was on top of a hill, but if this hill had come to visit Mohammed, he wouldn't have felt slighted. It was a respectable size, not quite as big as Windsor Castle and with fewer chimneys than Pittsburgh. Gardens and greenhouses stretched away down the hill. From the side of the house where we parked the cars, you could see half the Pacific Ocean. On a clear day, you might even spot hula girls in the distance.

My car was wheezing from the altitude. While it coughed itself into silence, I put my hands on my hips and tried to take in the scene. When I turned back toward the house, a first cousin of Bela Lugosi was standing in the doorway.

Mary Cantrell whispered to me that the Dracula look-alike was Hawkins, her father's personal valet. I decided that if I had to wake up every morning to see him laying out my suit, the only thing I'd have to be grateful for was that I wasn't in it.

It was a nice house. The front entry sent back echoes of our footsteps. If you were a bat, you'd always know where you were.

I'd instructed Mary to tell the staff that I was an insurance investigator. I figured I'd hint to them myself that I had undefined links to the lawyer's office that would be handling the will. That way they should be willing to cooperate and also be on their best behavior. Lawyers and insurance companies are notoriously reluctant to hand out money to the grieving relatives when they can't clap eyes on the corpse.

In a few minutes, Hawkins had assembled the whole staff in the drawing room. They weren't a pretty picture.

I went for the three women first. If that sounds mean, I'll have to live with it. Murder is pretty mean, too.

The cook was Dracula's missus. She looked like she might have an attack of severe *angst* any minute, so I started on her with a sharp jab. "Where's Cantrell's body?"

I said it out of the side of my mouth, the way you see it done in the movies. It's a good technique. People automatically know how they're supposed to react. Mrs. Dracula jumped like she'd just found a spider spinning a web in her mouth. Everybody else froze and looked extremely unhappy. I gave up any hopes of being voted Houseguest of the Year.

"I . . . I don't know."

It was a good answer and the others began to thaw out a little. I came back with more questions, to keep the temperature low, but I didn't expect to learn anything from this session unless one of them tipped something by accident. After about five minutes, I knew they were too good for that, or else they were all innocent. I went on with the questions, seeing to it everybody got a turn to be nervous, but I couldn't hope for anything more than to learn their personalities.

I learned a lot, all of it bad. These people had no loyalty to anyone but themselves. Cantrell had never been anything but a meal ticket to them, and now they were assured of eating regular for the rest of their lives, and doing it in style at Kirkdale. Maybe they weren't vampires, but you don't have to be a vampire to be a bloodsucking freak. I didn't trust them and I didn't like them.

In between questions and answers, I stole a few looks at Mary Cantrell. What I saw made my insides turn into a prizewinning macrame exhibit. She thought they all loved her.

It was a nice afternoon, so I spent a couple of hours by myself, taking the sun and snooping around the gardens and the grounds. All the place needed to qualify as a national park was a souvenir stand and a couple of bears.

Cantrell's favorite roses held my attention for a long time. They were the color of blood an hour after it runs out of a wound. If you were building a house, you could use the thorns and save yourself the price of nails. I looked at those bushes and thought about them for a while, then I decided there was nothing in it for me. Instead, I covered the ground all around them. That's when I found it.

There are clues and there are clues. Some of them only require one look for your day to turn into Christmas. Some of them never say a word to you. This one was the silent type.

It was a piece of dental floss about four inches long.

I kneeled over it as if I was thinking about

starting a religion. I didn't touch it for a while, just studied it in its natural state. It was twisted a little, and muddy, but its waxy surface shone in a couple of spots, so there was no mistaking what it was.

After a while, I picked it up and took inventory. I'd been right the first time. It was about four inches long. Johnson & Johnson. Flavored with cinnamon. And maybe with something else. I hoped the brown stains were only mud.

I needed two things very badly, a Baggie and a drink. I only had one of them on me at the moment, so I carefully put the dental floss in my wallet, where there was nothing to contaminate it, and pulled the bottle from its holster under my jacket.

"Are you going to keep that all to yourself?" a voice said softly behind me. It was the kind of voice that makes a man turn around with his eyes wide open.

It was Dracula's daughter, Elvira Hawkins, Mary Cantrell's personal maid and companion. She was wearing a black uniform that didn't insult her figure. It didn't insult my imagination, either. I'd had other things on my mind back in the drawing room, but I'd noticed her. You couldn't miss a profile like that, even in black, maybe especially in black, but I can concentrate on my job when I have to. Now I'd put in a few hours, interviewed possible suspects, inspected the scene of the murder, and filed what could be a clue. I was on my break anyway. I handed over the bottle.

She took it and drank without wiping off the top. That did something to me. I didn't want to admit, even to myself, what it was.

"What did you want to see me about?" I said.

"I'm curious about who you are."

"I'm an insurance investigator. Sometimes I work with lawyers, too. It depends."

"No, you're not. You're not with any insurance company. Insurance investigators have better suits," she said. "So do guys who work with lawyers."

I didn't even blink. "You can't tell by the cut of the cloth," I told her.

"I can," she said. "Only one thing had me puzzled."

"What was that?"

"You don't wear a hat," she said. "Private investigators always wear hats."

I gave her my most winning smile.

"I have a hat. I hate it. I hire a guy to wear it for me."

We grinned at each other for a while.

Then I figured my break was over and I went back to work.

I put my hand out and she put the bottle in it.

"Okay," I said, "I'm an investigator, private or otherwise. Do you have something I might want to investigate, or were you just thirsty?"

At some point in your relationship, a women who wears black is sure to turn nasty. I've learned that over the years.

"Listen, you shamus or shaman or shogun or whatever you guys are called, you've only horned in here where you're not needed or wanted. Kirkdale has always been safe from people like you. Isn't it bad enough that Mr. Cantrell was bitten by a vampire and murdered right here where he should be safe, in the comfort of his own home? Poor Mary is in her room, crying her eyes out. I've spent my life trying to protect her from the harsh realities of life, just the way her father wanted me to. Now all this has happened. Please, leave her alone! Your help can only make life worse for her, even worse than her father's death has already made it. Leave her alone! Leave us all alone!"

She didn't even say goodbye, but she was nice to look at in that black uniform running up the hill to the house. The only thing that kept me from enjoying the view completely was the fact that neither Mary Cantrell nor I had said word one to the staff about vampires.

I took Mary Cantrell with me when I left that place. She protested a little because she didn't understand why I was so worried about her. I reminded her that she was paying me to tell her things like this, even if she didn't like them. Especially if she didn't like them. She said she'd come with me.

Hawkins saw us to the door, but I could tell from his face that he wasn't hoping we had a nice day.

We left in separate cars. It was a while before we reached civilization. When I saw a diner that looked as if it might have evolved enough to have a telephone, I signaled to Mary and pulled into the parking lot.

"Sit tight," I called across to her. She nodded, looking very unhappy but very brave.

I went in and found the phone and called Danny Lavender.

"I have some night work," I told him. "Meet me at the office at seven. Bring your fists."

When I went back to the parking lot, Mary Cantrell was gone. They'd left her car there, with the driver's door open, as a souvenir.

3

I called Danny Lavender again, then sat by the window in the diner drinking coffee. When I saw

Danny's car roll into the parking lot, I signaled to the waitress and ordered two burgers.

He took the hat off but kept the glasses on when he sat down across from me. He didn't say a word, but the angle of his head told me he was eager to hear about the case.

"This one could ruin your appetite," I told him. "Wait till we eat."

The burgers were exactly what I expected. I added another star to the rating of Joe's Place.

We even risked the coffee. It was going to be a long night.

When I told Danny everything that had happened, he still didn't say a word but he nodded three times during the story. When Danny Lavender nods once, that means he thinks the case is really bad. I'd never seen him nod three times. I waved for more coffee and this time I added reinforcements from my holster.

"We have to get her out of there," I said.

Danny Lavender nodded again.

It's like when you see a guy ahead of you on the highway pass an exit, then stop and back up. You don't do anything at first. You just stare at him, trying to comprehend the fact that he's really doing this thing.

That's how it is when you suddenly get a break in a case. It's like the sun deciding to shine in your window at midnight. I stood there on the steps of the diner, staring at Mary Cantrell's car. The same car she'd driven when she led the way up to Kirkdale. The car that had the widget for the gate.

An owl could have found the gate again in about two minutes. To me, every tree looks like every other tree. I like them all right, but they have a tendency to stand between me and where I'm going. When we got to where I thought we were close, we had to kill the headlights and cruise in the dark. It took over an hour to locate that gate in the pitch blackness, with Danny leaning on the widget all the way.

Once we were inside, Danny rigged the widget to keep the gate open while I turned the car around so it faced out toward the road. I like to leave a place quiet and quick.

The moon was high above us by the time we hiked up to the house. When we reached the edge of the woods on one side, Danny pointed up. The whole house was in darkness, just a black shape against the black sky, except for a light in one window on the second floor. While I stood there, trying to convince my lungs to go back to work, I saw a shadow pass the window, then pass it again. I knew that shadow. It was Mary Cantrell.

Then I saw another shadow in the same window. I knew that shadow, too. I would have known it anywhere. It was Elvira Hawkins, and she was guarding the prize.

"It's my bet the door isn't locked," I whispered to Danny. "They'll rely on the gate."

He nodded. I couldn't tell if that was good or bad.

We walked up to the house, opened the door, and went in.

I put my hand on Danny's arm to hold him back a minute. I was afraid the pounding of my heart would sound as subtle as jungle drums in that silent house. When the noise slacked off a little, we started forward toward the stairs.

The noise of my heart drowned out the sound of footsteps behind me. The guy had a good grip on my Adam's apple from behind before I even knew what was happening. Nobody made a sound. The guy wouldn't let go. I saw Danny's dark shape turning toward me. I gave up trying to move the guy's arm from my throat, and reached inside my jacket to the holster. That holster has served me well. It earned another polishing that night. My hand closed around the neck of the bottle and eased it out. My throat was starting to hurt from where the guy was inconsiderately squeezing it, so I swung the bottle behind me and smashed the heavy in the mouth.

He went down like a thousand-year-old redwood, muttering, "My teeth, my teeth," but I didn't care. I came around in a hurry and hit him again, hard. He stopped worrying about his teeth then.

The jungle drums were going again pretty good after that, but we started back up the stairs.

At the top, I looked down the corridor. A blade of light was coming from under one of the doors. It was Mary Cantrell's room.

We went in there like a pair of matched bullocks.

Mary was sitting on the edge of the bed. Standing over her was Elvira Hawkins, and she was smiling.

Danny and I couldn't even manage a grin.

Beside the bed was an intravenous stand and hanging from the top of it was a clear plastic I.V. bag. I saw some others on the night table. There was about a mile of plastic tubing, too, all stretched out and hooked up and ready to go. Elvira had one end of it in her hand, and attached to the tube was a hypodermic needle. She was bending over Mary's arm as she smiled, taking aim with that needle, and that's the way she froze, looking up at us.

For a while, everybody just looked things over, not saying anything. There wasn't much to say. I figured there were two possibilities. One was that the vampires were packing refreshments for a picnic, but I didn't like that one too much. The other was more terrible than I had time to think about just then.

I said, "Hello, Elvira."

Her smile turned real nasty and she snarled at me.

"We're onto your little game," I said, very polite and respectful, "but the game just came to an end."

She straightened up then. I couldn't tell if she was still snarling because Danny Lavender was wrapping one of his hands around her head.

Then Mary Cantrell was in my arms and I wasn't thinking about Elvira any more.

She sobbed for a while and kept turning those eyes up to me. I gave her all the time she needed to get herself calm again. Danny kept himself busy with Elvira.

After a while, I told Danny I thought we'd overstayed our welcome and maybe it was time we left. Elvira looked very subdued. Danny had her tied up securely with the plastic tubing.

"So long, sister," I said.

She mumbled something but I couldn't catch it. The gag in her mouth didn't improve her diction.

Mary was steady on her feet as we went down the stairs. She didn't need any coaxing to leave the house this time.

At the bottom of the stairs, the heavy we'd left there was starting to come around and maybe even remember his own name. I advised him to see a dentist, then hit him again with the bottle so he'd have to.

We didn't dawdle after that and got across the open patch okay and into the woods. It was a lot easier getting down the driveway than it had been hiking up. When we finally saw the car sitting there in the moonlight, with the trees politely standing aside for us to leave, I figured we were home free.

We piled into the front seat quick and got out of there.

I liked having Mary Cantrell safe on the seat beside me, and I liked having Danny Lavender protecting her on the other side.

About a mile down the road, I switched on the headlights and picked up some speed.

From behind me in the backseat, a voice said, "Do drive carefully, Mr. Kendall. We wouldn't want to have an accident now."

It happens like that sometimes. I'm the most suspicious person I know. I even know some credit managers who aren't as suspicious as I am. I always check the backseat of the car. I didn't check it that time.

Danny and I had never rehearsed it, but Dracula back there, in the person of Hawkins, he of the beauteous daughter, didn't have time to figure that out.

I swerved the car sharp to the left, then sharp to the right, then left again. Danny had had his arm across the backseat, behind Mary's shoulders, because otherwise his own shoulders wouldn't have let the three of us in the seat. While I was making the car imitate an eggbeater, Danny planted his elbow in the vampire's face.

I heard Mary Cantrell gasp beside me, but I didn't have time to think about that. I screeched the car to a stop and threw on the brake.

Danny was already climbing over the seat into the back and making sounds like he wasn't having a good time doing it. His compensation was that Drac wasn't having a good time, either. I joined him in the back as soon as the car stopped rocking.

He had the situation in hand already. I like a

guy who thinks ahead and comes prepared for emergencies. Danny had kept half of that plastic tubing, and he was already getting Drac done up tight enough for special delivery.

"Put your finger there," Danny said, and pointed with his chin.

I put my finger there and held it till he pulled the last of the tubing tight.

"Okay," I said, and began to think maybe I'd take up breathing again.

"Look out!" Mary Cantrell cried.

I wished she'd been a little more precise, but in a second I figured out what was worrying her. The vampire was going for Danny Lavender's throat.

Danny snatched his head back just in time, but he continued leaning his arm against the vampire's chest.

"His teeth," Mary said. "You have to watch out for his teeth."

She was right.

Danny looked at me, without releasing his hold.

"Here," I said. I reached inside my jacket for the holster.

"Sorry I can't offer you a drink," I told Hawkins, showing him the bottle.

He said two words to me then that I don't want to write down. I used the back of my hand twice to make him regret each of them. After that he didn't say anything. It's not easy to talk with the neck of a booze bottle shoved down your throat and an angry Eskimo holding it in place.

4

After our little disagreement with Hawkins on the subject of neck-biting, we decided to sit out the rest of the night in the car and not risk driving while somebody held onto him. We found a road down to the beach and parked there, waiting for daylight. If everything went according to Hoyle, the vampire was going to go into hibernation at dawn's early light.

Danny Lavender was in the backseat, nursing our friend with the bottle. Mary Cantrell stretched out across the front seat, saying she only needed to rest her eyes for a bit, and dozed off right away.

That left me.

I spend a lot of time thinking things over. It happens I have a lot of time in which to do that.

Now I was thinking about vampires, and I didn't like the thoughts I was having. In my business you get used to having new thoughts, learning new things, but sometimes you have to learn something you didn't really want to know. The worst of it was the fact that I'd already been believing in vampires and acting on that belief for most of the day. And the day had been pretty long.

In any prison, fellow cons will call a truce and gang up very cosily to erase a child molester or a traitor. I wondered what that fraternity would do to a vampire.

But then a vampire could never be put in a prison. That was going to be kind of a roadblock for me.

I listened to the ocean some more and wished I could slow my heartbeat down to its rhythm. I kept myself occupied by kicking some sand with the toe of my shoe. It didn't help my thinking any.

I knew I couldn't kill him. I've seen lots of murders and I know lots of interesting ways to go about it, but stakes through thc heart just aren't in my line. I couldn't turn him over to the police. I couldn't kill him. I couldn't let him go. I had a real problem on my hands.

I kicked the sand some more but it just blew away on the breeze, like all my thoughts.

"I'm so sorry I got you involved in this," Mary Cantrell said softly at my side.

I turned my head and looked at her. People tell me I deal out the words pretty sharp, sometimes sharp enough to cut, but I didn't know what to be saying now. Also, I kept my hands in my pockets. If I'd taken them out, I might have been tempted to violate the client-investigator relationship. I looked at her, standing there in the silvery moonlight on the rippled sand of the beach, her skirt moving softly around her in the breeze from the ocean. She had her face tilted up to me. Those eyes. I looked away.

"I'll think of something," I said. I could hardly hear my own voice.

"I mean it," she said. She touched my arm with the tips of her fingers. "You're a good man, Mike Kendall. I can see that. You've already risked your life for me, and that's more than any fee can ever repay you for. I know you deal all the time with . . . with terrible people and the terrible things they do to each other. It must be awful, having to face that every day, having to face that knowledge. I've just learned something about that myself, so I understand a little of what you must feel."

I waved one hand to brush it all away. I didn't move the arm she was touching.

"This must be the worst thing you've ever had to deal with," she said. I could hear the sadness in her voice.

"I've seen worse," I said.

I hadn't.

I felt her hand tighten on my arm. I watched the ocean as if I expected Russian submarines to surface any minute. "I'll get us out of this," I told her. "I'll find a way."

"I know you will."

I spent some time trying to think of a way. I couldn't.

"Mike," she said. Just like that.

I turned to face her and we moved closer together. Nothing moved on the beach except the eternal ocean.

When we kissed, I could taste the salt on her lips.

Dawn can be beautiful in California, with the first pink light streaking up over the mountains, almost as beautiful as the red and gold and purple of sunset over the Pacific. This dawn wasn't beautiful at all. It was just gray and overcast and misty, but it was the best I'd ever seen.

The part of me that's mean wished I could take credit for solving the problem, but I couldn't. The problem solved itself.

About the time the first light began to touch the beach, the vampire in the backseat began making some unpleasant noises deep in his throat. He kept it up and after a while I heard Danny Lavender grunt. That wasn't a good sign, but if Danny had needed help, I would have known. Mary had gone back to sleep, stretched out like a child on the front seat of the car. I was still watching the ocean.

Then Hawkins started coughing as if he might choke, and I wondered if maybe Danny Lavender was forgetting his own strength. Besides, I was very attached to that particular bottle and I didn't want to lose it down the gullet of a vampire. I went back to see what was going on.

Hawkins had his eyes wide open and they were darting around in every direction, except he kept blinking madly, as if somebody were shining a spotlight into them. I thought he looked pretty pale, too. He was definitely not in the pink of health.

His tossing around and gurgling woke up Mary Cantrell, and the three of us studied him. I could see Mary's face filled with the most terrible sadness of all, the knowledge that someone you thought had loved you has now betrayed you.

Then something changed in the noises Hawkins was making. I wasn't expecting it from him so at first I didn't realize what it was. Then I caught it. There's a special kind of sound a man makes when he's gagged, not just the usual protests and faked noises of choking, but a sound that says clearly, if you've heard it before, that the subject has something to say and that maybe he's going to sing the song you want to hear. Danny Lavender was looking at me, waiting for a signal. He'd heard it, too.

"I think he wants to say something," Mary Cantrell said.

I looked at her and let my admiration show.

"Okay," I told Danny. "Uncork him."

Danny removed the bottle from the vampire's mouth, not taking too much care to avoid banging the bottle on his fangs. The vampire winced. I didn't like myself too much for it, but I enjoyed seeing that.

"You are all so foolish," were the vampire's first words.

The jungle drums started up again in my chest.

"So foolish," he said again, and started laughing. It was a weak laugh, but it was laughter. It made Mary Cantrell cry. I hit him for doing that.

His eyes glared at me, but the smile never left his face.

His voice was fading fast and his face was going more pale by the second. He was dying and suddenly we all knew it. But he was still smiling because he knew something else the rest of us didn't know.

Then he told us what he had to say and it was the worst thing I'd ever heard.

He told us everything, the whole ugly story. Nobody interrupted while he spoke. Dawn was getting brighter by the second, and he didn't have much time left.

"I want you to know this," he said. "Knowing that you have this knowledge will be the last and the greatest pleasure of my life.

"I know what happened in the bedroom upstairs. I know you left Elvira there, but rest assured that she has gotten herself free by now. She was always a resourceful girl. But she is not a vampire.

"You look surprised. No, she is not a vampire, nor are any of the other staff at Kirkdale, so you're safe on that score.

"It is true that I was planning to make them vampires, beginning with my dear Elvira, of course. And I was going to use your blood for that purpose, young lady. But that doesn't matter now. They will simply have to look out for themselves from now on in the lowly way of puny humans with limited human powers. And Elvira, I'm sure, will do well for herself. A good-looking girl can always do well in sunny California, eh?

"No, I was the only vampire at Kirkdale. And now I am dying. You have me and it seems obvious there is nothing I can do to escape. My powers are weakening. With every ray of dawning light that shines, I grow weaker. In minutes, I shall be dead."

His eyes were losing their gleam by the second, but as he looked at each of the three of us there was still a fierce light burning in them. And there was something else, too. There was amusement. I knew that with his last breath he was going to tell us something we didn't want to hear.

He looked at Danny Lavender a moment, then he looked at me, then he let his gaze come to rest on Mary Cantrell.

"I bit your father, young lady. Had you forgotten that? Oh, his blood tasted good. Quite rich and aristocratic and—"

"Stop it!" I said. "That's enough! You're having the last laugh anyway, so just get on with the story." I made a fist and showed it to him.

He smiled, but it looked as if it took almost the last bit of life left in him. He closed his eyes, then opened them again. He was still looking at Mary.

"Your father," he said. "I bit him. Now your father is a vampire!"

His eyes blazed for a second, but that was the end. California's vampire population went down by one.

The trouble was, California's vampire population had also gone up by one the day before.

Mary Cantrell's father was a vampire and we had to track him down before he killed others.

And if we found him, what were we going to do with him?

I didn't know. All I knew for sure right then was that Mary Cantrell was sobbing against my shoulder and I hated a world in which someone like her could be made to cry.

Pretty soon, the sun started doing ugly things to the vampire's body. Nobody said a word while we buried what was left. Then we got in the car and went away from that place.

5

We spent a little time going back up in the hills to the diner to get Danny's car and my own. They were still there. I hoped that might mean my luck was beginning to turn, but I knew better than to hope it too much.

Mary said she could drive her own car back to L.A. and my office. I let her. She needed some time by herself, but I could also see the set of her jaw and the old determination in her eyes. She'd had a bad night but she was going to be okay.

I told Danny Lavender to meet me at the office at dusk. I figured he'd be stirring again about the time Jonathan David Cantrell would be up and about. It was going to be a long day. But the day wasn't going to be as long as the next night.

Back at the office, I found Mary Cantrell sound asleep on the couch in my waiting room. That was more use than the couch had seen in years. It wasn't much but I was glad it was there for her. I reminded myself to dust it sometime. You never know when you're going to need a couch.

I locked the office when I left. I wanted to find Mary Cantrell there, safe and sound, when I got back.

My first stop was the local booze emporium. I wasn't taking any chances, so I bought a new bottle for my holster, plus another couple for good measure. It's a comforting feeling to know you're packing plenty of armament going into battle.

Then I went to Joe's Place and drank four cups of breakfast, black. I'm not usually an early type and Joe looked at me funny when I came in, but he knew enough to leave me alone and just keep the coffee coming.

I tried to think everything over again and figure where this road was leading us, but nothing made any sense till I started on the third cup. Coffee is important in my work. I think very highly of countries that grow it.

When Joe poured the fifth cup, he put a packet of Alka-Seltzer on the table beside the saucer. Joe is a good man.

I hated what I was thinking. I knew it was the only answer, the only way we were going to stop Jonathan David Cantrell, but I hated it anyway.

She was awake when I got there and one look at her face told me she'd figured it out, too. It didn't take a second look to tell me she was ready to go through with it.

"You know what has to be done," I said.

"Yes."

"I'm sorry."

"It can't be helped," she said. "I can do whatever I have to."

"You'll be risking your life. I wish there were some other way."

She shook her head. We both knew there wasn't.

Even a decent citizen who doesn't believe in vampires knows a lot about them. For one thing, they're creatures of habit, and that's the key to getting them. That was the first thing I'd realized, and that had led Mary and me to this conversation. I discounted all that stuff you hear about mirrors and garlic and dirt from the vampire's grave. Maybe it's true, maybe it's not. I didn't care. I only cared about what mattered most. And what mattered most and first was finding him.

In order to find him, we'd have to set a trap. But what do you lure a vampire with? Blood? Too easy. Everybody you pass on the street has blood. No, you have to use the one thing that pleases a vampire most, a chance to hurt the one person that vampire has most loved in life.

We were going to have to use Mary Cantrell herself as the bait to catch her own father.

That was pretty bad, about as bad as things can be. But there was still something else.

"I can't kill him," Mary said quietly. "And we can't just let him die, the way Hawkins did. I've already faced my father's death once. I can't face it again. We'll have to figure out something else."

"Yeah," I said. "I know. I just don't know what."

I didn't, either.

We didn't talk much during the day. Mary spent some time looking out the window, but it wasn't much nicer out than it was in. I kept myself busy studying the scars on my desk.

About one o'clock I had an idea.

"Tell me about your father," I said. "Tell me everything, whether you told it to me before or not. What I'm looking for is the things he cared most about. Besides you."

She started talking, telling me all sorts of things, the kinds of things that are awkward to talk about after somebody has died. Everything seems trivial in the light of the person's death. I listened carefully. I couldn't afford to think any of it was trivial, because somewhere in what Mary was telling me was the clue we needed.

I couldn't hear it. I listened, but I couldn't hear it.

"He had a lot of money," I said. "Did he give any of it away?"

"Yes," Mary told me. "He was very generous and supported a large number of charities."

"Who got the most?"

She thought about that. "There were all the

usual charities," she said slowly, "but there was one that he was especially fond of. Yes, I think they may have gotten even more than the others."

I waited.

"It was the zoo."

"The zoo?" I said.

"The zoo in Santa Bonita. It was only a small zoo for many years, and of course overshadowed by the San Diego Zoo. But the group of directors there wanted to expand it. I don't know if they went to my father or if he first approached them, but I know he gave them a lot of money in recent years." She looked at me. "A lot of money. He loved animals almost as much as he loved flowers. I'm sorry I forgot to mention that before."

"It's okay," I said. "We've got it now. Or half of it, anyway." I stood up. "Let's take a ride."

"Where are we going?"

"The zoo," I told her.

We got there just before closing time, and the guard at the gate didn't want to let us in. Mary asked him to call the head office and tell them she was there. I don't know if it was her voice or her eyes that got him to make the call. He was back in less than a minute, and in two minutes more that guard was riding us around on his motor cart, showing us all the sights.

I was looking for something, but I wouldn't know what it was until I spotted it.

After about fifteen minutes, we'd seen everything there was to see but I still hadn't seen what I was looking for.

"Let's go around again," I told the guard. He was pretty cheerful about cooperating. Overtime is good money.

We went a little distance and then I told him to stop.

"What's that?" I asked him.

He glanced over where I was pointing. "Not finished yet," he said.

I put my hand on his shoulder. He looked at me and I let him read my face.

"Oh," he said. "You asked me what it is, didn't you? Right. Well, in about a week's time, it's going to be the new World of Night exhibit."

I didn't want to look at Mary Cantrell.

"Tell me about it," I said.

"Well, you remember how they used to have, you know, the snake house and the rodent exhibit and like that? But it didn't work out so good because all those things sleep all day long and only go out hunting for food at night. Kind of like the graveyard shift of the animal kingdom. . . . Do you get it?"

I looked at him some more.

"Right," he said. "So in a World of Night exhibit, what they do is, they turn around day and night by putting all the lights on a different schedule. Fools the animals, see? When people are here in the daytime, it's dark inside, kind of like moonlight, but the animals think it's nighttime and they're all up and going about their business. Then at night, real night, when there's nobody in the zoo to see them, the lights are on in the exhibit and the animals all go to sleep. Works out fine."

"When is it supposed to open?"

"Next week. Everything is done except the finishing touches. And, of course, they have to bring the animals in. They'll start doing that tomorrow."

"What's it called?" I asked him.

"I told you that. The World of Night."

"Any other name?"

"Oh, you mean like a benefactor? Yeah, some guy gave a few million bucks to build it and they put his name on it to be official. Boy, some people just don't know what to be doing with their money. Building a new home for a bunch of rats and snakes. Boy!"

"Yeah," I said. "I know how you feel. Ain't it something?"

"Yeah," he said.

"Yeah. Listen, the lady here needs a private room with a telephone."

"Oh, sure," he said right away, and I could tell from the look on his face that he was suddenly remembering what the front office had told him about showing this particular lady around.

"Yep, some people with money are real generous, you know that?" he said.

"I know," I said. "The telephone?"

"Right over there in the main office. I'll show you the way."

"You know what I'm thinking," I said to Mary Cantrell when we were alone.

She looked at me. She knew.

I called Danny Lavender first and told him to meet us there as soon as possible.

I didn't have to tell Mary who to call.

She got the chairman of the Board of Directors on the phone and told him what we needed. She also told him that if anything ever went wrong or if a word of this ever leaked out, that zoo would never see another cent of Cantrell money. On the other hand, if everything went well, she thought that perhaps in a couple of years it might be time to expand the zoo's facilities further. She also allowed as how she was very pleased with the work he was doing himself, and that work as good as his deserved to be rewarded.

Money talks. It just talks a different language from the one I learned as a child. I listened to it the way I'd listen to somebody talking French.

Mary Cantrell was terrific. She didn't even

have trouble reassuring the chairman that her father was quite well but out of town for an extended period.

She put the chairman on hold, went to the door, and called in the security guard. He put the phone to his ear and listened for a few minutes and said, "Yes, sir," a few times.

When he put the phone down again, he looked very respectful.

"I'll have the keys to the World of Night for you right away," he said, and went out of there like a shot.

I thought it would break my heart to see that brave little girl sitting out there on that stone wall by herself in the darkness. She just sat there, waiting, her eyes searching all around. I felt like an oaf, clumsy and helpless. I knew from the angle of his head that Danny Lavender felt the same way. We were about a hundred feet away from her on each side. We waited. That's all we could do.

I kept thinking what a long shot it was. Maybe he wouldn't come here at all. Maybe he was off in some other place right now, sucking somebody's blood. Maybe he was, but I couldn't think about that now. We were betting he'd come here and we were using his daughter's life to bet with and I had to concentrate on that.

And then I saw him.

I was looking at the second vampire I'd ever seen. That's a lot of vampires when you didn't even believe in them thirty-six hours before. You learn quick in this business to keep an open mind.

He was stalking her. I can't describe it any other way.

She saw him about the same time I did. I looked over to where Danny was hiding but I couldn't see him. I wished I could, I would have felt better, but I figured he was up to something and that was okay.

I looked back at the vampire. He was standing behind a tree, watching her. Then he moved forward, to another tree. It was dark, but I thought I saw his shoulders shaking. He was laughing. He was laughing because he was going to wreak the ultimate damage on the very person he most loved.

I thought about the ironies of life for a second. Then there was no more time to think because the vampire was moving closer to Mary again.

I wished I knew where Danny Lavender was.

Danny and I had tried to work out a plan as soon as he'd met us there. I've mixed it up with the best of them—that is to say, the worst—and so has Danny, but we couldn't figure out how to handle this case. Clobber him, was the best I could come up with. My holster was loaded and Danny had his fists. We had no other weapons. Besides, anything else we might have used would have been about as useful as hair on a golf ball. We were going to play it as it came, and never mind the risks. Anyway, Mary Cantrell was taking the biggest risk of all.

I watched the vampire moving closer to her. The jungle drums were going a mile a minute.

There was still no sign of Danny. I kept wishing I knew where he was.

Then Mary Cantrell was standing up to face her father.

"Hello, Daddy," she said. Her voice sounded steady.

He laughed, right out loud, gloating.

"I know what you want from me, Daddy, but—"

Now he threw his head back in the moonlight and laughed at the night like a jackal. It was the worst sound I'd ever heard. The moonlight shone on his fangs. He started reaching for her.

I stepped out from hiding.

"Hey!" I shouted.

He swung around, distracted for what turned out to be a crucial second. He snarled and took a step toward me. I was glad to see Mary move backwards, away from him.

I didn't know exactly what I was going to do, but I went toward him anyway.

"Got the time?" I said.

He threw his head back again to laugh but the laugh was cut off short. We found out at the same time where Danny Lavender had been.

In that same second, the vampire turned even whiter than he'd been to start with and spun around in confusion, momentarily off balance. That moment was just enough for me to race across the pathway and caress the back of his head a couple of times with my favorite weapon. The vampire didn't go out completely, but he went down for the count without further protest.

I wasn't surprised that even the vampire was frightened for a second. I'd be willing to bet that anybody would be pretty frightened if nearly three hundred pounds of albino Eskimo suddenly dropped from a branch above him, naked in the moonlight except for his white cotton Fruit of the Looms, and yelling at the top of his voice some Eskimo words that he probably didn't learn at his mother's knee.

We didn't waste any time. Danny grabbed for the vampire's arms and I picked up his feet and we ran for the back door of the World of Night. Mary had kept her head through it all and had the door open wide for us.

We didn't have to carry him very far to the room we'd picked out, but I thought we'd never get there in time. I kept looking at those fangs.

Then we had him inside.

"Kiss the vampire goodbye," I told Mary Cantrell.

She did. On the forehead.

For her sake, I would have liked to put him down a little more gently, but there wasn't time for that. We dumped him and got out of there and locked the door behind us.

Mary slept on the couch in my waiting room that night. I slept with my face on the desk. The scars were rough to sleep on but none of that mattered.

When I woke up, Mary Cantrell was standing in front of the desk.

All she said was, "Thank you."

I waved a hand.

We went across to Joe's Place. Joe took one quick look at her and was very impressed.

"I just pray that it's a permanent solution," she said quietly after a while.

"It's as permanent as we can make it," I told her. "The Cantrell Foundation will endow the World of Night in perpetuity, with a provision that no changes can be made in the building without the Foundation's approval. Except for the new wall sealing off that room and a slight rearrangement inside the building. And if he ever does get out, it'll be in the daylight."

"Yes," she said. There was nothing else to say.

We went back to my office for a minute and she got out her checkbook and wrote me a check.

Then I saw her to the door and silently declared the case closed.

When I looked at the check, I saw it was for more than my fee. I split the difference with Danny Lavender. I owed him a lot.

* * *

That was the last I ever heard of Mary Cantrell, except for a note I had from her a few weeks later. She told me she had fixed things with the lawyers and her father was now officially deceased. The servants had all decamped for parts unknown, and now she was alone in the world. She was taking the money she inherited and going away someplace to start a new life where nothing would ever remind her of the past. I never saw her again.

The city is a jungle and I live in it every day, and like the real jungle, it's filled with wild beasts. But unlike those beasts, I have a memory. I know that Mary Cantrell is safe now and I know that she kissed me that night on the beach with the moonlight shining on her hair.

I must write myself a note to remember that sometime, to think about it. It'll be like a vacation. It'll be nice.

THE DOG

by Pauline C. Smith

Thc morning after Aunt Sue called, Trudy phoned her office. "I can't be in today," she said. "My uncle died and I must go back home. Could I have a week off?"

Her boss said of course. Was there anything he could do? He was so sorry.

There was nothing he could do and really nothing to be sorry for, thought Trudy. She had never liked Uncle Fred, her Aunt Sue's husband, and she was sure no one else had.

She packed her bags, had the Mazda gassed, and took off.

She thought about Aunt Sue as she rolled off the miles. They had given her a home during her last two years of high school and the one year of community college. Aunt Sue took the place of the mother she had lost, but Uncle Fred? Well, he was just someone married to Aunt Sue.

She arrived in the early evening and parked her car at the curbing. She leaned on the steering wheel and looked at the house she hadn't seen for more than a year. A small, white house, shaded by old oak trees and surrounded by a chain link fence.

She picked up her bags, opened the gate and walked up the path to the house.

Aunt Sue led her to the kitchen and talked about food.

"But I've eaten," said Trudy. "I stopped along the way."

"Oh well, then, some cake and milk?" urged Aunt Sue. "You had a very long drive."

With Aunt Sue's chocolate cake in front of her, Trudy asked about Uncle Fred.

"You know he'd been sick for many months," said Aunt Sue. "He knew he was going to die. He talked about it a lot. And he read everything he could get his hands on about death."

Trudy shivered. "He read about *death?*"

"Yes. He sent away for these books. Piles of them. And he read them all. He told me that after he died, he would be back."

"Be *back?*" cried Trudy.

"That's right," said Aunt Sue. "Those books he read on transmigration, reincarnation, and I don't know what all made him sure that he would come back somehow, some way. He said he didn't mind dying now that he knew he'd be back."

"Well," said Trudy. "Well, maybe that helped. Maybe it helped him face the end."

"Maybe it did," said Aunt Sue. She smiled. "I'm glad you came."

"Of course I'd come," said Trudy. "Have you made all the arrangements?"

"What arrangements?" asked Aunt Sue.

"For the burial. The funeral."

"Oh yes," said Aunt Sue. "It's tomorrow afternoon."

"What will you do now?" asked Trudy.

Her aunt looked startled. "You mean now that Fred is gone?"

"Yes, now."

"Well, I suppose I'll stay on right here. I've got thc housc and Fred's insurance. I'll probably do a little volunteer work at the hospital and the church. See people. Do things. Fred never liked to have me go anyplace or see anyone except him. Maybe I'll even learn to drive the car. . . ."

"Good," said Trudy.

"He never really wanted me to do anything except stay right here at home and take care of him."

"I know," said Trudy.

"Another thing—" Aunt Sue trembled with excitement. "You know what I'm going to do? I'm going to get a dog."

"A dog?" said Trudy. "For protection?"

"No, no, no," cried Aunt Sue. "I mean a dog to love. You know, I always wanted a dog. Fred hated them. That's why he built the chain link fence around the yard. 'To keep the dogs out,' he said."

It was during the graveside service the next day that the sky darkened and the thunder began to roll. The minister shortened his already short eulogy, and with a sympathetic pat on Aunt Sue's shoulder, he left just before the rain started.

Workmen in slickers stretched a tarp over the still-open grave and took off, at a run, for one of the buildings on the cemetery grounds.

Trudy hurried her aunt to their parked car. "Well," she said, "this looks like it's going to be a bad one." She turned on the motor and switched on the lights. "Imagine! It's almost as dark as night."

At that moment, the storm broke.

Rain came down in blinding sheets. Thunder roared. Lightning forked. Trudy switched on her wipers. She drove the cemetery grounds slowly, peering through the wiper swipes of her windshield, and came out on Cemetery Road.

"This will lead me to the old back highway, won't it?" she asked her aunt.

"Yes. Turn left here."

Trudy turned and crept along the road, the wipers swishing across the windshield. "Aunt Sue," said Trudy, "lean back over the seat and see if I don't have an umbrella there on the floor. I usually carry one."

Her aunt leaned back and reached down. "Here it is," she said.

"Good," said Trudy. "It'll help us a little when we have to run from the car to the—" and slammed on the brakes. The car skidded to a stop. A dog right-angled in front of her and galloped down the road.

"Oh boy," groaned Trudy, "where did he come from?"

The dog had become a blur in the downpour.

"He was there. All of a sudden, there he was." Trudy let out her breath and went limp. "I almost hit him." She put her foot lightly on the accelerator and inched forward.

She turned toward her aunt. "Did you see him?" she asked.

"I saw him," said her aunt.

They reached the old back highway. Trudy was relieved that there was no traffic. "Who'd want to be out in a storm like this anyway," she muttered. "Maybe a dog, though," her mind still on the dog she'd almost hit, "but the dog would just be trying to find a dry place. Right? I just hope he doesn't get killed doing it."

"He won't," said her aunt.

As they turned from the back road to Center, the rain slackened. "Not much, though," said Trudy. "Just enough so it isn't coming down in sheets. How do you feel, Aunt Sue?"

"What do you mean, how do I feel?"

"Well, now that the funeral is over—"

"It's over," said Aunt Sue. "That's all. At least I think it's over."

"What do you mean you *think* it's over?"

"Just that," said Aunt Sue. "Nobody can tell when anything's over."

"Of course they can," said Trudy. "Something happens. Something's done about it. Then it's over."

Aunt Sue did not answer.

Trudy turned from Center to First. Then onto Elm. "We're almost there," she warned. "Got the umbrella ready?"

Aunt Sue nodded her head.

"Front door key?"

"Yes," said Aunt Sue.

"All right." Trudy slowed to a stop at the curbing. "Now, make a run for it," she said.

Her aunt opened the door on her side and raised the umbrella. Trudy opened her side and ran around the car. Together, they unlatched the gate, squeezed through, and raced, bent against the rain, up the walk to the porch.

And stopped dead.

For there was the dog!

His brown coat was caked with mud, his mouth half opened in a fanged grin. He waited at the top of the porch steps just as if he belonged there.

"It looks like the dog that ran in front of the car," cried Trudy.

"It is," said Aunt Sue and took off, around the house and to the back door. Trudy followed at a dead run.

"Here," Aunt Sue threw the umbrella at her and twisted the keys on her key ring until she found the right one.

She unlocked the back door and yanked it open.

"But, Aunt Sue," cried Trudy.

"Get in here." Aunt Sue grabbed her, jerking her inside. The umbrella, still open, flew from Trudy's hand and rolled on the grass.

"Why did you *do* that?" demanded Trudy as soon as her aunt slammed the door. "Why did you tear around to the back? Look, you're soaked. So am I. . . . And my umbrella—"

"It was the dog," said Aunt Sue when she caught her breath. She was pressed against the door as if to form a barricade. "I won't go near the dog on the porch."

"Oh, come now." Trudy took off her aunt's coat and sat her down in a kitchen chair. She took off her shoes. "That dog won't hurt you. You said you liked dogs. Remember?"

Aunt Sue shuddered. "That's another thing," she said. "Maybe because I like dogs he became the biggest, meanest looking dog he could so I'd have something that scared me and something I didn't want." Aunt Sue started to cry.

Angrily, Trudy yanked off her own coat and stepped out of her shoes. "I don't know what you're talking about. Look, I'm going to make us some hot chocolate. Now you just sit there, Aunt Sue, and calm down. The dog'll go away. He was just trying to find some shelter from the rain. He happened to find your front porch."

"My front porch," said Aunt Sue. "There are many, many front porches between the cemetery and here, so he finds mine. Behind a fence and latched gate."

Trudy turned from the stove. "Maybe he jumped over the fence. And who says he came from the cemetery?"

"You did. You said, 'He looks like the dog that ran in front of the car.' And that was way out on Cemetery Road just before we turned off on the old highway."

Trudy turned back to the stove. "Lots of dogs look alike."

"Yes. Yes, they do," said Aunt Sue. "But this one left the cemetery right after we did. Then he ran in front of your car. Then he worked himself through a latched gate and found my front porch. Doesn't that mean anything to you? Don't you think he's telling us something?"

"No, I don't." Trudy felt a chill travel along her spine. "What's he telling us?" She poured the chocolate into two cups and took it to the table.

"He is telling us he's Fred," said her aunt.

The cups clattered. Chocolate spilled. A scratching noise sounded from the front door.

"He wants in," said Aunt Sue. "Fred wants inside his own house."

"Stop it!" cried Trudy. "He's just a stray mutt that wants in any house."

Her aunt shook her head.

The scratching became frantic. The rain beat down. Thunder roared. Trudy cleaned up the spilled chocolate. . . .

"You see," said Aunt Sue, "I learned a lot during those months your Uncle Fred was dying. I learned about reincarnation; that is when people come back as people. I learned about transmigration; that is when people come back as anything, a bird, a plant, an animal like Fred. Fred told me about it. He said I could never be rid of him. He said I'd have to go on taking care of him as I had always done."

The scratching was loud and grating as if the claws were digging deep into wood.

"Do you believe it?" asked Trudy.

"I didn't then," said her aunt.

"Now?" asked Trudy.

"Well, now I know that Fred is here."

The scratching stopped.

The rain poured. The thunder roared.

But the scratching stopped.

"Aunt Sue," cried Trudy, "the dog has stopped."

"For just a little while," said her aunt.

"I think he's gone."

"No, he isn't."

"I'll go look."

"Don't open the door," cried her aunt.

"I won't." Trudy raced to the front hall. She pulled the curtain aside and looked through the narrow window beside the front door.

She saw the dog as he stepped carefully down the porch stairs. She remembered how Uncle Fred always walked carefully down those stairs. He used to say: "They're dangerous. The risers are too high. The treads are too narrow. . . ." but Uncle Fred complained about everything. Anyway, this was a dog, not Uncle Fred.

She lost sight of the dog in the rain, and returned to the kitchen.

"He's gone," she told Aunt Sue.

"Did you see him go?"

"I saw him go down the steps. But the rain—"

"Well, he hasn't gone. Just wait."

They waited. And it came.

The sound of scratching. This time on the kitchen door.

Trudy screamed.

Then she jumped as the dog gave two sharp barks, sounding like "Gertrude," the name Uncle Fred used to call her, which she hated.

"I'm going to phone the dog pound," she told her aunt and slipped into her shoes.

"What for?"

"To come and get the dog," said Trudy. "There's a leash law, you know. That dog shouldn't be running around loose. The pound'll pick him up and that'll be the end of him."

"I hope so," said Aunt Sue. "But I don't think it will happen."

"It will. It's got to."

Aunt Sue put her shoes back on and walked to the window in the back door. She could look down on the dog as he scratched away. There was a bald spot on his head exactly like Fred's bald spot.

She walked back to her chair and sank wearily into it.

The storm gathered force. The winds blew.

Trudy walked from the kitchen to the hallway and flicked the wall switch. The lights did not go on. So—the electricity is out, she thought, and wondered if Aunt Sue had candles. Of course she did. The hall was dark. It was early evening, but black as night.

Trudy found the telephone on its stand. She inserted her finger in the last hole of the dial and circled it.

She told the operator she wanted the pound. "The animal-what-ever. The animal shelter."

"One moment please," said the operator.

Then—"Here's your party."

"There's a dog," Trudy said quickly into the phone. "He followed us—he's scratching at the doors. Can you come and—"

A streak of lightning brightened the hall and the phone went dead.

"No, no," cried Trudy and clicked the receiver. But the phone was gone.

She groped her way down the dark hall to the kitchen. There, gray light came through the windows.

"What happened?" asked Aunt Sue.

"The phone conked out."

"Of course," said her aunt. She cried out as if it hurt. "It's Fred. He won't let any outsiders in. The dog's even got a bald spot, Trudy. He's got Fred's bald spot. I looked out and saw it."

The dog growled from the back door. Trudy remembered how her uncle used to grumble when anyone reminded him of his bald spot.

"All right, Aunt Sue," she said. "Enough of that. You're bugging me. That's a dog out there, a common ordinary dog. If he's got a bald spot it probably means he's got the mange—"

The dog scratched at the door.

"Stop it," screamed Trudy. "Stop that. Go away. Get out of here." She turned to her aunt. "Look, Aunt Sue, I think we've got to get out of here. Go somewhere and get someone to come and take the dog away—"

"Not out there," cried Aunt Sue, horrified. "We can't go out there."

The rain was easing off. Lightning no longer flashed. The thunder did not roar. Trudy edged toward the door. She pressed her face against the window and looked down upon the dog. Sure enough, he had a bald spot . . . which doesn't mean a thing, Trudy told herself.

He scratched deeply on the door again and again. Then, abruptly, he turned and trotted away.

"He's gone," breathed Trudy. "This time, maybe he's really gone." She raced for the front door and, pulling aside the curtain, peered out, waiting for the dog to return to the porch.

He didn't come.

The rain had abated so that it no longer poured but dripped. But she was still unable to see as far as the fence, so she didn't know if he'd left the yard. Oh, he has, she thought—and back in the kitchen she told her aunt, "He's probably gone off to scratch on someone else's door."

Aunt Sue wasn't as sure, even after minutes passed without a sound of the dog. "What he's really done is he's gone off to figure out another way to get into the house."

"Oh, Aunt Sue, an ordinary dog can't figure out things like that."

"No," she agreed. "An ordinary dog can't . . ."

At that instant, a crash sounded within the house. Then a heavy thump.

Trudy tore across the room to the stove. She looked wildly about.

Aunt Sue sat straight in her chair. Not a muscle moved. "He remembered the loose screen in the bathroom," she breathed. "He climbed through the open window."

Trudy spied a heavy iron skillet and grasped it.

The dog bounded from the bathroom down the hall and sat, filling the doorway, the half grin on his face, fangs sharp and bright.

As close as he was, Trudy thought how much bigger he appeared—and fiercer.

The three were frozen in the faint light.

With the dog barring the way into the hall, Trudy and her aunt were trapped. If they tried to make it to the back door, the dog, in one leap, could mow them down and chew them to shreds.

Trudy didn't doubt but that he would do just that. His eyes blazed in the shadows of the kitchen. Spittle drooled from the sides of his mouth and turned to froth.

While the dog watched Aunt Sue, Trudy slowly lifted the skillet.

The movement, the deeper, shadowed movement, caught the dog's attention.

He turned and sprang.

Trudy hurled the skillet. She heard the crunch of bone. She felt teeth dig into her thigh and the spongy chill of froth slide down her leg.

The dog dropped. She edged around him and backed her way across the room. Thunder grumbled. The dog's body thumped convulsively against the floor. A lightning streak lit the windows. . . . In that moment and during that instant, the dog's body appeared to be haloed by that of a man which faded as the kitchen turned dark.

Trudy caught her breath and groped behind her for the table edge—something to hang onto, something to lean against. Thunder rolled through the sky again. Lightning flashed and the dog, just a dog now, lay quiet on the floor.

"So it was a dog after all. Just a dog," says Aunt Sue today.

"That's all." Trudy laughs with a quaver. "Of course, the dog happened to be mad and of course he happened to bite me so, of course, I had to go through all those rabies shots, but it was a dog after all. For that I am thankful. Just a dog."

"You said that all the time," says Aunt Sue.

"I did, didn't I?" Trudy answers. "I didn't know he was rabid, though, until I saw that froth. Then I knew," she shudders. "Hydrophobia means morbid fear of water. Did you know that, Aunt Sue?"

Aunt Sue nods. They had repeated this same conversation so many times that of course she knew. . . .

"So there it was—raining," continues Trudy. "The dog must have been *desperate* for a dry place. And *that's* the reason he followed us home."

"And we found him on the porch when we got there."

At this point in their reiterated discussion, Trudy wonders if her aunt realizes she has blown the practical, sensible, factual dog story all to bits and supplanted it with a theory, a legend, a myth of an Uncle Fred who, knowing where his home was, beat them to it.

She wonders.

She wonders if Aunt Sue saw the haloed image of Uncle Fred over that of the dog in the lightning flash that terrible funeral night.

Or did she see it herself?

She wonders if Aunt Sue sold her house and moved close to Trudy because she feared the return of something that might be a man.

She wonders.

She wonders about every stray animal she sees. Every plant her aunt buys and hangs in her apartment—the ferns with their fast-growing tentacles, the cacti with spines . . .

Trudy wonders and becomes impatient with herself for wondering. Because, of course, it was a dog. A stray dog looking for a dry place. A dog with mange. A mad dog. It just happened, that's all.

But still Trudy wonders.

And she wonders if her aunt wonders, too.

HOUSE BY THE ROAD

by Janet O'Daniel

" 'The night grew darker and a wind was rising as the storm howled around him. Trees bent and branches reached out toward him as he struggled forward along the lonely road. Suddenly a light shone out from a solitary house far ahead . . .' "

Irene put down the typed sheet. "Classic beginning, all right. Is it a spoof?"

Jane smiled. "I guess so. In a way. And I really haven't decided where to go with it. Want some more sherry?"

"Oh, I shouldn't—" Irene held out her glass. She had kicked off her shoes and was letting the fire warm her feet. "But why do it?"

"It's the irresistible first paragraph, isn't it? You just have to keep reading."

Irene yawned comfortably and sipped her sherry. "I'll take your word for it. You know about these things. Look, are you happy with the house? It's darling—I mean, I love what you've done with it, but somehow when you first told me you were buying it, I didn't think—you know—that you'd be moving in alone."

Neither did I, thought Jane, looking around at the room, its simple white curtains, its blue and white homespun covers, its old fireplace. There was a copper pot for firewood, there were blue

African violets in pots on the deep windowsills. A braided rug. She tried to see it with an impartial eye. Was it all too cute, too homey? Totally unsuitable for today—and for a man? A foolish affectation of simplicity and nostalgia? But he had never seen the house. That was not why—She heard again in memory the angry words, the slamming door.

"Is it something that's over?" Irene asked cautiously.

"Yes, it's over. He's gone to England for the summer."

"Well, possibly when he comes back—"

"No," Jane said shortly. "Not when he comes back either."

Irene asked no more questions and they went on talking, at ease with an old friendship, about times remembered, about the college where they both taught, about the summer that stretched ahead, neither of them probing deep where pain might hide.

"We'll be at the Cape for a few weeks. Come and visit," Irene begged.

"Too much to do here. I haven't even started on the yard and garden. It's a terrible tangle. And I plan to do a lot of writing."

"Sounds daunting."

"Well, a little. Which brings me to a problem. Do you know of somebody I can get to help—around the house, I mean?"

Irene frowned, concentrating on the problem. "I'll put out feelers. Is there just a drop more of that sherry?"

Was it important, Jane wondered, that you like someone who worked for you? Because at first meeting she didn't much take to Flora Hammel, a shapeless, dough-faced woman in green polyester pants, her short gray hair standing out stiffly.

She was what Jane thought of as a watcher. Her eyes slid narrowly around the room as they talked, taking in everything—curtains, furniture, Jane herself. Jane realized she had hoped for someone warmer, friendlier, perhaps a bit more reassuring. Still—

"I expect to be writing every morning in my room upstairs," she explained. "It's not a large house and there won't be a great deal for you to do. I was thinking perhaps two days a week? Then in the afternoons I'd like to work on the garden. I'll probably need a man to help with that. The place has been badly neglected for a long time. I don't suppose you know of anybody who does yard work?"

"Why do you need a man?"

"Why—no reason. I just thought—"

"Do it myself."

"It's fairly heavy work, some of it. Brush clearing, and I see a lot of brambles. Some dead wood that could be cut up for the fireplace—things like that. And I want to start a small garden of my own."

"I could give you a hand. Got all the tools, too. But suit yourself. A man would want more money," Flora said pointedly.

"Well, there is that." Jane gave a nervous little laugh because she could not quite picture herself working alongside Flora Hammel. She felt curiously trapped. "Suppose we give it a try then," she said weakly.

"Up to you," Flora said. Then she paused. "Writing what?"

"Mysteries. I write mysteries."

"Know a lot about that, do you?"

A lot about what? Jane wondered. Death, deduction, violence, evil?

"I teach English at the college," she said vaguely.

For the first time since she had entered the house, Flora Hammel's mouth twitched at the corners with something that looked faintly like amusement. "When do you want me to start?" she asked.

They decided on two days a week. Mornings Flora would work in the house; afternoons would be for outdoors. She was always prompt, driving up in an ancient blue Dodge, its fenders well corroded. She whipped through the house with her dusting, polishing, scrubbing, never making too much of it. The place was always immaculate by noon. Then in the afternoon the two of them would go out and work at clearing brambles and dead wood, trimming branches, routing last autumn's leaves which had never been raked. The little house, low and nestling close to the ground, stood on a slight rise, but the property behind it fell away in a broad sweep toward low ground which grew softer and boggier in its farther reaches. Jane had to admit that Flora was a capable worker. Also, the trunk of the ancient Dodge was loaded with tools.

"You need a grass hook for that," she would say. Or, "Wait a minute, I'll fetch the big secateurs. . . . Hold it now, we'll have to dig that root out. You got a spading fork? Never mind, I brought one. . . . Here, use the pruning saw for that limb . . ." She was bossy as a four-star general, but Jane, being a novice in such matters, listened meekly and did as she was told, learning as she went along.

"That there's mint—you'd better pull it up."

"Oh, but mint! And it smells so lovely."

"Never mind that. Look at the roots on it. Take over your whole yard if you let it."

"Could I dig it up and put it somewhere where it wouldn't be in the way?"

"Down there in the boggy part, maybe—where those ferns are. But only a sprig or two, mind. It'll spread."

Obeying meekly, Jane carried the fragrant plants down to the moist ferny corner, tucked them in and patted earth around them, reminding herself all the while that it *was* her house and her garden just the same.

One morning she came down from her study to find Flora dusting vigorously, shifting furniture around, tidying up piles of books and magazines in the living room. Something slid out from between the pages of a book and the woman bent to pick it up. Jane's face went warm and flushed as she recognized what it was. Flora regarded it with interest.

"Relative?" she inquired, glancing up from the picture.

"No, no. Just a friend," Jane said quickly. "I really don't know why I saved it."

"A nice-looking man," Flora said. "Except around the eyes."

Jane took the picture from her crossly. "What do you mean, around the eyes?" She glanced down at the face whose every expression had once spoken such a special language to her.

"Eyes give the show away. That's where you see the important things," Flora said, sliding one of her glances at Jane before she marched out of the room.

"Well yes, I've heard she's a little peculiar," Irene admitted with a grin. "But she seems to be doing all right by you. The place looks fine. In fact, it lifts my spirits, being here."

"Do your spirits need lifting?"

"Oh, not really. Only we broke up last week. He moved out."

"Oh dear. I am sorry."

"No, it's okay. Actually, there's someone else I've been seeing, which is why he moved out."

Jane wished inwardly that she could be as flip and easy about such things as Irene. Even loving the little house on the quiet road, she still felt pain on these soft spring evenings.

"Hey, how's the story going?" Irene asked. "The one with the irresistible beginning?"

"Oh—well, actually, I haven't had much time to work." But time was not the problem, Jane thought as a small worry prodded her. She seemed singularly devoid of ideas at the moment. Too much distraction getting the house settled, no doubt that was it. Only now she'd work regularly and it would start to come. It always had. . . .

Then one night there was a storm, wind and rain accompanied by enough thunder and lightning to make the living room and fire a nest of comfort. The lights blinked and dimmed but managed to stay on. It was enough warning, however, to prompt Jane to bring out candles in case they might be needed. She sat back cosily in her chair then and watched a television show in which fearless vice squad members in pastel outfits pursued malefactors and confronted them in crouching, two-handed gun stances. Jane kept dozing off and losing track of the plot.

The knock at the door startled her awake, and for a moment she felt muddled and fearful. This was a quiet road leading nowhere in particular. And on a night like this! She got up and approached the door cautiously, hesitated, then slid it open a crack.

The woman who stood there wet and disheveled was still unmistakably stylish. "I'm terribly sorry," the woman said. "I've probably scared you to death. But my car simply died out there on your road and I saw your light. I wonder if I could use your phone to call for help." She had a clear light voice, a cultivated speech that suggested to Jane private schools and a pony.

Jane hesitated for a moment, feeling the ricochet of her story bouncing around in her head, then peering behind the woman to see if accomplices lurked in the shrubbery, but the woman appeared to be helplessly, indeed wretchedly, alone.

"I don't blame you one bit," the woman said, and a held-back desperation sounded in her voice. "I just don't know what else to do."

It was the small catch in her voice that prompted Jane to throw the door open wide.

"Come in and sit by the fire," she said. "You look frozen."

The woman's relief was in her voice. "Oh, I am grateful. Perhaps I could telephone a garage in the village?"

"Yes, of course." Jane indicated the phone in the hall. But when the woman lifted it, "I'm not getting a dial tone," she said worriedly, turning to Jane.

"It's the storm," Jane said. "I'm sure it'll come back on. Why don't we sit here and let you dry out a bit and then you can try again."

"It's a terrible imposition," the woman apologized. "But I just can't say no. Your fire looks so lovely."

It had, in fact, died down while Jane dozed, but the coals were still hot and glowing. She added wood and it blazed up while she took the woman's wet coat. Jane took note of the handsome tweed skirt and the sweater that was surely cashmere. The coat had a Burberry label. The woman looked as if she might be thirty-five, but possibly forty; hard to tell. Long legs, slender feet, well-manicured nails. And dark hair caught back in a coil—not many women wore it that way any more. That marvelous look that Claire Bloom had always had, Jane thought. She poured sherry for both of them.

"I'm Anabel Starr," the woman said.

"Jane Gerard."

"This is really wonderful of you," Anabel Starr said. "And your house is an absolute dream. Have you lived here long?"

"Just moved in this year."

"I love it. Beautiful simplicity, and so tucked away and sort of out of things."

"Is there someplace you have to be?" Jane inquired. "I mean, will people be worried about you?"

"I was headed for the airport, and so of course I'll miss my flight, but that can't be helped." The woman seemed to hesitate. "No—no one's going to be worried about me."

Jane had taken note of a handsome leather case. "Traveling on business?"

"Yes. I work for the Pentelle firm. Cosmetics? I'm always flying someplace or other. I guess that's why a house like this appeals to me. So stable."

"To me, too," Jane admitted. "I fell in love with it. It's so right for one person."

Anabel's delicate eyebrows arched upward and Jane realized she had, without meaning to, admitted her solitariness. How had that happened? A vibrating tension of alikeness seemed to be thrumming between her and the stranger. She's alone, too, Jane thought.

"You live here by yourself then."

"Yes." Jane sighed. "I had thought—at first—that I might be sharing it with someone. It didn't work out."

"Oh dear, I didn't mean to pry," Anabel said.

"No, it's all right."

"Are you by any chance connected with the college? I noticed it as I drove past."

"I teach there, yes. In my free time I write."

"Really—what?"

"Mysteries."

"How wonderful! What power you must wield over all those lives you put on paper."

"I hadn't thought of it as power exactly," Jane laughed. "But yes, it is fun. Agonizing too, of course, when I get stuck."

They chatted lazily, sipping their sherry and confiding—just as she and Irene did, Jane marveled. Then Anabel got up to try the telephone again. "No luck," she said, frowning and holding out the lifeless instrument. Jane listened. "Oh well, not to worry," she said. "We'll try again in a while." She was, oddly, quite content to sit in the warmth of her little house with the strange woman, exchanging confidences and listening to the storm outside.

Presently in a quiet pause she said, "He's in England spending the summer. The one I'd thought might be sharing the house with me."

Anabel Starr nodded slowly. "I thought it might be something like that."

"Oh dear. Is it that obvious?"

"Only to someone who's been there." Both of them gave sad little laughs, and Jane got up to refill the glasses. In a curious way the mutual admissions had made them closer.

"Look," Jane said at last. "I'm afraid you're not going to get through to the garage tonight. And very likely they've closed up by now and gone home anyway. Why don't you stay here? I've a perfectly good spare room that no one's even used yet. You'd be the first. Then in the morning I'm sure we can get help for you."

"Oh, I couldn't!"

"Of course you could. Anyway, what else is there to do? And I'd love the company."

"It's really so—so very good of you."

Jane felt pleasantly satisfied as she showed Anabel to the small guest room tucked under the eaves with its sloping ceiling, its blue and white sprigged wallpaper, its candlewick bedspread.

"I think you'll sleep well here," she said with a mixture of shyness and householder's pride. "Here—you'll want this." She held out a nightgown.

"What a wonderful room!" Anabel cried. "I feel simply awful about this, but I know I'll sleep well. I can't thank you enough."

Jane herself fell asleep almost at once in her own room and slept soundly in spite of the roar of the storm and the rather exhilarating novelty of the situation. Now and then she dreamed—but of pleasant things like nutmeg and kittens.

In the morning the world was clear and washed, all its colors bright. Anabel Starr, after a night in a strange bed, still looked fresh and well groomed. The telephone was working, the local garage reached. By the time they had finished a breakfast of buttery toast and golden coddled eggs in blue bowls and drunk all the coffee down to the last of the pot, Mr. Kelly, the mechanic, had brought Anabel's car to the door, explaining that it was fixed, nothing serious, something about the distributor cap. And then Anabel was gone, leaning out of the car window and calling out, "Can't thank you enough, Jane—we'll keep in touch!"

Jane turned back to the house, feeling that the whole thing had in some curious way stretched her horizons. It had knocked out her classic story beginning, having turned out so well, but that was no matter. She would go to work on another idea that had been rattling around in her head.

Murder on campus. Possibly a visiting lecturer—she paused in front of the hall mirror. It was probably only the contrast with the stylish Anabel Starr, but she was looking downright seedy, she thought. Ragged hair in need of trimming and styling, and—she glanced down at her hands—those nails! Often she shucked off her garden gloves to get a better grip on something when she and Flora Hammel worked in the garden, and now her hands had a rough, worn look. Before she could change her mind she telephoned the beauty shop in the village and made an appointment for later in the day. Then she headed upstairs to straighten the spare room. Flora would not be coming until tomorrow.

As she pushed open the door it seemed to her that a faint smell of mold and mildew greeted her. She went to the window and threw it open, slightly embarrassed and hoping Anabel Starr had not noticed. Of course it was a little-used room and, too, there had been all that damp weather. But when she went to pull the bedclothes apart and remove the sheets for laundering, she took a backward step and put a hand on each side of her face.

The white sheets were smeared and smudged as if someone had crawled between them with unwashed feet. On the pillow where Anabel's shining-smooth head had lain were shadowy grease marks. The nightgown Jane had lent her was wadded up in a ball and stuffed under a pillow. When she drew it out she could smell the moldy smell again. For a moment she could only stare as the whole episode, which had seemed so pleasant, dissolved into something sour and unattractive. How was such a thing possible when someone looked so fastidious and well groomed? And how could she herself have been so completely fooled? So much for first impressions, she thought gloomily. There was something depressing about the incident that clung to her throughout the day. The little house, which had been so private, so much her own, seemed as soiled and violated as the sheets.

She kept her appointment at the beauty shop, although she had lost much of her first enthusiasm, and in the end she was glad, for her mood lightened as she began to see herself turning sleek and elegant. Her ragged nails were manicured, her hair shampooed and trimmed, styled into a bouncy short cut. She returned home to find the house smelling sweet and fresh once more, and this time her image in the hall mirror reassured her. Really, she told herself, she was much too quick to take things to heart. No real harm had been done. Even so, she slept less soundly that night. Soft animal footsteps padded on the roof, disturbing her. Living here she would have to get used to squirrels and raccoons, of course, she reminded herself. But in the morning as she dressed a new smell assailed her. Unmistakably, a mouse had died somewhere behind the walls. Oh well, that was country living, too, she supposed.

"What in the Sam Hill do you call this?" Flora scowled and held up a sheet. "Looks like you been having orgies."

"Oh that." Jane hesitated. How much of the story did she really want to explain? But how could she *not* explain with Flora standing there holding the grimy sheet? And what was there to be ashamed of anyway? She sighed.

"It was something that happened night before last," she said. "During that heavy rainstorm?" Flora listened, and Jane told the whole story as quickly and simply as possible, then waited for a reaction—a shake of the head, a derisive hoot of laughter—she had already learned that Flora expressed herself forthrightly. Instead, the woman remained impassive, her face bland and almost without reaction. "Well," she said at last. "Fancy that." She turned and stuffed the soiled sheet into the washing machine along with the rest of the linens, added detergent and turned the switch to *on*. Over the sound of the water rushing into the tub she asked, "What'd she say her name was?"

"She *said* it was Anabel Starr," Jane replied, qualifying it because after all, the woman had not turned out to be what she seemed; her name too could be suspect. "Said she traveled for some cosmetics firm called Pentelle."

Flora Hammel wiped her hands on the front of her flowered apron and headed out of the small laundry alcove into the kitchen. After a moment she turned back.

"Did you know you got a cat on your roof?" she asked.

Jane stood away from the house, shaded her eyes against the morning sun and peered upward. "So *that's* what I heard. I'll bet he's been there all night! Not much to look at, is he?"

It was a ragged black tomcat with a torn ear, bony and bitter-looking. His tail switched angrily and as the two women watched he got up, stalked across the roof peak and back, and sat down again.

"What's he doing on my roof?" Jane frowned. "Oh dear, the poor thing's probably hungry. Maybe I should feed him."

"You never get rid of an animal if you do that," Flora said, tucking her hands into her apron front.

"Well no. I suppose not. Still, I wouldn't mind having a cat. I'm sure there's a mouse dead in the woodwork somewhere. I smelled it this morning."

The cat let out a long drawn-out yowl and paced back and forth again. Jane shivered. "He's really not the kind of cat I want, though. I mean, I'd like one that looks a little friendlier. Maybe I should call the SPCA to come get him."

"Leave him alone," Flora advised. "Chances are he'll take off on his own." They started back into the house. "What about that mouse? What do I do about that?" Jane asked.

"Give that some time, too. Take a few days for the smell to go away. Ain't anything else you can do unless you tear down the walls."

Jane steered her mind away from the process which would take a few days. "Is it too wet for the garden today?"

"Oh, no, it looks pretty good to me. You could plant those things you bought. You know what I got out at my place? A tire—well, an old one—I white-washed it and planted geraniums in it. Maybe I could locate another one if you'd want it."

Jane gave her a nervous look. "Oh, I guess I'll just put them in those pots I found in the cellar—thank you anyway."

Flora shrugged.

It was a shady garden, but since Jane could not bring herself to part with venerable oaks and copper beeches, she set out shade-loving plants—hosta and impatiens, astilbe, ferns, lilies. She saved the one sunny spot, on the front doorstep, for a big pot of red geraniums. When she was done, she told herself that now that was off her mind she would get down to some real work on the new mystery. She spent several mornings sharpening pencils and cleaning her typewriter. She changed the ribbon and bought a fresh ream of paper. She checked prices on word processors.

Then she began making lists. One sheet was headed *Ideas* and another *Things To Look Up.* Then one morning she walked into her study and had just sat down at her desk when a large slab of plaster fell from the ceiling, landing in dusty chunks and crumbs on paper, books, and typewriter. Jane gave a loud, startled cry and jumped up, backed against the wall and suddenly started sobbing. By the time Flora got upstairs she had brought the tears under control and was looking angrily at the gap in the ceiling.

"Of all the messy, maddening—" she fumed. "I suppose there's a leak in the roof somewhere. Isn't that why plaster falls? Because it's gotten wet?"

"Could be," Flora agreed, but she was looking at Jane's face rather than at the fallen plaster. Jane saw the look.

"I'm all right, Flora," she said. "It's just that my work hasn't been going very well, and I can still smell that damned mouse and now this. I'm okay, honestly. I'd better go look in the yellow pages for somebody to fix the ceiling."

"I've done some plastering," Flora said, but absentmindedly, as if it were only a minor accomplishment in her catalog of skills. "I'll take care of it. Look, why don't you do something else today—go outdoors or something. Forget about work." There was a gentler note in her voice than Jane had heard before, and the stocky frame, the nimbus of wiry gray hair, the putty face, even the probing gimlet eyes, seemed to offer reassurance.

"Maybe I'll do that," Jane agreed weakly.

She glanced up at the roof as she went out, but the black cat had not reappeared. She walked around the house, inspecting the things she had planted, then returned to the front steps and sat in the sun near the geraniums, closing her eyes.

She could smell the faint spicy odor of the flowers beside her. But after a time the smell grew stronger, and instead of being pleasant it was sharp and rank, almost a smell of decay. She opened her eyes. A huge toad was sitting near her on the stone step, its bulging eyes staring at her.

I will not scream, she told herself firmly. Her gardening books said that toads were a gardener's best friend—they ate insect pests. It was just that this was such a very large one. Giddily her mind ran back over those silly horror-movie titles *he* had once made up to amuse her. *The Eggplant That Ate Chicago.* That sort of thing. *The Toad That Ate Jane Gerard.* She got up suddenly and went into the house. Flora was on her way downstairs with dustpan, bucket, and broom. Her eyebrows went up in a question.

"Biggest toad I ever saw in my life," Jane explained, managing to laugh. "It came right up and sat beside me on the front step just now."

Flora stood quite still for a moment. Her mouth was tightly pursed like a drawstring bag. At last she said, "Come on into the kitchen. You and me better have a little talk."

She made fresh coffee and sat opposite Jane at the round wooden table. Stubby fingers were curved around the white cup. After a long thoughtful silence she said, "What it is, you see—all these things happening—this place has a spell on it."

Oh my God, Jane thought desperately. She's absolutely mad. Here I am sitting in my own kitchen with a woman in an apron and lavender stretch pants, and she's crazy as hell.

"Haunted? Is that what you mean?"

Flora shook her head impatiently. "No, no. Nothing like that. That's a different can of worms entirely. Your unquiet spirits, your ghostly manifestations. No, this is another matter. And a really well-laid spell's nothing to take lightly, let me tell you. Give me unquiet spirits any time."

"But how do you know—about the spell?"

Flora Hammel sipped her coffee and set her cup down. "I've got gifts."

Jane, beginning to see the humor in it and to surrender to unreality, felt that she had definitely passed from the world of the rational. But what difference did it make after all? By this time next week the ceiling in the study would be fixed, the house would be aired out and life would be going on as usual. "What sort of gifts?"

"Oh—" Flora made a flinging gesture with one hand. "You know, seeing things, knowing things. And special things happening to me. During the great flood of '35 when it poured for two days, I went out and played hopscotch—came in dry. Things like that. It's a mixed blessing, of course." She paused, then added, "Actually, I could easily have been a witch."

"Really," Jane said dryly.

Flora nodded. "In fact," when I was younger I did have a go at it—briefly. I didn't care for it. You weren't supposed to miss any of your coven meetings—because of needing thirteen present, you know? Things like that. They got testy about it once or twice when I didn't show up and finally I said look, it's not for me. But the other things you never lose. The gifts." Her eyes narrowed as if to see into distance.

"And that's what makes you think—I mean, is that how you can tell a spell when you see it?" The woman nodded again. "But who's doing it?"

Flora sat back in her chair and gave Jane a direct, scrutinizing stare. "You went to the beauty shop the other day."

"What on earth has that to do with anything?"

"Sudden decision, wasn't it?"

"I thought I needed a bit of improving."

"Hair uneven, nails choppy—"

"Yes." The air in the kitchen grew still around them.

"Day after that woman stopped here, wasn't it?"

"She was so well groomed. I felt shabby. Later, of course—" There was a silence in which both of them thought of the sheets. Then Jane heard a buzzing sound and realized Flora was humming low, something droning and with no tune. Finally she stopped humming and said, "She cut off some of your hair and took some nail clippings while you slept."

Jane burst out laughing. "Flora, that's absolutely ridiculous! I slept very peacefully that night. If anybody'd crept in to cut off my hair and nails I'd have wakened!"

Flora said, "Hair and nail clippings, ball 'em up in hot wax, you got the start of a good spell."

"Well, if she's putting a hex on me she's doing it long distance. She took a plane out of here the next day."

Flora was shaking her head back and forth slowly. "She's right here. She never left."

Jane felt the room turn cold around her. The chair she sat in trembled slightly. Small hairs rose along her arms. "Oh come on," she said, but her mouth had turned dry and her voice cracked.

"They want this place, you see."

"They?"

"There's two of them. There's her—her real name's Bella. I know her from way back. And then there's Gloud."

I am really right down the rabbit hole, Jane thought helplessly. "Gloud—" she murmured.

"Actually, Gloud's higher up. He's giving the

orders. Bella never could do anything but follow instructions."

"Higher up?"

"Upper echelons. Much closer to the seat of power."

"Are you talking about—" Jane felt another quivering of her chair. The mouse smell seemed to be invading the kitchen.

"I recognized him," Flora said. "Very first time I saw him on the roof I knew we were in for trouble."

"On the roof. That *cat?*"

"And of course just now, when you were sitting on the front step—"

"The toad."

"That was Bella. She's not bright, but I will say she was always good at transmutation. For myself I think it's a little on the showy side."

"Why do they want my house?" Jane demanded suddenly.

"My guess is they've been living here right along and don't like being pushed out—it was vacant a good while before you bought it. And it's a nice out-of-the-way place, good hunting for Gloud down in the bog. I suppose it's not often they find a place that suits them so well. But actually, they don't have to have reasons." Flora took a swig of coffee. "I was suspicious when you told me that name, Anabel Starr. Stuck a bit of her true name in there—*bel*, you see, from Bella. And Starr, of course, from the pentacle. Five-pointed star—they always use that."

"And Pentelle Products," Jane added. Then, realizing what she had said, she scraped her chair back noisily and got up.

"I do appreciate your telling me all this, Flora," she said. "But for now I think we'll just let things go along as they have been. I'm sure it will all work out."

Flora finished her coffee and wiped her mouth on a corner of her apron. "Suit yourself," she said. "I better get to work on that plastering now."

Jane insisted on helping, but even with the two of them working, it took most of the day to make the repairs. Dropcloths had to be draped over everything, a ladder hauled upstairs. Putty knives, chisels, and plastering compound were produced from the trunk of the Dodge. When it was done, late in the day, both of them stood off and admired the smooth wet patch, Flora with chips of plaster in her bushy hair, her coverall apron smeared and dusty. "Not a bad job if I do say so," she said modestly, and Jane said, "Flora, you're unbelievable! It looks wonderful!" The new clean plaster smell was a reassurance. It was her house again, whole and right. And Flora might be a crazy old country type but who cared? What was a world without room for a little craziness?

"And I won't let you go home without something to eat," she said. "Not after all that work. Let's wash up and fix some supper." She glanced outside and saw that it was darkening. "Looks as if we may have some more rain."

Flora turned away and began picking up her tools, and once again Jane could hear her low tuneless humming. This time she was determined not to let the situation slide away from her. "I took a nearly defrosted chicken out of the refrigerator a few minutes ago," she said. "We'll stick it under the broiler and make ourselves a nice salad to go with it."

She picked up the dropcloths and shook them out the window, noting as she did so how the wind was rising. Another stormy night, she thought, remembering the last one.

"There now." She closed the window and

folded the cloths, snapping them firmly and making sure all the corners matched. Because things should be orderly. Corners should meet and edges should be straight, and if you saw to that, why everything would be perfectly all right— She stopped herself quickly. "I'll go down and get that chicken started," she said.

Flora followed her down the stairs, carrying tools. It seemed to Jane that with each step the house grew colder. The front hall held a damp chill that made her shiver. She marched with military resolution back to the kitchen, and the cold seemed to follow like a cloud, moving when she moved. She saw the chicken on the counter by the sink where she had left it, and then in the next instant saw that it was not a chicken. And screamed. She could hear her own scream crashing off the walls with a shattering sound. The dropcloths fell to the floor. Flora set down her tools with a clanking sound and stepped over to the sink. Jane stood frozen in the center of the room, hugging herself to hold things together, to keep her whole body from flying apart.

"Don't touch it!" she screamed. But Flora had already lifted the severed hand, using two fingers. She dropped it smartly into the kitchen garbage pail and let the lid bang down over it.

"Nothing to get excited about," she said airily. "It's just the old severed hand dodge. Easy trick. Some Ajax will take care of that stain." She proceeded to clean it up, sponging and sudsing lavishly. "Now then." She folded her arms and frowned, making what seemed to be an executive decision. "We'll have to get down to business. Actually it's a good thing this happened. Brings matters to a head. I was wondering when they'd make their move. Now I'm sure it's going to be tonight."

"What are they going to do?" Jane asked in a hoarse whisper.

"Try to get you out of here. A power struggle, is what it is."

Jane grabbed a chair and lowered herself into it stiffly. For a moment she sat there, rigid. Then at last she said in a low bitter voice, "Well, they can have it as far as I'm concerned. I don't know who they are—who's doing all this, and I don't care. I don't want to live in a place where people do such awful things."

"Going to just turn it over to them? Shoot, now, you don't want to do that, do you?"

"It's wicked and it's evil, whatever's going on here, and I won't stay, that's all. I'll sell the place and get out."

Flora's shoulders suggested a faint shrug. "Well, that's up to you. But meantime, there's tonight."

"What do you mean?"

"Well, I mean—here we are, aren't we?"

Jane looked at her, then at the sheltering walls and windows of the little house, all of which had seemed up to now so safe. Now they pressed in on her, imprisoning her. They no longer seemed straight, but leaned slightly as if from outside pressure. She closed her eyes and then opened them and the walls were straight again.

"What can we do?" she whispered.

Flora strode back and forth across the kitchen, shedding plaster dust as she went. "I have an idea. But I'll need some things from my car. And that may be a trick. Once I'm out they won't want me to get back in."

The door was hinged to swing outward, and even with the two of them inching it open carefully, the wind grabbed it from their hands and sent it all the way back, whacking against the house. While Flora made her way down the walk to where the Dodge was parked, Jane managed to get it shut again. She leaned against it and watched as Flora took from the trunk a large burlap bag, bulging and tied with rope. As she slammed the lid down and turned to start back, a gust of wind bent the trees wildly and struck her head on, causing her to stagger and go down on one knee. She got to her feet and plodded on, clutching the bag. The wind tore at her with every step. Her gray hair stood on end. By the time she reached the house she was bent almost double. Jane waited until the last minute before opening the door. Once again it was pulled out of her hands, but Flora tossed the bag inside quickly and the two together were able to pull the door shut. "Aroint thee!" Flora gasped. "Aroint thee, dammit!"

At once she pulled herself together. "Well now. So far so good," she said. "Let's start a fire in the fireplace."

But smoke billowed out into the room when Jane lit the kindling. She backed up, coughing. "Something's blocking the chimney!"

Flora, busy untying the rope from around the sack, gave the fireplace a glance. "I expected that," she said with a short nod. "No matter. Two can play that game." She began pulling from the bag sticks, twigs, and some dried plants that had a stiff, moribund look.

"What *is* all that?"

"Oh—hemlock, henbane, adder's tongue, nightshade, moonwort, wolfbane—a few other things."

"Do they grow around here?"

"Some, and some grows far afield, but I know their secrets, I mind where to seek 'em out." Flora's speech was slipping in and out of archaic cadences, Jane noticed. She pulled out a small dried cluster of dusty gray and held it up.

"Angelica," she said solemnly. "It's a holy plant."

She began tossing them in small handfuls into the struggling fire. "Bring some candles," she ordered Jane. "We'll lay 'em out in five points."

Jane hurried to obey, and placed the candles according to Flora's instructions. The room was filling with smoke, but it no longer made her eyes and throat sting. It was a cloudy mist now, fragrant and soft, and it moved around her in slow swirls. Flora had pulled from the bag a rusty black cape, badly wrinkled, which she threw around her shoulders, and she ordered Jane to sit beside her once the candles were lighted. "Adder's tongue and penny-royal," she intoned, "elder, alder, work to spoil. Darnel, bryony, leopard's-bane—" She broke off and said fussily, "We really could use some good horse dung, but I don't much like carrying it around in the trunk—oh well, no matter, we'll make do. *Tán hlyta, tán hlyta—*"

"What is it we're doing exactly?" Jane asked.

"It's a form of fumigation, I guess you'd say—turning their own bag of tricks against them, actually. Of course the words count, too." And once again she began mumbling, phrases that Jane could not make out. Jane closed her eyes and listened, finding a curious peace and reassurance in the aromatic smoke and in Flora's mumbling.

A sheet of rain hit the windows with a crashing sound and thunder made the little house tremble. There was a rumbling overhead followed by a roar as something hit the roof. Jane guessed that the chimney had gone over. A brick came crashing down into the fireplace, scattering sparks. Outside, voices that sounded disembodied began to moan and wail. A window shattered, flinging glass across the floor and creating a draft that blew outward rather than in, so that Jane began to feel herself drawn toward the opening. Her eyes widened. She looked around in alarm and saw that the wall above the fireplace had cracked. Blood was running from the crack and streaming downward. The draft pulling Jane toward the window grew stronger. "Flora!" she shouted, and reached out for the older woman's hand. But when she touched it, it was cold and dead, a corpse's hand. Jane let out a wild scream and dropped it, but then felt Flora's arms grab hold of her and hang on tight, pulling her back. The wails from outside rose in pitch and Jane could feel a dizzy whirling sensation as if she were being turned round and round fast. But Flora's grip on her did not falter. The smoke from the fire seemed to wrap them more and more tightly in its thickening substance. Slowly the voices from outside grew fainter. At last, after one fierce feline yowl, they faded altogether. Silence moved in around them and Flora's grip loosened. Into the sudden stillness came a loud knock at the front door. Jane, rubbing her arms against the cold, looked around. "Do I dare answer that?" she whispered. "Is it—I mean—could it be—"

Flora held up a hand for silence, squinted with concentration and listened as the knock came again. She gave a curt nod. "It's all right. You can open it."

"I'm terribly sorry," the man said, standing in the doorway with rain dripping from his disheveled hair. "I've had a blowout down there on your road and it's sent me into a ditch. I'm afraid I'm going to need a tow. Could I possibly use your telephone to call someone?"

Jane thought of the lean stalking cat on the roof. Gloud. He was obviously good at transmutation, too. Quite capable of assuming a pleasant shape like this tall rangy man, capable of smiling an apologetic one-sided smile. She scanned his face, studying it carefully. She saw how the eyes crinkled up at the corners, how blue they were and how straight and clear their gaze. *Eyes give the show away. That's where you see the important things*—She took note of the damp red sweater he was wearing; one sleeve was out at the elbow. She thought that he did not know about the hole in the sleeve, and that seemed curiously touching.

"Please come in," Jane said.

He still looked apologetic. "I hope I didn't scare you. It's a bad night." Once again their eyes met.

"No, it's all right." Jane turned and led the way in. Her head had gone light and fuzzy. The house spun around her in a smoky haze as if it were righting itself, making adjustments. Slowly, carefully, she put one foot after the other, trying to remain in the real world.

"The phone's on the hall table," she said, enunciating clearly. "Kelly's garage is the place to call. Do you see the number right there?"

"I do, yes." And while he stood in the little front hall dialing, she went back into the living room.

The haze had cleared; the fire was snapping on the hearth, drawing strongly up the chimney. Chairs were sitting correctly, the braided rug lay smooth across the floor. Walls stood straight; the polished windows gave back her reflection. On the deep sills African violets rested solidly in their earthen pots. Not cute or quaint at all, Jane thought, assessing the room. Strong and simple—it even had a certain rough charm. A place that would suit a man quite well.

Flora, broad and solid in her lavender stretch pants, was bending over from the waist, puffing a little and stowing something in a bag—an ordinary shopping bag, it appeared to be, the kind one used at the A&P.

"Well now," she said crisply, "I'll be getting along."

Jane felt memory slipping away from her. She tried to grasp it and hold on. "Flora, is it all right?" she whispered anxiously. "I mean—did you get a look at his eyes?"

Flora nodded. "Looked safe enough to me. Anyway, you see how the room's cleaned up."

"What do you mean?" Jane tried to remember something. Candles and blood and broken glass were in her head, but jumbled and unclear.

"Love," Flora said. "The first impact can do a lot of that transformation business—pretty basic stuff. But it's no match for a really well-laid spell." She picked up the shopping bag, drew herself up straight, and gave Jane a severe warning look. "For that you have to call in a pro every time. And don't you forget it."

THE GHOST OF MONDAY

by Andrew Klavan

By Friday, it was gone. Fletcher read the paper on his way home from Wall Street, and there was not a sign of it. The blackout at Grand Central Terminal had replaced it on the front page. Within, it had given way to an anti-import demonstration in the garment district and a drug-related shootout in the Heights. It amused him. After all his worry, all his wrestlings with the inner angels of conscience and fear, it had not even been news for a week. In the great tidal wave of events, it was a droplet. It had vanished without a trace.

He threw the newspaper away before he got on the elevator. He rode upstairs with his hands folded in front of him and his eyes trained on the doors. A corner of his mouth twitched upward: the suggestion of a smile. Other than that, he betrayed nothing.

He loosened his tie as he entered his apartment. He kicked off his shoes as he shut the door. He liked the feel of the shag beneath his stockings. He tossed his briefcase down by the bar and poured himself a drink.

He drank standing by the window, looking down on Fifth Avenue. He watched the string of green traffic lights running away into the crystal darkness. He watched the cabs' red taillights weaving beneath them, and beneath the golden crown atop the Crown Building, and the solemn iron cross atop the red brick steeple of the Presbyterian church, and between all the avenue's towering, concrete walls, which narrowed to the vanishing point.

The tapping annoyed him. This was the third day he had heard it. He knew it was coming from the bathroom and suspected it was in the pipes, but he wanted to make sure before he called a plumber. It was probably a steady thing, but it entered his consciousness now as if it had just begun again after a pause. He flinched and turned toward the noise just in time to see a flutter of tan skirt disappear around the hall corner.

"What the hell," Fletcher said. He put his drink down on the coffee table. He walked to the hallway.

He called: "Hello?" Then he snorted. "Good, Fletcher, talk to yourself," he said aloud.

Still, he went down the hall. There were three doors down there. The bathroom was to the right, the bedroom to the left, the closet straight ahead. He flicked on the bedroom light, glanced in. Nothing there. Of course there was nothing there. He tried the closet, feeling silly. Finally, he hit the bathroom light, and went in.

The tapping seemed to come from someplace right next to the tub. He couldn't pin it down exactly. It was a steadily repeated rap, muffled, like someone knocking on the door of a neighboring apartment. All the sounds of the building traveled through the bathrooms. You could never tell which apartment they were coming from.

He stood looking down at the tiles beside the tub, he noticed an odd smell. Faint, but thick, swampy. The tapping must be caused by something backing up in the pipes. He thought: Tan skirt. She always did dress well. But blackmail is blackmail, all the same.

The thought was unbidden. He shook it off. He turned to go. But as his eyes crept across the mirror over the sink, he had an odd sensation. It seemed to him for a moment as if his reflection had paused while he turned. Paused to stare at him and smile while he continued to turn away. He wheeled back to it. It was just as it should be. Everything was just as it should be.

Irritated, he grimaced at himself in the glass. He killed the bathroom light and stepped across the hall to the bedroom again.

He decided to get undressed. He'd get into bed, maybe give the Walker papers another once-over. There was not a thing wrong with them, he knew that, but it would put his mind at ease. It was a special trust, after all. The boss had assigned it to him personally. The boss would have handled it himself, in fact, if he hadn't been so distraught about his wife.

He went to the bedroom closet and opened the door. There was a man standing inside, waiting—a man with wild laughter in his eyes and an axe in his hands. The man stepped forward, raising the axe above his head. Fletcher had time to let out one high-pitched shriek, and then the man buried the blade in his brain.

And was gone. He seemed to pass right through Fletcher. The blade did not bite flesh or smash bone. It simply dissolved on contact and disappeared. Fletcher reeled backward. He sat down hard on the bed. His face sank into his hands. He felt sick at his stomach. The man with the axe: it had been he. It had been Fletcher himself.

Slowly, he looked up, looked around him at the empty room. Had he really had such madness in his eyes? He hadn't felt mad. He had felt very calm, very logical. Remembering the old camping axe like that. He hadn't used it in years.

The tapping began again, louder now. And drifting from the bathroom with it came that rancid smell. He tried not to take it in, but it crawled into his nostrils. It seemed to drip, viscid, down the back of his throat.

He cursed: a small, strangled noise. He stood. His fists clenched, he strode into the bathroom. He paused there in the dark, the smell thick all around him, clogging his senses, the tapping louder, clouding his mind. He held his breath. With an angry sweep of his hand, he snapped on the light.

The tub was filled with blood again.

"Damn!" He growled it now. A single step took him to the tub's edge. He reached down for the chain on the drainage plug.

Her hand rose, dripping, out of the bath and grabbed him. Her fingers wrapped tightly around his wrist. He felt the dampness of them. As he tried to pull free, he saw the diamond on her engagement ring flash in the light. Crazily, he thought: Had she been anyone but the boss's wife. Had she just not threatened to tell.

The strength of the hand was preternatural. It dragged him toward the blood-filled tub. The tapping was like thunder now inside his head. He cried out and pulled free.

The hand sank down, out of sight. The tapping ceased. Only the blood remained. He wanted to close his eyes, to make it vanish. He couldn't. He was afraid.

Instead, he stood staring as the blood began to drain away. It drained slowly, with a soft gurgle. He kept staring as the level sank lower and lower. It was low enough so that nothing could be hidden beneath, but he kept staring. Finally, the last of it spiraled down. The tub was empty.

The tub had to be empty. He had seen to it, had scrubbed it thoroughly when he was finished. The hand, the arm—all the pieces—he had loaded them into the trunk, one by one. It had made him gag to do it, but he had gotten it done. Loaded them into the trunk and thrown the trunk in. . . .

All at once, the tapping returned. It was a pounding now. It was right beside him. He spun around. The trunk had come back. It was sitting on the bathroom floor again. The pounding came from inside it. It grew louder and louder. The top of the trunk began to shudder with the force of it. The top of the trunk began to rise.

Fletcher was babbling as he ran from the apartment. He was laughing as he tore down the firestairs; out into the lobby; out into the night. He was still laughing when the cop found him. He was sitting under a streetlight, hugging his knees and laughing. When the officer leaned toward him to check him out, Fletcher looked up at him and smiled. He crooked his finger at the cop, and the cop leaned closer.

"Nothing vanishes," Fletcher said, giggling. Then he told the whole story.

The cop was spellbound.

SITTER

by Theodore H. Hoffman

It's shortly after you've checked on the kids again that you hear the first noise.

You're sitting on the couch, sipping Diet Coke. Their Diet Coke; it tastes funny, somehow. Minutes ago you'd tiptoed up the stairs, peering in on the kids, hoping the light from the hallway wouldn't disturb them. Even in such dim light you could see the bruise on little Brian's cheek. A fall, Mrs. Redgrave ("Oh, please call me Cam!") had said. But you'd watched the way Brian had held back from his parents, clinging to Samantha. None of the standard histrionics (hooray for vocabulary tests), the tears and the "don't go's." It had seemed like shyness, normal in kids when around strangers. Now, you realize it had been fear. Fear of Mr. Redgrave, mostly, with his marble eyes and too-moist grin. A man who wanted things his way, and was willing to use force to get them. Yes: You can see it now in your mind's eye, more clearly than when it happened, when they walked out the door ("We'll be back by eleven! Take care of our babies!") and climbed into the BMW (of course) and zipped off to their little party. Then, you had been pleased that Mrs.—Cam—had not gone through that little speech the other mothers all did, "the emergency numbers are right next to the phone" (with that distant look of suspicion in their eyes). You'd thought that meant she trusted you. Now, you understand it meant she didn't care.

The kids were terrific, just as Nance had said. Quiet kids. The kind you want to have someday. Not like some of the brats you've sat for (usually just once), not weird like in the movies where they crawl out of your womb with bloody claws and hate in their oversized brains. . . .

They'd gone to bed right when they were supposed to. You tucked them in carefully, humming to them. At five and two and a half, so pure, so simple. So helpless. You'd asked Brian about that bruise, and he hesitated only a moment before echoing his mother's story about The Fall in the Front Yard. But hesitated nonetheless. What did he have to be afraid of, you'd wondered; and then Mr. Redgrave rose in your mind's eye like a vampire at dusk.

And now you've heard a noise.

—)scruff(—

Frozen, holding your breath, can of soda angled so near your lips, you strain to listen. (DDDUU-Uhhhnnnn . . . swells the trembling pipe organ in your head.) Nothing; even the silence is quiet, for once. You let out your breath, and wonder if you should have a look around. Check on the kids. ("Why don't you check the children," and there's Carol Kane, getting the phone call from the police telling her that those murderous, obscene phone calls have been coming from *inside the house* and the door to the kids' room is creaking open and)

(STOP IT.)

Silence. You sit back. Smiling. You're not going to be like the girls in those stupid movies, going to investigate every sound, usually with (HA) a stupid candle, and the psycho whose escape from the nuthouse you'd heard about on the radio (never never play the radio or TV while babysitting, too much chance you'll hear or see something unpleasant, stick to the cassettes, Barry Manilow and Bon Jovi), the psycho is waiting around the corner with nail clippers, waiting to do ungodly things to you. . . . Then again, there are the fools in the war movies, the sentries who hear something and shrug and go back to their card game, and wind up with an extra mouth gaping between their eyes. . . .

Damn it. (Why do you do this, why do you do this every stupid time?)

You get up. Pace. It's a lovely house, big and soft and bright. (Jack Nicholson could get lost in here, too) (now STOP it.) You listen to your breathing, settle it down, grip the can more tightly. Walk over to the photos on the fireplace mantel. Yup: the Grand Canyon (Hello! you mouth to the frozen family waving to you, Cam cradling little Brian as though to pitch him over the side). Niagara Falls (why do parents let their kids so near the rails? You can see the headlines—*dead*lines, that voice inside your head says—"KID FALLS TO WATERY DEATH AS STUPID PARENTS

—)click(—

—now what *was* that.

You listen, stock-still, and the silence seems to be whispering now, but your mind tries to comfort you: Hey. Houses, even new ones, settle at night. Calm down. They have a cat, remember? You haven't seen it since you put the kids to bed, and it hasn't come near you, it's scared, remember? The doors and windows are locked. You've checked. Calm down.

You let out your breath. You feel it empty from your lungs, inflate your cheeks, rush over your lips; and you do it again just to replay the feeling. There's something reassuring about it.

(Yeah—the dead can't breathe) (oh now just STOP it!)

Quiet.

Quiet.

(TOO quiet, your mind says, and you think SHUT UP! and your mind does, angrily and reluctantly.) You realize you are in a vulnerable position. They could come from so many directions. From the hallway to your left. From behind the wall obscuring most of the foyer, which leads to the kitchen. (Is that where the sounds are coming from? The kitchen?) (. . . knives . . .) (TOLD YOU TO SHUT UP!) From the window behind you, with that flimsy lock you keep checking. From the fireplace. (THE SANTA CLAUS MURDERS, the deadline screams, and they get Jamie Lee Curtis to play you in the movie and it's called *Santa Claws,* and at the climax there's a slayride, and there's Jamie Lee on the living room floor with her face sheared off and the blood isn't pouring or spurting my God it's *bubbling* like when you blow through a straw into a strawberry shake, and out in the woods the masked killer is cupping your face in his hands and it's still alive, your eyes blinking and your mouth trying to form words, and he's leaning to kiss you with his leathery wet lips and his tongue curls inside your mouth, licking his palms, and HIS EYES ARE MR. REDGRAVE'S) and there's a pounding, someone at the door? behind the wall? upstairs in the kids' bedroom (oh my God not there, anywhere but there) . . . ? And you whirl around before you realize the pounding is your heart, just seventeen years old and trying to work itself into a coronary (like Daddy's and) (damn it) (*he* lived). . . .

—)Scruff(.

You hear it. It's not like the other times, the

other houses. You *know* you hear it. You still don't know what it is—your mind's not even goading you with guesses any more—but it is a noise and it seems to be coming from the kitchen and it is caused by something. *Some*thing. (Or some *thing,* that voice adds, smiling wickedly, but you expected it to say that) and you shake your head and, aloud, say, "No."

The sound is swallowed by the house, tasted, passed quickly from corner to corner, room to room, chair to rug to banister to front door. "No." You hear it whispered hungrily around you; and you know you do not hear it, and you listen until it fades away.

In that eye of stillness, you do what you always do, what you must do. You devise escape routes. Contingencies; that's what they're called in those war movies. You consider every scenario (now where'd you get *that* word?) and work out an escape. If they come through that window—and you edge over to check the lock again; yes—then you'll LEAP OVER THE SOFA, FLINGING THE LAMP BEHIND YOU WITH YOUR LEFT ARM, AND HEAD FOR THE STAIRS, GRABBING THE VASE AS YOU RUN, YELLING BLOODY MURDER (oh *Jesus* what a stupid phrase), YELLING LIKE MAD AS YOU RUN, READY TO DO WHATEVER YOU HAVE TO DO TO SAVE THE CHILDREN. . . .

And you feel better as you stand there, working out escape routes. Refusing to hear any more noises. You roll your shoulders, flex your fingers, stretch. Not much longer now. The Redgraves, whatever their other problems, are a prompt couple; that's what Nance told you, anyway.

But then you'd probably have taken the job no matter what she told you (like about Mr. Redgrave's eyes and lips). Because you've missed it. Babysitting. After that last time, word had gotten around, and none of the mothers would call you any more. That bothers you, how mothers can be so stupid, that they can't see how you'd give your life to protect their kids (something your parents would never do). Anything you'd done was done with their precious little children in mind—most of them brats anyway. Not like these kids, Brian and Samantha. They're so . . . vulnerable. And having to grow up with that ugly name. Redgrave—sounds like where Communist vampires come from. (Mr. Redgrave rises in your mind again, teeth bared now.) These lousy parents couldn't even get their *name* right.

Or their house. You hug yourself, looking around slowly. Too big, too empty. Why don't they have an alarm system? This may be a nice neighborhood, not much riffraff (now you're talking like Daddy); but still, this is the kind of place you'd think the really good burglars would try to hit, especially on such a big lot, fenced in so the neighbors can't see in (JESUS WHY DO YOU DO THIS TO YOURSELF EVERY, SINGLE, TIME). You are getting mad. Less and less at that stupid voice in your head, more and more at the Redgraves. Running off to their little social functions, leaving these sweet kids with strangers and bruises. (Nance has already sat for these people *six times* since they moved in. And she may be a terrific friend—she got you this job, didn't she?—but you *know* she doesn't care about the kids as much as you do. She wouldn't put her life on the line for them. She can't even keep her eyes open for half of the best moments in the horror movies you take her to!) You smile, and wonder if there is a gun in the house—

)Click(.

—and your nerves are shrieking again, your mind racing (what the hell is that what the hell *is* that!). "Scruff click?" What makes a noise like that, you wonder, backing from the entrance leading to the kitchen, where the sounds are definitely coming from. What? Maybe the cat eating from a dish? One of the kids sneaking a midnight snack? (Oh God is it really that late?—No, no, just ten forty-five, hold on, hold on, they'll be back by no later than eleven, that's what Cam said, "no later than eleven," that's what she promised. . . .) Maybe the refrigerator coming on? Maybe a hooded strangler easing the window open with blood-bloated eyes (Mr. Redgrave's eyes) and piano wire in his raw meaty hands and

(STOP THIS RIGHT NOW!)

. . . and you realize you are pacing the room, choking a pillow from the couch, walking dangerously near those entranceways. . . .You take an angry breath, and you turn as though to march right into that kitchen and prove to yourself that it's just happening again (memories flare in your mind like those flashing lights on the police cars), you're overreacting to your stupid imagination, just like Daddy says, you're being silly, inventing murderers and monsters, probably inventing the noises—

)Scruff click(.

—no you're not.

The phone. You back to it, trying to swallow, ready to throw the pillow and go for the andirons or whatever the hell you call those fireplace pole things—

And suddenly you see yourself in your mind. It's like a movie. The way the sounds come just at the most quiet moments. The way the house is set behind dark fences. The stairs (*Psycho*. . .). The kids ("Why don't you check the children," and was his name really Brian or was it Damian, is she really Baby Jane . . . ?) (JUST SHUT UP!)

No alarms. No emergency numbers. Redgraves. Red. Graves. Eyes and lips. Bruises.

You reach for the pole (poker, a poker, that's what it's called, CALM DOWN), and it feels oh so solid in your hand; yet it accelerates your fear, because holding it means you're serious, you really think there's somebody in the house and you've really got a weapon in your hand and you've really, finally, got to protect the children. . . .

)Scrick(.

Your free hand wavers over the phone. You *can't* call the police. What if it is (but you KNOW it's not) another false alarm? You can't stand the thought of everyone looking at you again, like they're scared of you; or making fun of you like those creeps in school. More lectures from Daddy, even Nance acting different around you . . .

No. Hold on. "No later than eleven," and that means she thinks they'll probably get home BEFORE then, and it's nearly eleven now, and there's just not enough time for someone to be stabbed strangled butchered (SHUT UP) raped burned (PLEASE SHUT UP!). . . .

Nance. She's home. (Thank God for grounding! Bless you, Mr. Piper, you jerk!) And you pick up the receiver and start dialing, awkwardly holding the poker with your little finger against your palm

—)SCRUFF(—

and ignoring the noises

—)CLICK(—

and when the cat runs in, an orange blur, you can't help it you SCREAM and Jamie Lee Curtis could *never* duplicate that, and the damn cat changes its mind and heads right on back out of there!

And it's all so silly and stupid that yes, you

laugh, just the way the script would say to do; and you look at the poker you've somehow held onto and you feel—moronic, a scared little schoolgirl (and hoping you didn't wake the kids). You toss the poker onto the plush rug the way the girl always does in the movies, and it lands so softly, as softly as the footstep behind you as the hand that covers your mouth as the hand that wraps around the phone receiver warm and hairy, and almost as softly as the chillingly familiar voice that says, "That's a good girl," then stays quiet no matter what those terrible hands are doing. . . .

. . . except . . .

Except:

Before any of that can happen you get your hand around the back of his head (my God his breath in your ear is so *hot*) and you grab a handful of mask and the hair beneath it and YANK and somehow he's flying over your shoulder, you hear him gasp and his painful grip is gone; and before he can even land you're leaping over the couch, flinging the lamp behind you with your left arm, and heading for the stairs, grabbing the vase as you run; and you are about to scream because you hear him thundering up behind you, thundering through the plush silence of the rug with certain murder in his eyes (oh how you know those eyes) but he's got to get by you to get at the children so you raise the vase and turn to brain him . . .

No one.

You let your breath run wild and glance around madly (where is he where *is* he); and you jerk around because maybe somehow he got on the stairs above you, but no one—

—and somehow it's worse, not being able to see him, not knowing where he is (even though you know WHO he is), waiting for him to JUMP

OUT AT YOU KNIFE RAISED TEETH BARED and chills and shivers rack you, you stab out a hand to turn on the lamp next to the stairs, and the light chases the shadows; and you feel a stirring of triumph, because he can't get you in the light; these psychos they need the darkness, and you skitter through the room, vase at the ready, and turn on every light you can!

And you catch your breath. Your thoughts. Survey the situation. Form your escape routes. And somehow you know he is going to try to do the unexpected; going to try to get at you through the least likely way.

The front door. (The last thing you'd ever suspect.) (HA!)

You gather what's left of your courage and let it propel you into the living room again, to the poker. It seems to jump into your hand. You toss the vase onto the couch (so quietly it bounces . . .).

You're ready.

A calm fills you. A sense of confidence. Of justice. You take your place behind the front door, away from the window (locked? yes) that would give you away. The poker is firm in your grasp. You're *not* going to be like one of those girls in the movies. You're *prepared.* Your escape routes are *planned.* You glance at the stairs—how the psycho would get at those lovely kids. You won't let that happen. They're going to make it. So are you. As the glare of headlights cuts through the window, you steady yourself, and raise the poker.

—And in the breathless silence, there is another voice.

The voice you have heard so many times before, at moments like this. A calm voice, soothing yet insistent. The poker wavers.

(No. Not yet. Not here. Not them.)

Distantly, you hear a car door slam. Light laughter.

(Yes. The poker down. Softly, hurry. Back in its place. Yes.)

The muffled rhythm of shoes on a driveway.

(Quickly. Lights, off. The vase. Good. The lamp. Yes. Everything is all right. Remember always your ultimate escape route: the appearance of normality. Never let them know what happens behind these eyes.)

The rustle of a key, struggling to fill a lock.

(The time will come. Patience.)

You are sitting on the sofa, finishing the Diet Coke when the door opens. You look up, and smile. Cam smiles back. So does Mr. Redgrave. And you see how much, in this light, he looks like Daddy.

"Well! Here we are, right on time! Everything go okay? Samantha or Brian give you any trouble?" Cam asks, handing her wrap to Mr. Redgrave, looking around the room.

"Not a bit," you say, standing. Walking toward them, over that mute rug. "Straight to bed, and right on time. They're lovely children—Cam."

She smiles, lightly squeezes your shoulder. "Well, thank you. And from what I can see, Nancy was right: You are a very sweet and dependable young woman. Don't you think, David?"

"Looks that way," he says, and looms over you for a moment. "Looks as though you've certainly earned your money. Cam and I are grateful. Well, suppose I should get you home. Got everything?"

(Yes.)

As you get your purse, you wonder if you should ask to see the children one more time, to make sure they are okay. Their faces dance in your mind briefly (like sugarplums) and you glance around to make sure the shadows hiding at the corners of the room are empty.

"Ready," you say.

(Yes . . .)

Cam waves. "We'll let you know when we need you again, honey—

(. . . soon . . .)

—and, really, thank you again. You'll hear from us soon. I'm afraid poor Nancy may have talked herself out of a job!"

(. . . YES . . .)

You follow him to the car. He even opens the door for you. As you sit back in the soft seat, he says, "There's a concert next week Cam and I were planning to attend. Are you doing anything Wednesday night?"

You close your eyes. Smile. "Not a thing." And you wait for thc screen to fade to black.

GHOST IN THE HOUSE

by George Sumner Albee

Want a beer, darling?" asked Henry Decker, home from the office at 5:30, now comfortable in slacks and a pale-blue polo shirt. "Or a martini?"

"A martini," said Deborah firmly. "Henry, I don't know how to tell you this—but there was a ghost in the house this afternoon!"

Henry stirred the cocktails in the monogrammed pitcher she had bought for their fourth anniversary, and they went out onto the screened porch that overlooked their small but trim back yard.

"That darned grass is four inches tall," observed Henry. "I'd swear I mowed it only a couple of days ago. Tell me about your ghost."

"It isn't a bit funny. It scared me out of my wits," said Deborah from her aluminum chaise. She smoothed her candy-striped summer skirt. "I thought I heard someone in the living room, so I went in, and there it was."

"In broad daylight?"

"Broad daylight. It was a pudgy little man, about forty, in a chocolate-brown suit with a pin stripe, a tan shirt, and a dark red tie. His shoes looked as if they'd just been polished. He had a brown hat with a narrow brim, shoved back on his head, and there was perspiration on his upper lip."

"I never knew that ghosts perspired," said Henry, with a chuckle. "Who was it?"

"I'm not joking!"

"Oh, come on, darling. But how did he get in? I told you to always keep the front door locked."

"I don't know how he got in. He was twirling a key around one finger, on one of those chains made of tiny silver balls—I suppose he got in with that. He took out a notebook and began to make notes in it, and I said, 'I beg your pardon,' and he paid no attention to me. I asked him who he was, but he just went on writing, and then he started down the hall to the bedrooms. 'Hey, where do you think you're going?' I said to him. And then"—Deborah faltered—"I reached out to take hold of his arm, and my—my hand went right *through* him."

"You're serious, aren't you?" Surprised, Henry put down his cocktail glass on the yellow plastic top of the aluminum porch table. "You must have a fever. Maybe you have this one-day virus everybody is catching."

"I took my temperature, and I feel fine," Deborah said impatiently. "But there *was* a ghost in the house this afternoon, at exactly twenty minutes past three. I saw him just as plainly as I see you right now."

"I can see you're upset, and I don't blame you a bit," said Henry. "All right, the thing to do is to look at it scientifically. First, we have to assume it was a real man. He could have been any number of things—an appraiser, an inspector from the Fire Department who got the wrong address and happened to have a passkey that opened our door. Those guys do have passkeys, you know. He didn't hear you because he was so wrapped up in what he was doing. Or maybe he was sent out to repossess somebody's furniture, and he thought you were the owner and was trying to get in and out of the house without having you scratch his face with your nails or throw a vase at him. That would explain his pretending not to listen to you."

"It doesn't explain my hand going through him. You don't understand. I stuck my arm in front of him—as if it were a fence, or a gate—and he walked straight through it. My hand went in at his chest and came out through his back as if he were a soap bubble."

"You were excited and upset, darling, so it just seemed that way to you," Henry reassured her. "It was a hallucination, Deb. Even normal, healthy people have hallucinations sometimes. I must have told you about the time I thought the barn was following me, that time I drove nonstop to Florida. It was so real I could see the cracks between the boards, and a sign on it advertising a baking powder."

"My hallucination smelled of talcum powder and bay rum," said Deborah, unconvinced. "From a barber shop. And he was chewing gum. Anything that real, I'd as soon call a ghost and be done with it!"

Henry laughed. "Okay, so we have a ghost in the house," he said. "He didn't do anything to hurt you, did he? He didn't even say 'boo'? Let's have a drink to him."

Deborah lifted a forefinger. "Shhh—"

"What?"

"There's somebody in the living room right now. I hear voices."

"I don't."

She was pale. "He's back! My God, Henry, he's back!"

"Nonsense. You sit here, and I'll go see."

"I'm coming with you."

With Henry leading they sped silently along the hall to the living room. Just inside the front door, which was open, stood three people—the man in the chocolate-brown suit, precisely as Deborah had described him, and a younger man with extraordinarily dark, heavy eyebrows and a girl of twenty or so in a green silk maternity blouse and white sandals.

"This is the one I think you should take," the pudgy little man was saying. "Two bedrooms. An all-electric kitchen. The price is twenty-three-five, but the bank has taken it over. Give me a good down payment and I think I can get it for you for twenty-two."

"Look here, folks," Henry broke in, "I think there's been some mistake—"

The three paid not the slightest attention to him.

"What about the furniture?" asked the young wife. "It's lovely. Wall-to-wall carpet, too."

"That's the special inducement I mentioned," said the pudgy real-estate man. "It's all paid for, but used furniture doesn't bring much at an auction, which is the way the bank would have to sell it. You folks tack on a thousand—making the total price an even twenty-three—and I'm sure you can have the furniture. It will represent a big saving for you."

"Listen," said Henry, raising his voice as he grew angry, "I don't know whose house you think you're in, but this place is not for sale."

With an exclamation, Deborah turned and ran back down the hall. The door of the rear porch slammed. Henry hesitated, then decided he could deal with the intruders later—Deborah's fright was more important, for the moment. He followed her, calling her name.

"I'm out here, dear," she answered. She was standing on the lawn, close to a panel of plastic screen, where a trumpet vine hid her from the house. "Oh, I'm so frightened—"

"It's all right," Henry reassured her. "There's nothing to be afraid of. It just came to me. You know what? They're deaf. That's what it is—all three of them are deaf."

"But they're talking to each other."

"Deaf people talk to each other. They're reading each other's lips."

"But they saw us! We were right in the same room with them!"

"No, we really weren't. We were at the front end of the hall, and it's dark there. Their eyes were still dazzled from the sunshine outside. They simply didn't see us."

"They're ghosts. I tell you they *are*."

He kissed her. "Ghosts don't sell real estate, sweetheart. They don't wear maternity dresses, either—not any ghosts I ever heard of! You stay here now, and I'll go in and get rid of them."

"Don't leave me!" cried Deborah in terror. "I—I haven't told you, but I've felt strange for days. Oh, darling, I'm afraid I'm losing my mind!"

"Then I'm losing mine too," said Henry comfortingly, "because I saw your ghosts and they didn't scare me a bit. Deb, you know perfectly well there's no such thing as a ghost."

"I'm coming back inside with you."

"I wish you wouldn't."

"Please—"

They found the three strangers, evidently after a tour of the two bedrooms, in the kitchen. The husband was agreeing that the house was a bargain, furnished, and saying he could pay five thousand dollars down in cash.

"This house belongs to me," said Henry. He raised his voice to a shout. "This house is not for sale!"

"I'm sure that will be satisfactory," said the real-estate man to the husband, "and since you're dealing with the bank that holds the mortgage, it'll be a simple matter to transfer the papers."

The young wife was so happy to know the house was hers that she pirouetted out of the kitchen into the living room, and on through the living room to the front door. Smiling, the two men followed her.

Jaw thrust out, Henry went after them doggedly. He caught up with the realtor just as, key in hand, the pudgy man stepped out onto the red brick stoop and turned to lock the door. "I've had about enough of this. Now you listen to me," Henry said, and put his hand heavily on the man's brown worsted shoulder.

It sliced right through.

"The young couple that had this place would be glad to know you like it so much," the real-estate man was saying. "They were just about your age. It was a terrible thing. A trailer truck sideswiped their car on the thruway. They never knew what hit them."

BEHOLD, KRA K'L! The Bohemian Demon of Gardenia Street

by Richard F. McGonegal

George had three passions: reading Dostoyevsky, doting on a ballerina named Trudi (short for Trudulobov or some such surname), and conjuring demons.

By contrast, I had none—at least none of those.

Although we were both graduate students, George and I had met not as classmates, but as neighbors—two refugees who had fled to the residential section of Gardenia Street to escape the perpetual pandemonium of campus life.

George lived upstairs in the tidy two-story across the street. I had been to his place only twice in the three years we had known each other, both times on Saturday nights when Mrs. Medvedsky—the Czechoslovakian landlady who lived on the main floor and imposed a strict "no visitors" rule—routinely went to church.

I had tried to make friends with Mrs. Medvedsky, hoping for an exemption from the "no visitors" rule. I was tired of constantly playing host to George or, more often, both George and Trudi. But my smiles and "hellos" yielded nothing more than an impassive scowl. The only real exchange I ever had with Mrs. Medvedsky was the time she whacked me with a broom while I was leaning against her white picket fence, waiting for George. "You breaking it" were her only words when I looked at her, dumbstruck. I learned later from George that the scowl was a fixed feature and that she added *-ing* to every verb in the English language.

In time, I accepted my role as unrequited host and even began looking forward to George's erratic visits. He would come at any hour of the day or night, sometimes as often as three times a day, other times as infrequently as every two weeks.

It was toward the end of one of those two week spans when I heard his familiar knock.

"I need your help," he said abruptly, pushing open the door and parading in, followed by Trudi. Whenever I saw Trudi, I always marveled at how a girl so tall could weigh so little.

"Name it," I said, motioning for them to take seats at the kitchen table.

George sat down, Trudi sat down. "I need you to help me conjure a demon," George said.

I sat down. "Why me?" I asked.

"It takes two people," George replied.

I looked at Trudi.

"Too dangerous for her," George said, misinterpreting my look. I wasn't trying to volunteer her, I was trying to determine if George was serious. Her expression revealed nothing.

"Wait a minute," I said. "Just how dangerous are we talking about?"

"Oh, it's no problem—as long as we do it right," George replied.

"Have you ever done this before?"

"Well, I've tried a few times, but I haven't had any luck yet."

"Luck?" I asked.

"Okay, success," he said. "You know what I mean."

I stared at him for a long, silent moment. "I don't think so," I said finally.

"Why not?"

"Uh-uh," I said, wagging my finger at him. "The question is 'why?' Why should I?"

George leaned forward, folded his hands together and placed them on the table. "To prove," he said in a slow, measured voice, "that God exists."

"By conjuring a demon?"

"Sure," George said, emphatically. "People are always trying to conjure God, have been for centuries. They go to church, prayer meetings, even go on TV. But what have they proved? Nothing. So I say, why not try another approach? You see, if we can conjure a demon, then we prove Satan exists. And if he exists, then God must exist. And the bands of angels, the whole works. Otherwise, Satan would have taken over a long time ago and we'd all be totally evil instead of just working at it."

He paused a moment, then added, "It's not a new idea."

Trudi and I looked at each other, equally baffled.

"Well," George said, after a long pause. "What about it?"

"I don't know," I replied. "I mean, you've got my curiosity aroused, but I need to know a lot more about what's involved and what I'm in for."

He proceeded to outline the entire plan and, in the end, it sounded so implausible I agreed.

"Now remember," George said as he rummaged through a heap of papers and assorted junk in the corner of his room, "her name is Kra K'l." It was Saturday night, Mrs. Medvedsky was at church, and we were preparing to conjure.

"Krackel," I repeated.

"Not crackle," he said. "You make her sound like a breakfast cereal. It's Kra K'l: Like Raquel, but with a K and a slight hesitation between syllables."

I repeated the name and he nodded approval.

If Kra K'l dealt in chaos, I thought as I surveyed George's apartment, she was going to feel right at home here. The place looked as if someone had detonated a dozen garbage bags filled with books and papers within its confines. The only semblance of order was the photographs of Trudi, who arabesqued, pirouetted, and pas de chevaled across the far wall in tights, toe shoes, and diaphanous tutu.

"And you say you don't know what she's going to look like?" I asked for the umpteenth time. I was nervous.

"No way to be sure," George said. "She can take any number of forms. Aha!" He straightened up and displayed a brown sandwich bag. "See those four tape marks on the floor?"

"I see three," I replied.

He handed me the bag, then pushed aside a stuffed chair littered with books, revealing the fourth mark. "Take that stuff in the bag and sprinkle it from mark to mark so you make the outline of a diamond," he said.

"What is it?" I asked, sniffing cautiously at the contents: a gray-green powdery substance.

"Just some stuff I mixed up," he said. Then, with a wry smile forming at the edges of his mouth, he added, "But I wouldn't sneeze in it if I were you."

I jerked my nose away from the bag. "What's it for?" I asked. I was beginning to realize that although I had asked a lot of questions in advance, George's answers had been very general. I was also beginning to realize that because I had never done anything like this before, I had overlooked a lot of questions.

"It forms a kind of barrier," George said. "We'll get Kra K'l to appear inside the diamond and that's where she'll stay."

"Are you sure it's supposed to be a diamond?" I asked. "I always thought it was supposed to be a pentagonal."

"Pentagram," George corrected. "But that's for your Assyrian, Mesopotamian, and other Middle Eastern-type demons. Kra K'l is Eastern European, Bohemian actually. For them, it's diamonds."

I began spreading the powder on the floor, making straight and steady lines from mark to mark. If this was going to be Kra K'l's cage, I wanted it to be secure. "What's Bohemia now?" I asked, nearing the halfway point of my task.

"Czechoslovakia," George said.

I shuddered, leaving a zigzag of powder. "This doesn't have anything to do with Mrs. Medvedsky, does it?"

"Well, she's kind of like the bait, in a way," George said.

I stopped spreading and looked at him, but he was stooped over behind the chair.

"In the old days they used candles at the corners," George said, "but today . . . *voilà.*" He held up in each hand a large flashlight with rectangular bases and handles that had a red blinker on one end and a flashlight cowl on the other. "I've got a couple more of these around here someplace," he said, poking his head behind the chair again.

"What do you mean, Mrs. Medvedsky is the bait?" I asked.

"How can I explain it?" George mused aloud as he shifted his rummaging to the area behind the sofa. "Kra K'l is kind of like a scout. Think of Satan as the big chief. He doesn't go out on his own and look for people to possess and stuff like that. He has scouts for that sort of thing. What we're going to do is make Kra K'l think there's a Christian soul who has lost faith—specifically Mrs. Medvedsky. And when Kra K'l comes to scout it out . . . wham, we trap her."

I looked George straight in the eye to determine whether he was putting me on. He wasn't—an observation that made me wonder if any other demonologist had ever invoked the "big chief and scout" metaphor to describe the craft.

I continued spreading the powder while George rounded up the remaining flashlights. "Know what this is?" he asked. He held up a shallow, cylindrical clear plastic dish.

It looked like the kind of thing I kept my pet turtle Scooter in when I was a kid. "Looks like one of those turtle house things," I ventured.

"Exactly," George said, smiling. "Except it's called a turtle aquarium."

"In case Kra K'l shows up in the form of a pet turtle, right?"

"Go ahead, poke fun at a demon," George said. "Very courageous."

He was kidding, but his comment made me nervous, nonetheless. Despite the sheer ludicrousness of the whole scene, I could not dispel the anxiety I felt. As much as I tried to tell myself that nothing could possibly come of this charade, I could see George was absolutely serious. He was eccentric, maybe even a little batty, but he was serious about this.

I finished my spreading. It looked pretty good. I was contemplating ways to tell George that I was bailing out, quitting, giving up the cause—but something held me back.

George had a flashlight at each point of the

diamond and began adjusting the beams toward the center.

"George," I said, hesitantly, "where'd you pick up this stuff?"

"Catalogues," he replied.

"Catalogues?"

"Mail order," he said. "I got a hell of a deal on the flashlights."

His choice of words amused me. "No," I said, "I meant the conjuring stuff."

"Oh, that," he said as he waddled around the diamond, refining his adjustments to the light beams. "Books mostly. But I've had to improvise a lot."

"We don't have to sacrifice anything, do we?" I asked. "I mean, you know, like animals?"

He looked at me with a blank stare. "What'd you have in mind?"

"Nothing," I replied. "Just asking."

He shook his head slightly and rolled his eyes, then resumed his rummaging.

Although I was a little miffed, I felt somehow relieved. His confessed improvisations—the powdery whatever, the flashlights, the turtle aquarium—suddenly all seemed laughably harmless.

"What are you looking for?" I asked, as his rummaging grew more frantic.

"The damn woodblock," he said, flinging papers in the air and sweeping books off the sofa.

I held up the woodblock and stick he had given me earlier. "I've got it."

"Okay," he said, "let's run through this last part one more time. Now, all you need to do is chant 'Kra K'l' over and over while you hit the woodblock on each syllable. Kra K'l, Kra K'l, Kra K'l," he chanted while clapping his hands with the rhythm of the words. "Try it."

"Kra K'l, Kra K'l, Kra K'l," I repeated.

"Slower," he advised, then chimed in, "Kra

K'l, Kra K'l, good, Kra K'l, Kra K'l, okay." We stopped.

"Now, while you're doing that," he said, "I'm going to be reciting the 'Lamentation of the Lost.' It's real arhythmic, but don't let it throw you off your tempo. This is the lamentation that Christians used when they had a breach of faith. Your chant is like a homing device which lets Kra K'l know where we are, and my lamentation is kind of like the drawing card. You see, all those religious artifacts Mrs. Medvedsky has downstairs give off an aura that this is a Christian house. What we're going to do is try to trick Kra K'l into thinking Mrs. Medvedsky has lost faith and is calling out in distress. Got it?"

"Got it," I said.

"Good," George said. "Now the main thing is that you don't stop the chant once we've begun. It may take some time, but don't stop unless I do. No matter what you see, or hear, or sense, don't stop the chant. Okay?"

"Okay," I replied.

"It's important," he said.

"Okay!" I said, abruptly. "I understand."

George positioned me on the outside of the diamond at the angle nearest the door. He put the turtle aquarium inside the diamond at the angle farthest from me, then poured some gooey liquid into it from a Tupperware pitcher. He placed his feet just outside the far angle, surveyed the scene for a moment, and gave the starting nod.

We began. After about a minute, I found that if I closed my eyes, I could concentrate better in the face of his shrill, obnoxious lamentation. I chanted, he lamented, for five minutes, then ten, then twenty, then forty. Occasionally, I opened my eyes to look at the clock and to look at George, hoping for some sign from him that we could quit soon. I was bored and sweaty, and his lamentation was making me irritable.

A cool breeze carrying a faint, sweet odor swept over me, and when I opened my eyes, I could see the vague outline of an image forming inside the diamond. My eyes widened, my heartbeat quickened as I watched the image take the shape of a woman. She was tall, thin, and angular. She wore white robes like the ones women wore in Hercules movies, and her face was shrouded in a translucent white veil. Although I couldn't discern her features, she looked unmistakably like Trudi.

I glanced at George, who gave me a furtive look that signaled not to stop the chant.

I looked back at the woman, straining to see the features behind the veil, convinced now that it was Trudi and that they were playing an elaborate joke at my expense. What baffled me was what kind of trick they had used to make her appear out of thin air.

The woman spoke in a language totally foreign to me, and her voice was deep, ponderous—nothing like Trudi's.

"I do not understand your language," George said.

The woman turned toward him. "Who summoned me?" she demanded.

"You have been summoned by the 'Lamentation of the Lost,' " George said. "Speak your name."

"I am known by many names," she said.

"Is Kra K'l among them?" George asked. His voice was steady, resolute.

"Perhaps," she said. "Why do you summon me?"

"I call upon you to tell me from where you came," George demanded.

The woman turned toward me and approached,

stopping just at the inside edge of the diamond. "This has gone too far," she whispered. The voice was undeniably Trudi's. "I'm sorry we played this trick on you. I didn't want to do it, but he talked me into it."

"I knew it," I shouted. I was angry, confused, resentful.

"Don't listen to her," George screamed, scurrying around the edges of the diamond. "Whatever she said, don't listen to her. What did she say?"

"C'mon George," I said. "I know who it is. The joke's over."

"No, it's a trick," he yelled, grabbing me by the shoulders.

"Yeah, it's a trick all right," I said. "And I fell for it."

"Just break the line," she whispered to me quietly. "Show your anger. Break the line."

I moved forward, but George pushed me back. "Are you crazy?" he cried. He looked back at the woman and he seemed genuinely confounded at hearing Trudi's voice.

"See that," I said. "How can she look like Trudi and talk like Trudi, if she isn't Trudi?"

George stared blankly for a moment. "There," he said suddenly, pointing to the photographs on the wall. He looked back at me. "If that's Trudi in the diamond, she could cross the line." If George was acting, he was displaying a talent I had never seen before.

"Dammit!" George said, as we both heard the sound of the front door opening downstairs. "Mrs. Medvedsky's back."

A whirlwind swept the room, a bone-chilling cold wind that scattered papers and rattled the walls as a noxious odor filled my nostrils. The figure within the diamond had become a blur of motion, hazy and indistinct. I clutched George's arm as I watched the new image take shape—three-toed claw feet, four long arms with sharp talon fingers, two dragon-like wings folded behind her shoulders, a sharp flaring snout, glistening ivory teeth set in deep blue gums, eyes like blue flames and a body covered entirely with blue-green scales. The creature was both horrible and breathtakingly beautiful.

"Behold, Kra K'l!" George cried out. He turned to me and whispered, "Christians seem to bring out the worst in them."

The footsteps came rapidly up the stairs, the apartment door burst open. Behold, Mrs. Medvedsky—broom in hand and a pissed-off scowl on her face.

"I thought I telling you no visitors," she said adamantly.

The demon snorted, hitting us with a cold, stinking blast.

"You," the landlady said, turning on the demon. "What are you being here looking like that?" She swiped at the demon with the broom, missed, and scattered the powder about the room.

Kra K'l lunged from the broken diamond and Mrs. Medvedsky turned like a second baseman and whacked the demon across the backside with the broom. Kra K'l bolted down the steps.

"And you," she said, wielding the broom in a threatening gesture as she turned to me.

I cowered; George gripped his hair. "Jesus," he said. "Mrs. Medvedsky, I'll explain everything later." He turned to me. "C'mon."

I followed him down the stairs in a run.

"We did it!" he shouted exuberantly, on the front porch, raising his arms and looking toward the heavens. He put his hands on my shoulders. "We did it."

I was speechless.

"We've got to find her," he said. He headed for the street.

"Wait a minute," I said, catching up with him and walking briskly beside him down Gardenia Street. "What are we going to do when we find her? I mean, how do we get rid of her?"

"We can cover more ground if we split up," he said. "You go that way and I'll . . ."

"I'm not going off on my own," I said. "I don't know how to get rid of her if I find her. How do we get rid of her?"

"I don't know."

"What do you mean you don't know?"

"There are a couple of ways," he said, "but I don't know how well they'll work. This is my first demon." He paused a moment. "Anyway, first we've got to find her."

"She can't keep changing forms like that, can she?" I was scared, nearly hysterical, and I was hoping for a firm "no."

"As a matter of fact, she can."

"Great," I said. "Just great. You realize she could be anybody. Or anything. She could be a dog, or a squirrel, or an alley cat."

"Don't worry," George said. "I'll know her when I see her." He sounded confident.

I followed him. I had no choice. We searched everywhere—streets, alleys, garages, under porches—to no avail.

After several hours, we came to a wooden bench at a bus stop and George collapsed onto the seat. I climbed up on the backrest, dangling and swinging my feet above the seat as I scanned the empty streets.

"You realize what we've done?" I said, musing out loud.

George chuckled quietly.

"What's so damned funny?" I asked. I was dead serious.

Between chuckles, he said, "I can't believe Mrs. Medvedsky smacked her with a broom." His chuckles turned to quiet laughter.

It was contagious. There we sat—the two guys who had just turned a demon loose upon the world—laughing out loud.

After a few moments, we both stopped and looked at each other, as if we were sharing the same thought.

"George," I said, "now that we know He's up there, do you think He'll forgive us for this?"

In the week following the conjuring, events went from bad to worse, culminating with a visit from George. Under the circumstances, his appearance seemed somehow appropriate.

I hesitated at hearing his customary knock, then relented and opened the door.

Instead of whisking into my kitchen, he stared at me across the open portal. "What happened to you?"

"I got into a nest of hornets," I replied, assuming he was referring to the prominent red welt on the tip of my swollen nose.

"You look like Bozo the Clown," he observed.

"Oh yeah, what happened to you?" I asked, gesturing toward the sling which held his left arm at a Napoleonic bent.

"Fell down the stairs," he replied.

"C'mon in."

We took seats across from each other at the kitchen table. George sniffed the air unceremoniously.

"Grease fire," I explained. "Nearly burned up my kitchen."

"My toilet overflowed," George countered. "It was a mess."

"I had hit-and-run damage to my car."

George pondered a moment. "We're in deep."

"Any ideas?" I asked. "You're the expert."

"Two possible explanations," George said. "Either Kra K'l is having some fun at our expense, or the guy upstairs is kind of pissed off at us."

"The guy upstairs?" I repeated.

"You know," George said, refusing to be baited by my sarcasm. "Either way, it doesn't matter. All we need to do is dispatch Kra K'l and we're in the clear."

"Simple as that?" I asked. "Okay, where is she?"

George shrugged.

"You don't know? You have *no* idea?" I grew more upset as I spoke. "She could be anyone. She could be one of our professors, she could be the cashier at the bookstore, she could be Trudi, she could . . ." I paused in mid-sentence, a sudden convulsive shiver spiraling up my spine.

". . . be me," George said unflinchingly, completing my thought.

I eyed him suspiciously. Then I backed into my bedroom, grabbed the crucifix I had hung on my bedpost, returned to the kitchen, and advanced toward him, brandishing the cross in my outstretched hand.

George bellowed—a laugh which stopped me in my tracks. "She's a demon, not a vampire, for crissake."

I tossed the crucifix on the table, humiliated: "I don't know, George, it's just that . . . what?"

He was staring out the kitchen window, his gaze intense. "There." He pointed.

I looked. Nothing seemed awry. My front yard opened onto the street. A car passed. Across the way, there was no activity, with the exception of Mrs. Medvedsky, who was sweeping her front porch.

"What?" I repeated.

"Mrs. Medvedsky," he said, his tone grave.

"So?"

"So, it's Saturday night. She should be at church."

"Maybe she decided not to go."

He stared at me. "She always goes."

"Always?"

He flopped back in the chair. "It makes sense," he whispered, as if thinking out loud. "They're so clever, but so arrogant. Of course Kra K'l would come back for her, after that broom thing. Jeez," he said, slapping himself on the forehead with his unfettered hand.

"You're sure?" I asked.

He nodded.

"I thought you said you'd recognize her when you saw her," I said. "You've been *living* with a damned demon."

"Kind of spooky, isn't it?" he said. "But never mind that now. We need to move."

"What are we going to do?"

"I've been doing some more research," he said. "I've got a plan."

It was my turn to think out loud. "Oh, no," I said.

"Now remember," George said as he wheeled the lawn spreader out of the shed. "I don't have the ingredients for any more powder, so don't lay it on too thick."

It was nearly two A.M. on Sunday morning—almost six hours of preparation after our revelation.

"You're sure the lines won't be too thin to hold her?"

George crossed his fingers. A prayer would have seemed more appropriate, but I felt—and I suspected George shared my feeling—that we were on our own until we squared things.

I tied an end of twine to one of the four stakes we had pushed into the soft turf and handed the twine ball to George, who headed across Mrs. Medvedsky's yard, unraveling it as he walked. He looped the twine around the second stake, pulled it taut and disappeared around the side of the house. As instructed, I followed with the lawn spreader, carefully guiding the wheel along the twine outline and leaving a trail of powder in my wake.

"What about the lights?" I asked, as we surveyed our handiwork—a perfect geometric diamond surrounding the house.

"Don't need 'em," George said. "The lights and the other stuff are only for conjuring." He pointed to the house. "We've already got Kra K'l trapped. Now all we need to do is get Mrs. Medvedsky out of there."

"And then we dispatch Kra K'l?"

"Right," he said.

"You're sure Mrs. Medvedsky is in there?"

"I'm sure," George said, irritably. I had posed the question before, and he had explained that Bohemian demons were shape-changers, not possessors. "If Kra K'l is assuming Mrs. Medvedsky's form for an extended period," he had reasoned, "she can't afford to have the real Mrs. Medvedsky running around loose, can she?"

"How do we get her out?"

"We go get her." He stepped across the edge of the diamond and headed toward the porch.

Using his key, George unlocked the front door. We entered cautiously and faced the door to Mrs. Medvedsky's apartment. George tried the knob—locked.

"Got a credit card?" he whispered.

I shrugged. "Try your student I.D."

He removed the laminated card from his wallet, wedged it between door and frame, twisted the knob and pushed. It yielded with a squeak.

We winced simultaneously and waited. Silence reigned. George entered first; I followed, shining my flashlight along the bare walls, vacant fireplace mantle, and naked bookshelves.

"Her stuff's all gone," George whispered.

I had never been in Mrs. Medvedsky's apartment, but I assumed the missing "stuff" was her religious paraphernalia.

Motioning for me to follow, George led the way down the hallway. We paused at the first doorway and peered into the room. Mrs. Medvedsky was lying on her back beneath the covers of a queen-size bed, snoring loudly.

"I'll get her," I said.

George grabbed me by the collar, nearly choking me as I started into the room. "Not her," George whispered. "That's Kra K'l."

I shuddered and backed out of the room.

"C'mon," George said. We tiptoed down the hall, searching the second bedroom, the bathroom, laundry room, and kitchen. Within the confines of the walk-in pantry adjoining the kitchen, we found Mrs. Medvedsky. She was seated on the floor, her wrists and ankles bound with shredded sheet and a wad of partial pillowcase stuffed into her mouth. I stopped and began working at the knots.

"Don't untie her," George said. "She'll just make a fuss. Wait till we get her out of here."

I placed an arm behind her back, another below her knees and heaved, staggering under her weight. Her eyes widened as I straightened, but she made no attempt to speak.

We emerged from the pantry, crossed the kitchen and began retracing our steps down the hall.

A sudden shadow loomed in our path as the

imposing figure of the demonically-inspired Mrs. Medvedsky stepped from the bedroom.

"What are you being here in my apartment doing?" she asked, her voice a remarkable impersonation of the landlady.

"Back door," I yelled, wheeling around and preparing to run, not knowing if there was a back door but fully prepared to create one.

Again George grabbed me by the collar. The sudden resistance to my burst of momentum yanked me off my already-unstable balance. I collapsed to the floor beneath the copious weight of Mrs. Medvedsky.

"Just a second," George said. "I'm not so sure."

"Not sure," I cried. I looked up at him, then down at the woman lying in my lap.

"Too easy," George said, as if thinking out loud. "What if Kra K'l saw us spreading the powder." He pointed to the woman whose weight had me pinned to the floor. "What if she's the demon."

The four of us exchanged suspicious glances; then George pulled a crucifix from his pocket and thrust it toward the upright Mrs. Medvedsky. She eyed him curiously. He turned the cross on my Mrs. Medvedsky. Her reaction was similar.

I frowned at him, recalling the vampire remark. Then I sensed the faint odor of something akin to sewer gas. I sniffed, traced it to the nostrils of the woman in my lap. The warmth of her body was increasing dramatically; the sheeted bonds and pillowcase gag began smoldering.

"Run!" I screamed, lurching and grappling unsuccessfully to free myself from the weight of the disguised demon. Disregarding my command, George lunged at the shape-changer, dislodged her with a block from his good shoulder, and sent her rolling into the bathroom. I slammed the door, George grabbed the real Mrs. Medvedsky by the hand and, together, we ran from the house.

The savage splintering sound of the bathroom door giving way reached us as we momentarily wedged ourselves—three abreast—in the front doorway. I yielded; George and Mrs. Medvedsky hurried through. They stopped abruptly as Mrs. Medvedsky grabbed the broom leaning against the porch railing and clutched it menacingly with both hands. George grabbed the broomstick with his able hand and they tugged back and forth, each trying to wrest it from the other.

I was attempting to maneuver around George when Kra K'l—transformed into her horribly beautiful blue-green self—suddenly perforated the exterior walls of the house and flew wildly into the yard. George released the broom, careened backwards, and knocked me over the porch railing. I landed unscathed, but cracked a juniper bush and crushed four yellow mums. Mrs. Medvedsky cried out. Kra K'l twisted her head to glare at us as her momentum carried her toward the diamond outline and—like a sparrow hitting a picture window—she crashed into the demon-barrier and crumpled in a heap.

We stared silently at the inert demon. "Quick," I yelled, regaining my senses after a momentary lapse, "the chant."

George began chanting; Kra K'l flinched. She arose unsteadily, bared her ivory teeth, flexed her scaly wings, and bolted into the air. We watched as she ascended like a bottle-rocket, smashed into some invisible ceiling, and dipped into a tailspin.

"Aha," I cried, my optimism premature. Kra K'l recovered from the plunge before hitting the ground. She dived at us like a screaming kamikaze—mouth agape, claws unfurled. Mrs.

Medvedsky flailed erratically with the broom, failing to make contact but warding off the demon. Kra K'l punctured the facade of the house, and the sounds of interior destruction prompted George to chant more loudly to compete with the din.

The demon exited by piercing a hole in the roof, but when she appeared to us again, her scaly skin seemed ablaze with blue-green sparks. She landed on the sidewalk in front of us, her rapidly-dissipating form clouded in greenish haze. The vague outline of her mouth tried to form a word, but no sound emerged. It seemed as if she were asking: "Why?"

When the haze lifted, no trace of Kra K'l remained. The house, however, yielded visible proof of her destructive departure. Around us, lights had come on in neighboring homes, people watched from their porches and yards and—in the distance—we could hear the sound of approaching sirens.

George looked at the smoldering perforations in the facade of Mrs. Medvedsky's house. "Looks like we're going to have a little explaining to do."

"Amen," I said.

FUN AND GAMES AT THE WHACKS MUSEUM

by Elliott Capon

He had two windows, one on each side of the main entrance door. Both were draped in black and purple fabrics. In the window to your left was a life-sized likeness of President Kennedy, waving and smiling and looking like he did right before he was shot. The workmanship was so extraordinary and the tragedy so recent that ninety-nine out of a hundred people who walked past the window would swear that the president was standing there, breathing and looking you right in the eye. In the other window was a fantasy creation, a person sort of split into two people, like Siamese twins. One half was an astonishingly lifelike representation of Anthony Perkins holding an axe, and he sort of melded into the other side of the figure, which looked like Anthony Perkins dressed as his mother, and she was wielding a large knife. It was because of this statue with its deadly cutlery that me and Pat Carter and Vince Riposo and all the other kids referred to the place as Berrigan's "Whacks" Museum.

All this took place in the town of Bellerive,

which was French for Pretty River, though of course the French had sold the place to John Adams or Andrew Jackson long before the rubber processing plant turned the river into a thick syrupy mess. Bellerive wasn't a particularly small town—we had a population of around twelve thousand—but it was the kind of place where everybody kinda sorta knew each other. We had four Protestant churches, a Catholic church, an A.M.E. church, even a reform synagogue. We had a VFW, a Knights of Columbus, an American Legion, an Elks Lodge, volunteer first aid squads at each end of town, and any number of PTA's. Everybody belonged to something or other, and everybody, if not known by everybody else, was at least known by *somebody* else. Several years later, I read a book called *Siege* by Edwin Corley, and one line has stuck with me for almost thirty years now: "He was aware of being black, just as Les Clayton was aware of being a redhead; so far it had not meant much more than that." That pretty much describes Bellerive. My father was chairman of the Brotherhood at the synagogue, and my best friend, Pat Carter, was colored, and my other best friend, Vince, went to Catholic school. But the differences didn't mean anything. There *were* no differences. To describe Bellerive as One Big Happy Family would be to sugarcoat the truth, but there was a great sense of community, of "Belleriveness," if you will.

That, I think, was one of the reasons a lot of important people did not like Mr. Berrigan.

Berrigan's Wax—or, if you were less than fifteen years of age, the Whacks—Museum might have been swallowed up in, say, New York or Los Angeles or Chicago, but in Bellerive it was quite a magnet. We had a halfway decent state park nearby, no great shakes in and of itself but coupled with a trip to Berrigan's, a day at the park made it worth packing the family in the car and driving for an hour or so to Bellerive. So especially on weekends, and during the summer, a lot of cars would come into town, people would visit Berrigan's, and then they'd hop back in their cars for the quick ride to the park. They came from within a fifty or sixty mile radius, from towns much like Bellerive, just to see the Whacks Museum; no one came out of Berrigan's and then unloaded major shopping dollars on Frémont Street, the main shopping drag, because there was nothing on Frémont that wasn't on *their* Main Streets. The mayor, the municipal judge, the members of the Town Council—all basically decent people, I must point out—they owned a lot of the stores and businesses that adjoined Berrigan's, and you'd see them looking out their windows or biting their lips or making disgusted faces as all these people would come, pay their dollar to get into Berrigan's, and then zoom out of Bellerive without stopping off at any of the other shops along Frémont. Biggy Piggy's Family Restaurant did a little ex-Berrigan business, but most of the tourists had either packed picnic lunches or got something at the concession stand at the state park. Not that the Whacks Museum was hurting anybody, mind you, but the powers that be were resentful. That was part of it.

The second part was that Mr. Berrigan didn't belong to anything. No one knew much about him, not even us kids. He lived alone, atop the museum, and we never knew if he was a lifelong bachelor, a widower, or divorced. He didn't belong to the VFW or the Elks, would come into church (sometimes the Methodist and sometimes the Baptist) usually only on Christmas Eve, and just generally did not participate in the spirit of

Belleriveness that we all held so important. He never went to Town Council meetings and never attended the volunteer fire department picnic fundraisers. Parents would drop an occasional odd remark that us kids'd pick up, and we got the impression that most of the grownups considered him an "odd fellow" or a "queer duck."

The third thing that, we gathered, the adults did not like about Mr. Berrigan was the rear room of the Whacks Museum, the one where us kids practically lived, me and Pat and Vince and all the other kids.

No one could then, or could now, deny that Mr. Berrigan was a genius at creating lifelike wax figures. He had an Elvis Presley and a John Wayne and Marilyn Monroe (with that dress blowing up) and a Superman and old Mahatma Gandhi and Jane Russell, you name them, they were there. His statues were remarkably, astonishingly lifelike. I think Vincent Price did about a dozen movies where the wax sculptor pours wax over living people and puts them on display, but Mr. Berrigan's statues were even better than that. The man was a superlative artist; and a dozen times a day someone would inadvertently catch himself saying "Excuse me" to or asking a question of one of the statues.

That was great for the old people and the tourists, but us kids always plunked down our dollar and ran right for the rear display room, the one you had to pass through the black curtain to get to, the one with the sign that read CHAMBER OF HORRORS.

He had Frankenstein and Dracula and the Wolfman and the Mummy. He had an empty pedestal with a plaque that said "The Invisible Man." He had the Creature from the Black Lagoon and Jack the Ripper and one of the Its: either "It, The Terror from Beyond Space" or

"It Came from Outer Space," I could never tell them apart. He had what were claimed to be authentic torture devices from the Spanish Inquisition on which realistic victims screamed and stared at us in agony and hopelessness. He had giant spiders and bats and rats and owls whose glass eyes glittered in the indirect and dim light. It was spooky in that room and it was unnerving and it was sometimes, when your imagination got to running away with you, downright frightening. We loved it. The place was rarely without two or three or ten kids, screaming in delighted fright and joking and chasing each other with pretend claws extended. There was always the one with the morbid sense of curiosity who would stand for hours staring at the torture scenes. One of those, a kid I knew only peripherally, named Larry, would, sixteen years later, murder his parents and his in-laws and his wife and his sister-in-law, but I think that was just coincidence.

Kids at that age, roughly ten to fourteen, all go through the horror/SF phase. We all collected and traded comic books and *Famous Monsters of Filmland* magazine and saw the latest Japanese monster movie every Saturday afternoon at the Bristol. And nobody thought much about it.

But then people, probably important people, started whispering things, things about how the back room of Berrigan's had items that were too unnerving for young, impressionable minds to be exposed to. The whisper probably started with the mayor and the other business people along Frémont, who passed it on to their wives, who brought it up at PTA meetings, where it got to all our parents, and then to us. They couldn't shut Berrigan's down, they couldn't prevent him from portraying movie monsters in his museum (they did shut down the dirty book store in less than two weeks), but they could prevent us kids from going in, from enriching Mr. Berrigan by thirty kids times a dollar a day two or three days a week. Our parents just simply refused to give us a dollar to get into the Whacks Museum, and the only way me or Pat or Vince could get in would be to save our total allowance for four weeks. And what, do without new comics or Heinlein paperbacks for a whole month just to see again the same statues? Sure, we loved the back room at Berrigan's, but we weren't willing to make that kind of sacrifice.

I don't know that Mr. Berrigan was being edged close to bankruptcy by the loss of revenue, but he must've been hurting, because most if not all of his mid-week cash came from us kids. It didn't take a genius to figure out what was the cause of his sudden decline in attendance. A few weeks after the ban went into effect, Mr. Berrigan took that statue of President Kennedy out of his window and replaced it with one of Mr. Hubert, the mayor. Mr. Hubert was somewhat overweight, and tended to perspire heavily. He also had a very heavy five o'clock shadow, usually by noon. The statue Mr. Berrigan put in the window was so true to life it was uncanny. Except that the statue was a *little* more overweight than Mr. Hubert, and there were big drops of perspiration so cleverly crafted they were astonishing, and the beard stubble was just ever so slightly more pronounced than on the original model. I think if someone had signed the name "Michelangelo" on the figure, it could have stood proudly in any museum in the world.

He also turned the Norman/Mrs. Bates statue around in the other window so that it was *looking* at Mr. Hubert.

Everyone thought it was a very funny joke, everyone except the mayor, of course. But there was nothing he could do about it. Mr. Berrigan even took an ad in the *Courier*, the daily paper that covered the entire county, announcing the new display as a tribute to our fine and respected mayor.

About a week later, Pat and me (Vince wasn't there because Catholic schools were open that week, the week before Easter; he'd be off next week, when me and Pat were both back in the hell known as sixth grade) were lounging in Boston Alley, a narrow street that ran behind and parallel to Frémont. The backs of the businesses on Frémont and those of First Street were all there was on Boston Alley; it was nothing but service entrances and garbage cans. We liked to sit there because no one ever came down it and we could pretend anything we wanted to.

This day we were playing FBI, looking for a Commie spy who had made off with the plans for the secret moon rocket and had eluded us by ducking down this alley. We were trying all the doors to see if he had entered one of the buildings. (He was going to have entered the Printrite Shop, where we were going to chase him into a vat of sophomoric acid and chalk up another victory for J. Edgar Hoover.) Pat turned the doorknob on the service entrance to the Whacks Museum . . . it turned. He pushed the door open and he looked at me. We must've looked like a negative and a print of the same picture: eyes and mouths wide open, torn between curiosity and flight. Pat decided it.

"Let's go in," he whispered.

It being a school holiday, we knew that there would be a trickling of tourists in the place, keeping Mr. Berrigan busy. So we went in. We were on a small landing, with a few steps leading up to a door we knew led to the Chamber of Horrors, and a longer flight of stairs leading downward. Mr. Berrigan knew us, of course, and if he saw us in the museum he'd know we hadn't paid to get in, so we both naturally headed down the stairs. I carefully closed the door behind us, making sure it didn't snap locked.

The staircase took a turn, and as we rounded it both of us gasped. We were in the basement of the Whacks Museum, and it looked like the dream mad scientist's laboratory.

There was a giant vat of what I assumed and still assume was wax, or paraffin, or whatever the figures were made of, heated with steam coils and gently simmering. There was a table the size of the *USS Lexington* with the tools of Mr. Berrigan's trade: knives and scrapers and spatulas and wires and glass eyes and wigs. But more important, more impressive, more absolutely, incredibly, sixth-grade *wonderful* were the works in progress. All over the room there rested heads, arms and legs, and torsos. A half-finished President Johnson head sat on a table; there was a headless and armless body that was dressed in cowboy clothes—Marshall Dillon, I presume? Or maybe Bat Masterson? Hideous monster faces stood on wire bodies or hung from hooks on the wall, including one that would, some twenty years later, bear a striking resemblance to one E.T. I picked up a fully formed scaly arm from the table and growled, thrusting it at Pat; he responded by holding an alien's head up in front of his own and lunging at me. We laughed, but then quickly strangled the noise. We just wanted to look, and we certainly didn't want to get caught. We examined, explored, gaped, and exclaimed for about a half hour, until we heard a creaking that frightened us. We bolted up the stairs and back out into Boston Alley, congratulating ourselves on our feat of bravery and derring-do, the Commie spy having blithely made his way back to Moscow with the secret plan.

That Saturday we took Vince with us, and the three of us crept back down to the workroom. The cowboy turned out to be an astonishing likeness of Nick Adams, "The Rebel." Again, we stayed for a few minutes, touching but not removing anything, and skulked out.

We discovered that the door was never locked, at least not during the day, and Pat and I, or Vince and I, or Pat and Vince, or Pat and Vince and I, or sometimes just me alone, went down there to marvel and explore several times over the next few weeks. We weren't allowed to see Mr. Berrigan's finished products, but we liked them even better seeing them as works in progress.

The mayor, in the meantime, was fit to be tied. He couldn't shut the Whacks Museum down on an obscenity charge, and he couldn't sue Mr. Berrigan for libel or slander since the wax figure in the window was a tribute to His Honor. Of course most of the town was laughing at him, which was obviously, but not *legally* Mr. Berrigan's intent. But Mayor Hubert came up with an idea and at the next council meeting he got up and introduced a measure to rezone Frémont Street so as to exclude shows and displays and businesses where merchandise is not purchased nor food consumed. The council, all his buddies and fellow cronies, of course passed the amendment unanimously, and Mr. Berrigan was informed the next day that he was in violation of the town zoning ordinance and had sixty days to vacate the premises of his wax figures. Of course, he could *sell* them, that would be within the spirit of the zoning change, but he couldn't charge anyone to just come in and *look* at them. He could've put price tags on them and *pretended* to sell them, but he still wouldn't be able to legally charge the admission fee.

Mr. Berrigan didn't have a leg to stand on. The proposed amendment was posted in the legal ads in the *Courier*, as was proper, and all parties in opposition were invited to attend the council meeting. Mr. Berrigan, as mentioned, never attended the council meetings, which were all open to the public, and no one else—all parents and Bellerive residents and PTA members—saw fit to rise in his defense. As Vince put it, Mr. Berrigan had been screwed, blued, and tattooed. In two months, he had to be out.

Our parents all reluctantly gave us one last dollar and let us go in to see the exhibits one more time. We all—us kids, I mean—told Mr. Berrigan how sorry we were, but he didn't say anything, just shrugged and shook his head. We knew how he loved that museum and all the statues, but we also knew that he wouldn't want to cry in front of a bunch of kids.

About six weeks after the council vote, the American Legion chapter had its annual dinner-dance at the Legion Hall, an ex-Masonic temple that was also used for most of the weddings and bar mitzvahs in town. Over a thousand people attended; the AL dinner-dance was *the* social event of the Bellerive calendar, since a sprinkling of everyone—the Protestants and the Catholics, the Jews and the Negroes—all came together under one roof for friendly and patriotic socializing.

I wasn't there, of course, but the *Courier* the next day had the story in such graphic detail that I might as well have been:

People started drifting out between twelve thirty and one A.M. Among them was Mayor Hubert, flushed with the congratulations of a cross-section of Bellerive society for his masterful handling of the Whacks Museum affair. The mayor was crossing the gravel road that separated the Hall from the grass parking lot when all of a sudden this big black car—a Cadillac, by all witnesses' descriptions—comes zooming down the road, spitting rocks in all directions, and catches the mayor right when he's in the middle of the road. The impact sent him flying fifty feet, and he was dead before he hit the ground. The car kept speeding, didn't slow down, just made jelly out of poor Mr. Hubert and kept going.

But what made the story even more interesting was that as the "death car" (so named in the *Courier*) passed in front of the Legion Hall, spotlights used to illuminate the night shone directly into the vehicle, and no fewer than seventeen witnesses gave the exact same description of the driver. He was a middle-aged man, balding with a pronounced widow's peak, a good thirty or forty pounds overweight, with wireless glasses and a small mustache, like the one Gale Gordon on the *Our Miss Brooks* show wore. But what was more remarkable was that all the witnesses agreed that the driver had a look of fear or horror on his face, which he had *before* he hit the mayor, and which didn't change *after* he struck him. Speculation was that the guy's accelerator was stuck, he couldn't control the car or stop it, and after he accidentally hit Mr. Hubert, he panicked and just kept on going. The state police were asked to help in the investigation, but as of the afternoon paper there were no suspects and no leads. An artist's rendition of the driver appeared in newspapers all over the state, and even the network affiliate in Little Rock showed the picture. After all, Mr. Hubert was the mayor of a town.

Well! I can tell you that when Pat and I met the next day in Boston Alley, we had little else to talk about. We had small sympathy for the loss of the mayor, since he had cost us Berrigan's Whacks Museum, but still, a crime of such brazen audacity deserved punishment. We spent a long time coming up with appropriate torments for the perpetrator, influenced no doubt by but surpassing some of the exhibits in the building we sat against.

Pat's father worked for a local moving company, and so he knew that on the following day a big truck had been reserved to start taking Mr. Berrigan's statues to their new home . . . a dead storage warehouse two hundred miles away. Having run out of ways to punish the mayor's killer, we decided to take one last, loving tour through Mr. Berrigan's basement.

Things hadn't changed much down there in the past few weeks. It was as if Mr. Berrigan had given up creating those magnificent works of his, and who could blame him? In fact, the last few times we'd been there we'd seen virtually *no* changes of any kind. It'd been like walking into a photograph. But this time, something struck me immediately, something that was on the large table, amid the lumps of wax and unfinished heads and knives. I walked over to it, and picked up one of those cheap cardboard "periscopes" with two little mirrors that were going at the five and ten for ninety-nine cents. You could use them to peer over fences and around buildings without being seen by the enemy, which came in handy while we were playing *Man from U.N.C.L.E.* But what would Mr. Berrigan be doing with one of them?

Pat had walked over to the other side of the room, where a draped figure stood. "I don't remember seeing this," he stage-whispered to me.

"Neither do I," I whispered back.

"I'm gonna see what it is," Pat said, and he pulled at the tarpaulin.

It was the figure of a middle-aged man, overweight, balding, with glasses and a Gale Gordon mustache. The hands were out, as if grasping a steering wheel. The face was frozen in a rictus of shock and fear. I think I gasped, but I know for a fact that Pat yelled and stepped backwards, tripping over his own feet and pulling the tarp completely off the figure. The statue tottered for a moment, then righted itself.

"Pat!" I hissed. "That looks like the guy who was driving the car that hit the mayor!"

Pat was still sitting on the floor. I could hear his heart pounding from across the basement. "Dummy can't drive no car, dummy!" he said.

I brandished the periscope. "No, but what if someone put the statue in the car to make it look like it was driving, and then sat on the floor and worked the gas and used this to see over the dashboard—" I paused to gulp a breath "—so he could see where to steer!"

"Are you saying—" Pat began, but then we both froze at the sound of rapid footsteps coming down the stairs.

"Who's there?" we heard Mr. Berrigan call. They were the first words we'd heard him say in weeks.

"Hide!" I breathed, and ducked behind some boxes and crates. I hoped Pat had found himself a place to hide too, but the blood rushing through my eyes had sort of made everything black.

I heard the sound of adult feet hitting the stone floor of the basement. "Who's there?" Mr. Berrigan asked. "Come out of there, I know you're here!"

I started to get up. After all, I was guilty only of trespass, not breaking and entering or burglary. Only later did it occur to me that Mr.

Berrigan would have been better off with no witnesses to his culpability.

As I rose behind the cartons, I was facing the driving statue. Mr. Berrigan was between me and the statue, his back to me. I was about to say something when the wax figure with the horrified expression moved forward an inch. From somewhere behind it, a deep voice said, "Berrigan!"

He jumped, and so did I, but then I recognized the voice as the one Pat used when he was imitating his father. What was he up to?

"Berrigan!" the "statue" said again, and it moved forward another inch. "What you did was wrong! Turn yourself in!"

I almost said, "Pat, are you crazy?" but the words died in my throat. If he had an idea, let him go ahead with it.

I could see the hairs on Mr. Berrigan's neck stand up, along with a few on his head. "Wh-wh—" he said.

The wax figure's hands began to move up and down. "You can't get away with this," Pat's father's voice said. "You can't live with this. Turn yourself in!"

The figure moved forward another inch, and began to sway gently. Mr. Berrigan was gulping, choking, trying to form words. Finally, he managed to spit out a sentence: "He—he t-took you all away from me! He took you!"

"We are just wax, Berrigan," the driver said. "We are nothing. You took a human life." The voice grew louder. "You've committed a grave sin, Berrigan! You made me help you! Go to the police, now! Turn yourself in!"

I'll be screwed, blued, and tattooed if Mr. Berrigan didn't fall to his knees right there on the floor and begin to beg the figure's forgiveness. I actually started to laugh, but he was babbling so he didn't hear me. One of the statue's arms pointed toward the staircase.

"Go!" Pat's father said. "Now!"

I couldn't believe it as I saw it happening, but Mr. Berrigan got himself up and dragged himself up the stairs and out the door, apologizing and babbling all the way.

The tension and fear and I don't know what were released in me then, and I burst into uncontrollable laughter. By the time I stopped, Pat was standing near me, his eyes wide. He was shaking.

"Oh," I said to him, "that was great." I put a hand out. "Slap me five, jive," I said.

He didn't slap me anything. He said, in a small voice, "I didn't do nothin'."

"What do you mean?" I asked. "You scared Mr. Berrigan into going to confess."

Pat gave a little shake of his head. "I told you, I didn't do nothin'."

We both turned and looked at the wax figure. Then we both bolted up the stairs and out the door and down the alley in the best Three Stooges tradition.

Because, you see, when we'd both turned to look at the wax statue . . . it smiled at us.

THE THEFT OF THE HALLOWEEN PUMPKIN

by Edward D. Hoch

Nick Velvet first saw the big multicolored hot-air balloons at an autumn rally on a farm in upstate New York one pleasant weekend when he and Gloria were driving aimlessly through the countryside.

"Oh, *look,* Nicky! Let's stop!" she cried—and since he was at least as interested as she was he pulled off the road into a field where other cars were parked.

There were about a dozen of the big balloons in all, crowded onto a farmer's field and looking a bit like some weird October crop come suddenly to maturity. Nick and Gloria walked among them, watching preparations for what was to be a cross-country balloon race. "Could *you* go up in one of those things?" Gloria asked.

"If I had to," Nick decided, viewing the gradually inflating balloons a bit uncertainly.

"They're perfectly safe," a freckle-faced young man assured them, overhearing their conversation. "Man has been flying in hot-air balloons for two hundred years."

"Is this one yours?" Nick asked.

"I don't own it but I fly it." He held out his hand. "My name's Roger Enfield." His red hair and a thin red mustache went well with the freckles. Nick guessed he was still in his early twenties.

He introduced himself and Gloria and Nick shook the young man's hand. "Where are you racing to today?"

"Where the wind takes us," Enfield answered with a laugh. "But we hope to head southeast across the Hudson and come down in Dutchess County."

"Can't you steer these things?"

"Oh, a little. You can go up and down by turning the burner on and off, regulating the amount of heated air in the balloon. Sometimes you can catch a stream of faster air aloft that's going in your direction. And we can always drop ballast if we have to. But a lot depends on the wind."

"Ready to go, Roger?" a tall man asked, striding through the crowd like an officer inspecting his troops. He wore riding boots and a tan-leather jacket reminiscent of the sort pilots wore during the barnstorming Twenties.

"Yes, Mr. Melrose," Enfield replied, and both of them climbed into the little gondola beneath the candy-striped balloon.

"That's Horace Melrose, the publisher," Gloria whispered. "I read somewhere that he's a nut about ballooning."

Melrose was snapping out commands as the ground crew released the ropes holding the balloon in place. Gradually it began to rise, clearing the trees and hovering for a moment as if seeking its way. Then a draft of air took it and it began drifting southeast toward the river.

"It looks like he's right on course," Gloria remarked as they strolled back to the car.

* * *

That was the first weekend in October, and Nick thought no more about Melrose, Enfield, and the balloon rally until three weeks later when he was far away, sunning himself on the beach of an expensive Acapulco resort. It was a nice place to visit in late October when the weather around New York began to turn damp and rainy, but Nick wouldn't have chosen it on his own without the urging of his latest client, who gave her name on the telephone as Rita Spangles.

"I can't come up there," she'd informed him. "And I can't do business over the telephone. Fly down here for a couple of days and I'll pay your expenses, in addition to your regular fee."

"All right," he'd agreed. "I'll phone you when I get in."

"No. Be on the beach the day after tomorrow. Have you got a bathing suit?"

"Yes."

"What color?"

"You get your choice of black or red trunks. Like a roulette wheel."

She laughed. "Wear the red. I always win on red."

"What will you be wearing?"

"A white maillot. I'll look for you around one o'clock."

So there he was, a half hour early, basking in the sun with a copy of yesterday's *New York Times*, looking, he hoped, like a typical businessman on vacation. Then he saw her, a few minutes before the appointed hour, strolling across the sand in her white one-piece bathing suit, carrying a striped beach jacket over one shoulder.

He tried not to look up too obviously as she passed, and she paused at his feet to ask, "Velvet?"

"Hello there," he said, glancing up with a smile. "Join me on my blanket?"

She sank down beside him. "From what people told me about you, I expected a younger man."

"Don't let the grey hairs fool you. I'm in disguise."

"I see." She picked up a handful of sand. "You steal things, right?"

"Right. Nothing of value. No money, art works, or securities. Worthless stuff only. My fee's twenty-five thousand."

"I know all that. Would you steal a pumpkin?"

"What kind of pumpkin?"

"A Halloween pumpkin. A jack-o-lantern. Next Sunday's Halloween."

"So it is. Where will the pumpkin be? In a store? In a farmer's field?"

"On the front porch of a friend of mine."

Nick rolled over on his stomach. "Miss Spangles, pardon me for mentioning it, but you could hire a couple of neighborhood kids to steal a pumpkin off somebody's front porch. They'd probably do it for a couple of candy bars."

"Not from this porch, they wouldn't. It's on an estate that's surrounded by a wall and has guards and dogs patrolling the grounds."

"Then why do they bother with a pumpkin if they don't encourage visitors?"

"A family custom. I think it's his wife's idea."

"Where is this place?"

She'd uncapped a plastic bottle and was spreading suntan lotion carefully along her firm thighs. Her hair was blonde and her complexion fair. She probably burned easily. "Dutchess County, north of New York. Do you know the area?"

"Sure."

"He's a publisher, name of Horace Melrose. He owns a chain of newspapers in cities around the country."

"I've met him briefly," Nick said.

"Can you do it? Steal the pumpkin from his porch on Halloween night?"

"It sounds easy enough. What's your connection with Melrose?"

"We were friends—" she began, and then corrected herself. "Hell, I was his mistress for eight years. Now I'm in exile down here. He pays the bills as long as I stay away."

"And the pumpkin?"

"That's a personal matter. You don't need to know any more."

"You want me to steal it as a sign? To remind him you're still around?"

"Something like that." She looked away, out to sea. "Just bring me the pumpkin."

"Is it a real one, or—"

"I know they use the same decorations every year, and then store them away. It's probably plastic or something." She reached into the drawstring bag she carried with her. "Here's a check for your travel expenses. You'll get your fee when you deliver."

Nick Velvet nodded. She was the sort of woman he liked to deal with, and not just because of the way she looked in a bathing suit. "You'll have it the day after Halloween," he assured her.

Roger Enfield was having a beer in a Poughkeepsie bar when Nick found him. It took a moment for recognition to dawn. "Sure, I remember you. At the balloon race. You had a nice-looking woman."

"Gloria will be happy to hear that," Nick murmured, signaling the bartender. "Who won the race?"

"Fella from New Mexico. Hot-air balloons are a big thing down there. They have races all the time."

"You work for Horace Melrose?"

"Hell, no! He acts like I do sometimes, though. For the races he hires the balloon *and* me from the promotion company I work for."

"Then your balloon's for hire?" Nick said with interest, ordering a beer for himself.

"Sure. What'd you have in mind?"

"A sort of promotion. On Halloween night."

"I don't take it up after dark. It's too easy to get tangled in power lines."

"Late afternoon, then. Just before dark." Nick hoped the pumpkin would be out on the porch then. It was a chance he'd have to take. "I'd want to go up, touch down at a certain spot, and then go up again. Could you do that?"

"Sure, if the weather cooperates. I don't go up if it's rainy or windy."

"The pay would be good," Nick assured him. "I'd want you to land on the Melrose property."

"What—on Halloween?" Enfield's voice rose in alarm. "Not a chance, mister! Not after what happened there last year!"

"Oh? I wasn't aware anything happened there last year. Why don't we move over to a booth and you can tell me about it."

Enfield wiped the foam from his red mustache and picked up his half-finished beer. "Sure, I'll tell you. It's no secret. It was in all the papers." They settled down in one of the wooden booths where there was more privacy and Nick ordered another round of beers.

The story Enfield told him was simple enough. On Halloween of the previous year, a man had been shot on Melrose property near the front porch of the house. A security guard had mistaken him for a prowler, and when the man started running the guard had fired. The man's name was Tom Reynolds and he was a sportswriter for a Philadelphia newspaper. He'd died at the hospital a few hours later. No one ever established what he was doing on the Melrose property.

"So you see what I mean about Halloween," Roger Enfield said. "If I landed that balloon there Sunday night, the guards would probably pump it full of holes."

"What's Melrose got to hide?" Nick wondered.

"Nothing. He just likes his privacy. He told me once he's around so many people every day he likes to get away from them on weekends."

Nick was struck by a thought. "He's a newspaper publisher. Did this man Reynolds work for him?"

"No. Melrose doesn't own any big-city papers. They didn't even know each other. That's why no one could figure out what Reynolds was doing there."

"Did the police bring charges against anyone?"

Enfield shook his head. "The Melroses are pretty important people up here. And Reynolds was trespassing, after all."

Rita Spangles had mentioned a wife. "What about Mrs. Melrose?"

"Jenny? She's a fine woman—very involved with social issues. She serves on a lot of committees."

Nick finished his beer. "Are you sure you won't change your mind about the balloon?"

"On Halloween? Not a chance! Take my advice. If you don't want to get shot, stay away from the Melrose place. If anything, those guards are more trigger-happy now than they were a year ago."

Until then, it had seemed like a simple and uncomplicated assignment. In fact, it had seemed so simple that Nick had dreamed up the balloon landing to spice it up a bit. The idea of using a hot-air balloon to steal a pumpkin and then escaping the same way appealed to his sense of the dramatic. If it couldn't be done, there were plenty of other ways to accomplish the theft. But the news about the man named Tom Reynolds being shot and killed there the previous Halloween bothered him. What if Rita Spangles had hired Reynolds to steal the plastic pumpkin, too? What if the whole thing was some sort of bizarre ritual to lure someone to his death each Halloween?

Later when he told Gloria of this idea, she scoffed. "Honestly, Nicky, you get the craziest ideas sometimes! You should be writing these horror movies the kids like so much. You could call this one *Halloween* 4½ or something."

"I suppose I did let my imagination go too far," he admitted. "But Tom Reynolds is dead, there's no denying that. And he was trespassing on their property, the same as I'll be doing."

"Can't you find out if there was any connection between Reynolds and this woman who hired you?"

It was a good suggestion and he wondered why he hadn't thought of it. "I've only got a few days but maybe I can find out something," he decided.

The following morning Nick was in Philadelphia, calling on Tom Reynolds' former editor at the newspaper office on Market Street. The editor's name was Paul Karoski, and his thin hair and pale skin indicated that his was a sporting life spent mainly indoors.

"Reynolds was one of the best young sportswriters I had," he told Nick. "It was a shame what happened to him."

"Exactly what did happen?"

"He was onto a story of some sort. He never did tell me what it was. It brought him to the

Melrose estate for some reason and he got himself shot. That's about all I know."

"The story must have been involved with sports somehow," Nick reasoned.

"Sure. Football, I think, because for a couple of days before he died he kept replaying a videotape from the Eagles-Rams game of a few weeks earlier. I even looked at it myself after the shooting, but I couldn't see anything unusual on it."

"Do you still have that tape?" Nick asked.

Karoski thought about it. Then he got up and shuffled through a stack of videotapes on top of a filing cabinet. "Maybe I erased—no, here it is. Eagles-Rams, from last October."

"Could I borrow it?"

The sports editor frowned at Nick. "What's your connection with all this? Are you a detective or something?"

"An investigator. I'm working on another matter and someone suggested I look into Tom Reynolds' death."

"All right," Karoski decided. "Take the tape, but bring it back. Give me a receipt for it."

"Gladly." Nick slipped the video cassette into the briefcase he'd brought along and reached for a pen. "One other thing. Did you or Reynolds know a woman named Rita Spangles?"

Karoski thought about it. "I don't, but I had no way of knowing all Tom's friends. He was a good-looking fellow, unmarried— Hold on. Wait a minute. Rita Spangles—I think that was the name of the woman at the hospital."

"What woman?"

"After he was shot, Reynolds lived about five hours. The hospital phoned me because they found his press card on him. I drove right up there, but he was dead by the time I reached the hospital. It was about a three-hour drive. They told me the only person he'd seen was this woman, and I think her name was Rita Spangles. I saw her only briefly, as she was leaving the hospital. I figured it was one of his girl friends."

"Did she seem upset by his death?"

"Yes. But she didn't talk to me."

"I'll get this tape back to you," Nick promised, giving Karoski his asked-for receipt as he left.

That evening he played it on their machine at home. Gloria looked in from the kitchen and sighed. "Don't we get enough football on Sundays and Monday nights?"

"This is work. It's a tape Reynolds was studying before he was killed."

"It looks like any other football game to me," Gloria said after watching it a while.

"That's the trouble," Nick agreed. He sat through the entire game—nearly three hours of it—without seeing anything unusual. It was just like any other football game.

On Friday night he looked for and found Roger Enfield in the same bar. "Are you back with your balloon plan?" the young man asked.

"A new one this time. You don't have to take me up, and you don't have to land the balloon. But could you fly over the Melrose place Sunday evening, just before dark?"

Enfield thought about it. "Daylight Savings Time ends Saturday. It'll be dark a little after five o'clock on Sunday."

"All right—around that time, then."

"Where'll you be?"

Nick took some money from his wallet and slid it across the table. "I'll be around. You just come in low and attract lots of attention."

The following morning Nick drove up to the Melrose place, stopping along the way to phone Jenny Melrose for an appointment. He represented himself as a free-lance writer wanting to interview her for an article he was preparing on gracious living in the Hudson Valley. He suspected that would perk her interest and it did.

She was a pleasant woman in her late thirties, a bit younger than her husband but with the same commanding personality. The sunny living room in which she greeted him had been decorated in expensive good taste—a bit old-fashioned by Nick's standards but still attractive. "Where will your article appear, Mr. Nicholas?" she asked, arranging herself on the sofa opposite him.

"I'm hoping for *The New York Times Magazine*, or perhaps *Country Gentleman*."

"I see."

"Could you tell me a bit about your style of living here?" Nick asked. "How you celebrate holidays, Halloween, for instance, since it's coming up tomorrow. Do you get any trick-or-treaters here?"

"Heavens, no. The gate is closed and there are guards. My husband is very security-conscious."

"How about decorations? Do you do anything special?"

"For Halloween?" She smiled at his question, perhaps at the absurdity of it. "No, no special decorations."

Nick pursued doggedly, "Not even a pumpkin?"

"Oh, we put a couple out on the porch with candles in them. They can be seen from the road. But that's as far as we go."

"I'd like to get a picture of those if I could."

She spread her hands helplessly. "I don't even know where they're stored. I must remember to have one of the servants get them out tomorrow."

"Perhaps I could come back then. The front of

your house is so lovely it would make a very effective picture in my story."

"I'm afraid tomorrow wouldn't be convenient."

"I wouldn't have to disturb you. You could just leave word at the gate that I'm expected. One of your security men can stay with me while I snap a photograph of the house on Halloween evening."

"Very well," she agreed. "I suppose there's no harm in that."

Nick forced himself to remain for another forty-five minutes, pursuing his line of questioning about holiday celebrations. Then he departed, confident that he had prepared the way. She had surprised him when she mentioned two pumpkins, but that wouldn't stop him. He'd steal them both.

Halloween proved to be a crisp autumn day in Dutchess County, with the last of the leaves drifting down through sunlit skies. Wearing a black turtleneck sweater and slacks, Nick arrived back at the Melrose estate a little after four o'clock, let himself in the chained entranceway, and drove up the curving driveway. He was just taking a camera from his car when Horace Melrose, coming around from the side of the house, accosted him.

"What are you doing here?" the publisher asked.

"Nicholas is the name," Nick said, extending his hand. "I had a most informative interview with Mrs. Melrose yesterday and she gave me permission to return today for some pictures of the outside of the house."

Melrose ignored Nick's hand. "There's supposed to be a security guard with you. We've had trouble before with reporters."

"I'm not a reporter, Mr. Melrose. I'm a free-lance writer doing a magazine article."

"Nevertheless, no one's allowed on these grounds unaccompanied." He walked quickly down the drive to speak some brief harsh words to the security guard on duty. The man came hurrying up to Nick.

"Get your pictures and be on your way, mister," he growled.

"The lighting has got to be right," Nick answered, looking at the sky. Enfield's balloon was due any minute.

As Nick fussed with the camera, Jenny Melrose appeared in the doorway with two large glowing plastic pumpkins. "Here they are," she announced. "I'm sorry to have kept you waiting." She placed one on either side of the wide steps and inspected the scene with a critical eye. "Can you get them both in the photo?"

"I think so," Nick said, looking through the viewfinder and taking a step backward, thinking ironically that the pumpkins were reasonable copies of the real thing and would actually photograph very well. "Let me just move them slightly," he said, noticing that Horace Melrose was no longer on the scene and the guard was taking only a casual interest in the proceedings. He lifted the nearer pumpkin, careful not to disturb the flickering candle inside. There seemed nothing unusual about it to make it valuable to Rita Spangles or anyone else. A grease-penciled number on the bottom—274—seemed to indicate what its price had been.

"What's that?" the guard said, pointing at the sky.

"It looks like Roger Enfield's balloon," Jenny Melrose said. She and the guard moved out beyond Nick's car for a better view. "I wonder what he's doing up so late in the afternoon."

Nick had a look at the second pumpkin by then, but there was no price marked on it. While Mrs. Melrose and the guard watched the descending balloon, he blew out both candles and tossed the pumpkins through the open window of his car.

"I think he's trying to land," the guard said, unsnapping the holster at his side.

The big striped balloon, settling toward the front lawn of the Melrose estate, did indeed look as if it might land. Nick climbed quickly into his car. "Thanks a lot," he called out to Jenny Melrose, "I've got my pictures!"

"What?" She turned, startled. "Already?"

Nick was already wheeling the car around the circular driveway. He heard her say something about the pumpkins, and then the guard shouted at him, but he kept going.

His car hit the slender chain across the gate and snapped it like a string. He saw a little puff of white in the rearview mirror and thought he heard the bark of the guard's gun fired after him. Overhead, Roger Enfield's balloon lifted high into the twilight sky, out of harm's way.

"What did *you* do for Halloween?" Nick asked Rita Spangles the following day, gazing out of her hotel-room window at the golden sand of the Acapulco beach.

"Trick or treat, like everyone else," she answered. "The treat was a bottle of French champagne in a nice man's room." She lit a cigarette and studied the two plastic pumpkins on the table in front of her. "Don't think I'm paying you *fifty* thousand just because you stole *two* of them."

"The second one's on me," Nick said generously. "I didn't know which one you needed."

She continued staring at them. "To tell you

the truth, I don't either. How come the heat from the candle doesn't melt the plastic?"

"They make it with a high melting point for uses like this."

"You think there's something inside the candles?"

Nick shook his head. "I checked on that. They're solid. Look, maybe I can help with your problem if you tell me about it."

"Is that included in your fee?"

"Sometimes."

"All right," she agreed with a sigh, sitting on the edge of the bed. "As you know, I was Horace's mistress. I still am, I suppose, though I haven't seen him in a long time. Just over a year ago, this reporter named Tom Reynolds, a sportswriter and photo editor for a Philadelphia paper, started nosing around. That's when Horace sent me out of town. Reynolds tracked me to Florida and started asking questions."

"What sort of questions?"

"Horace's firm wanted to buy a paper in the Midwest and someone out there tried to block the sale by claiming he had links to organized crime. They said he was a business associate of Norman Elba, who's involved in illegal sports gambling."

"The sports connection—that's what interested Reynolds!" Nick remembered the videotape of the football game. Luckily he'd brought it in his suitcase on the off-chance Rita knew something about it.

"I suppose so," she agreed. "Anyway, Reynolds asked me about Horace, about what we did on certain dates he named. At first I clammed up, but later, when I knew Horace was about to ditch me, I started talking. I didn't have any solid information about Norman Elba, though."

"What was Reynolds doing at the Melrose home last Halloween?"

"He'd learned something and he went to confront Horace with it. Horace thought it was a routine interview and agreed to see him. I told Reynolds he should have settled for a statement over the phone, but he wanted to see Horace's face. He saw it, all right, and got a bullet for his trouble."

"You were at the hospital when he died," Nick said.

She looked surprised. "How did you know that?"

"His editor told me."

"Yeah, well, I went up there with him. You know. He was a handsome guy, young."

"Then you saw the shooting?"

"Not really. I was waiting in the car out on the main road, so Horace wouldn't see me. I followed the ambulance to the hospital and told them I was his fiancée."

"Did he talk to you?"

"Just a few words before he died. He said to get the pumpkin. 'It's on the pumpkin.' Those were his exact words."

"*On* the pumpkin, not *in* it?"

"*On*. I'm sure of that. But the next day when I returned to Horace's place, the pumpkins were gone—stored away for another year. Horace didn't want me snooping around with his wife there—he sent me away and warned me not to come back. He promised to send me money, and he has, but I keep remembering Tom Reynolds, a nice guy who didn't deserve what he got. And I keep remembering the dirty deal Horace handed me. When another Halloween rolled around I decided I should try to even the score, for Reynolds and me both."

Nick turned over the orange plastic globes,

searching again for markings. "There's only the price on this one. Unless—"

"What is it?"

"This 274 scrawled on here with a black grease pencil. You said Reynolds was a photo editor besides being a sportswriter. He might have carried a grease pencil to mark photos, and when he saw the Melrose security guards drawing their guns he managed to mark this number on the pumpkin."

"I thought it was the price," Rita said.

"So did I. But $2.74 isn't a likely price for it. And there's no decimal point. It's not a price at all, but a number."

"A date?"

"February 1974? I doubt it. He'd have had time to put a line or dash separating the numbers if he meant them to be separated."

"Then what could it be?"

"Something important to him. The key to whatever he'd uncovered about Melrose and Norman Elba. I wonder—"

Nick was interrupted by a knock at the door. "Room service!"

Rita Spangles looked blank. "I didn't order anything."

"Open the door slowly," Nick whispered, slipping behind it.

But as soon as her hand turned the knob the door sprang open, propelled by a brawny man who barreled forward to grab Rita and cover her mouth before she could scream. Nick shoved back on the door, knocking a second man off balance, then dove for the one holding Rita. As they toppled, wrestling, to the floor, the second man recovered enough to shout, "Get the pumpkins!"

Rita snatched up a lamp and brought it down on the head of Nick's adversary, stunning him. Then she turned toward the man who had spoken. "I know you," she said, "you're Norman Elba!"

The gambler smiled and reached inside his jacket. Nick moved fast, almost by reflex, hurling the broken lamp at Elba's head just as a snub-nosed revolver appeared in his hand.

It was a brief battle. When it was over, Nick and Rita had Norman Elba and his henchman tied hand and foot with a haphazard collection of pantyhose, neckties, and a torn-up pillowcase.

"Melrose knew where to find you," Nick explained to Rita. "He guessed you hired me to steal the pumpkins and sent Elba after you." He turned to the gambler. "Isn't that right?"

"Go to hell!"

Nick held up the pumpkin. "What does 274 mean?"

"You tell me. You wanted it bad enough to steal it."

"It was Tom Reynolds' dying message, hidden for a year after his murder, and somehow it ties you and Melrose together."

Elba merely smiled. Rita appealed to Nick. "We can't hold him here forever."

"No," he agreed. There was a sound from the room next door. It sounded like a football game on television, and he remembered that the games from the States were shown here on cable. It would be Monday evening back East. Then he thought again of the videotape Paul Karoski had loaned him. "Of course—that's it!"

"What is?"

"Does the hotel have a video recorder somewhere?"

"There's one in the lounge downstairs. They play tapes of horse races in the afternoon and the guests make small wagers."

"Come on," Nick said. "I've got a tape in my room I want to play."

The lounge was unoccupied when they reached it and he slipped the tape into the machine. Then he turned on the set and pushed the FAST FORWARD button on the video recorder.

"What are you doing?" Rita asked.

"These machines all have digital counters to indicate the relative position of programs or scenes on a tape. See it there? It's almost to one hundred already. When it nears 274 we'll stop it and play the tape at its regular speed. I think we'll see something interesting—something Reynolds' editor missed because he didn't know where to look."

He waited another moment and stopped the tape at 270. Then he pushed the PLAY button. "But they're not even showing the game," Rita complained. "The camera's panning over the crowd in the stands."

"And there it is!" Nick quickly pressed the PAUSE button and the image froze on the screen. It was a picture of Horace Melrose and Norman Elba with their heads together in deep conversation. "There's the proof Tom Reynolds spotted! When he confronted Melrose with what he had, Melrose ordered his security guards to shoot him. But Reynolds managed to scrawl that number on the pumpkin, and to tell you about it before he died."

"But why didn't Horace try to recover this tape?"

"Reynolds may not have been that specific about the nature of his evidence. Or Melrose might have figured it was better not to call attention to the tape at all. If he led Karoski to believe it was valuable, he could have gotten another copy easily enough and looked at it a bit more carefully."

"What should we do now?" she asked.

Nick thought about it as he rewound the video tape. "Phone Paul Karoski in Philadelphia and tell him what we've got. Then we'll turn Elba and his friend over to the local police and I'll be heading home—as soon as you pay me my fee."

THE NIGHT WATCHMAN

by David Braly

He had walked the sidewalks of Sawyerville at night for as long as anyone could remember. He never hurried, never strolled, just proceeded in a slow but businesslike manner from one door to the next, turning each knob to make sure that every store in town was safely locked. To think of Sawyerville at night without thinking of its watchman was impossible.

And yet, while he was familiar to everyone, it was as an old building or weathered face is familiar, not as is a living, breathing person. People readily recognized his tall, lean figure, his slouching wide-brim hat, his low-strapped holster and gun, and his long, lead-handled flashlight. They knew his lumbering walk, his habit of staying close to the walls, within the shadows. They were familiar with all these things about him, but not with the man himself.

Somebody must have interviewed him for the job, must have shown him around the town when he first arrived, but no one could remember who. For in the whole town of Sawyerville, there was not one man or woman who claimed personal knowledge of the watchman. Where he lived and what his name was were as unknown as were his origins and past life. No one claimed him as their kin, friend, or acquaintance. No one could say what color his clothes or hat might be, although almost everyone assumed they were dark colors, just as they assumed that his skin, eyes, and hair were dark. His features were unknown, his face forever hidden by the night and by the slouching brim of his hat. In fact, there was even an argument about his features in the Golden Star Tavern one night in 1964. One man claimed that the watchman looked like Jimmy Stewart, another said that he resembled Anthony Quinn.

After that argument, when men saw the night watchman making his rounds they looked closely, trying to see the features of his face. But the night and the slouching hat and the distance prevented them. Perhaps if they'd walked up to the watchman they might have seen his face. And yet no man ever approached him. Nor, by some coincidence, was any person ever approached by the watchman, although he never appeared to avoid anyone. Every night he followed his route down the dark sidewalks and back alleys and no person ever happened to be directly on that route either by accident or by design.

What annoyed people about the watchman was that he wasn't satisfied to walk that route. He could and did go anywhere he wanted, and no one knew from one night to the next where he might be. Old men staggering out of the taverns on Main Street would see a shadow moving against a building on the opposite side of the street and think that it was he. Young men whistling as they walked home from the bordello on the edge of town would suddenly feel that they were being watched, and they would think that he was there, somewhere, in the night. Women hurrying down the dark sidewalks would feel his eyes following them. Teenagers sneaking down the deserted alleys after curfew would suddenly notice that the watchman was standing in the distance, looking at them. Small children were afraid to venture out of their yards after dusk, fearing an encounter with him, and they would imagine that every movement in the darkness was he.

For all that, the watchman was never a subject of much speculation or conversation. He was there, he'd always been there, people wondered who he was and where he lived, and that was all.

However, there was one person in Sawyerville who wondered more than the others about the watchman. Even as a child Thomas Perkins had wondered. He continued to wonder as an adult. His curiosity increased, and occasionally he voiced it to his friends in the bank or at whatever tavern he happened to be patronizing.

Thomas Perkins was the last member of one of Sawyerville's pioneer families. Amos Perkins, his great-grandfather, had come there from Missouri in 1878. He had originally ranched on land nearby, but over a period of many years he had by hard work and cunning opportunism built for himself and his family a great enterprise based upon land and livestock but also embracing several mercantile stores, two gold mines, and a freight line. The Perkins fief was shattered by the Great Depression, and by the time Thomas Perkins inherited its ruins, all that remained was five hundred acres of land along the creek, leased to a neighboring farmer, and a half interest in an abandoned cinnabar mine inhabited by bats.

There also remained the faded green three-story house on Walton Street, its steep grey roof and half-dozen chimneys towering above the nearby elms and the neighboring houses. A meter-high fence of slender green pickets enclosed its yard, that was planted with shrubs instead of grass. Thomas Perkins lived there alone. The only other person who ever went into the house was the old cleaning woman who busied herself there every day while Perkins was at the bank, where he had secured employment as a cashier. Early in the evening, after the sun had gone down but before the sky had blackened, Perkins would sit in his chair atop the high, covered porch of the big house, a tall, thin young man with black hair and piercing brown eyes who was overdressed in a blue three-piece suit, looking out at the front gate, at Walton Street, and out toward the center of town that was half a mile away and obscured by the nearby houses and trees.

When night came, Perkins would walk the several blocks to the taverns on Main, or drive his beat-up old Chevy to one of those at the edge of town. There he would drink whisky and talk with other men. Usually he talked about sports, politics, or local affairs, sometimes he talked gossip, and occasionally he talked about the watchman. Rarely his subject was the watchman, yet he talked more than any other man about him.

As time passed, Thomas Perkins warmed to his subject. Each year he talked more about him than the previous year, until men noticed that speculating about the watchman had become his favorite activity. His talk increased their own curiosity about the watchman, but mostly it caused them to wonder about Perkins himself, about why he was so absorbed in the subject.

Eventually the cashier became obsessed by the watchman. Never an evening passed that Perkins didn't mention him at some tavern. His attitude, the way he would spring mention of him into any conversation on the slightest pretext, revealed the depth of his obsession. It was clear to almost everyone who knew Thomas Perkins that the young man was thinking about the watchman during the whole of his days, and possibly dreaming about him at night. Old friends avoided him because they were tired of hearing his pointless speculation, and one or two men were heard to say that they feared Perkins was losing his mind.

Perkins probably noticed that he was driving away his friends. But apparently he could not stop himself. And their indifference to the mystery annoyed him.

"What's the matter with you people?" he exploded one night. "Don't you understand? Don't you see how strange it is? As long as the oldest people in this town can remember, that night watchman has always been making his rounds. Don't you realize how old he has to be?"

"Now, Tom," said his friend Carl Lockwood. "We both know that the watchman those old folks remember and this man can't be the same fellow. There must have been another one before this man."

"When was the current watchman hired?"

"I don't know."

"And who does he work for?"

"Why, the merchants of course."

Thomas Perkins wasn't satisfied by these answers. During his spring break in 1981 he decided to conduct his own, private investigation. It involved going through the files of the *Sawyerville News* and the records of the municipal and county governments, as well as his questioning people of knowledge and authority in the sheriff's department, the Sawyerville police department, the Chamber of Commerce, and the Sawyerville Merchants Association. What he learned was that there was no record or recollection of *anyone's* having ever hired the watchman.

Perkins reported his findings to his friends and to others who were willing to listen. Almost everyone he talked to expressed interest, but no one appeared to be alarmed by what he had discovered. Carl Lockwood listened attentively while Perkins revealed his findings, then shrugged his shoulders and suggested that Perkins write a letter about it to the editor of the newspaper.

Herb Sudbury had a better suggestion. Sudbury was a short, heavyset, bald man in his early sixties who had once been a millworker but who now did all sorts of odd jobs around town in order to earn enough money to pay for his shabby second-floor room at one of the old boarding houses on Thompson Street and an inadequate supply (to his own way of thinking) of whisky. Sudbury was also the father of the girl Perkins had almost married and one of the few friends he had who for brief moments could halfway match his interest in the mystery of the watchman. And his suggestion to Perkins was simple: "Let's follow him and see where he goes."

The next night Perkins and Sudbury huddled together beneath the bridge that spanned the creek. From his investigation Perkins knew that many nights the bridge was the last place where the watchman had been seen. And so they waited there, listening for footfalls on the pedestrian walk above, hearing for the most part only the creek water splashing over rocks. Occasionally they did hear someone walking on the bridge. When they did, Perkins would sneak out onto the south bank where he would stare from behind a bush until he was certain that the person he was looking at was not the watchman.

Finally, at eleven o'clock, Perkins recognized through the leaves of the bush the tall, lean, hatted figure of the watchman. He turned east after he left the bridge, walking down the narrow road that bordered the north bank. Perkins slipped back under the bridge, where he whispered to Sudbury that their quarry had arrived. Sudbury, sober for once, only reluctantly followed Perkins up the north bank and onto the road.

Just as they stepped onto the road, the watchman turned full around and switched on his flashlight, pinning Perkins and Sudbury in its beam.

"He sees us," gasped Sudbury.

"Stay calm."

"Calm, nothing. Man-oh-man!"

Perkins stared into the light. He didn't move.

Sudbury moved, but not much. He looked down at the bank, calculating his chances if he tried to escape. He knew that he was old and weak, that he could never outrun any man who had a reservoir of strength, and still less could he outrun a bullet. He remained where he was, anxious to flee but afraid to move.

Perkins started walking toward the watchman.

"What're you doing?" whispered Sudbury.

"I'm going up to him and look him right in the eye."

"Are you crazy? Come back ... Tom ... Tom!"

But Perkins continued to walk down the leafy road toward the watchman, eighty feet distant from Sudbury. Soon Perkins was so close that his body shielded Sudbury from the flashlight beam.

Sudbury stared, horrified, afraid to speak or to move. All that he could see was the shrinking black form of Perkins's back, outlined by the watchman's light. All that he could hear was the splashing waters of the creek and a gentle breeze swaying the upper branches of the elms and willows that lined its banks.

Suddenly the light disappeared.

Sudbury assumed that either Perkins was now so close to it that his bulk completely blocked it out or else the watchman had switched it off. Eventually he decided that the latter had happened. No matter how close Perkins was to the flashlight some of the light would be visible unless the watchman had switched it off.

Sudbury squinted in an effort to see what was happening. He could almost make out the form of Perkins standing on the road, but the watchman wasn't visible. The night was late, and dark, and its blackness was alleviated only by the quarter moon, the stars, and the light that came from the windows of a few houses on the other side of the creek through the elms and willows.

For ten minutes Sudbury waited for something to happen. Nothing did. And during the time of his wait his panic subsided, until finally it vanished altogether. He came to believe that Thomas Perkins and the watchman were standing on the road ahead talking to each other, maybe even having a good laugh about the way the cashier had thought the watchman so strange and mysterious. Yes, and he, Sudbury, was missing the conversation.

He began walking down the road, slowly at first but faster after he got his legs working good. He walked toward the black form of Perkins's back, listening for the conversation, for the laughs, but hearing only the splashing water and the swaying leaves.

Sudbury was less than ten feet from Perkins before he realized that the cashier was alone.

When he did reach him, he found Perkins staring straight ahead, wide-eyed, his mouth half-open and his face immobile.

"Where is he? Tom? Where's the watchman? . . . What happened? . . . Tom? . . . What's wrong? . . . Tom!"

Thomas Perkins never said a word to Herb Sudbury. And, although he did recover his ability to speak during the months that followed, he refused to talk about what had happened on the tree-shadowed road.

The watchman made his rounds as usual the following night, and all the nights that came after. Several police officers were heard to say that he would be questioned about what had happened the night Perkins suffered his breakdown, but they never did get around to doing it. Certainly no one else has tried to question or even approach the watchman, who still makes his nightly rounds down the sidewalks and back alleys of Sawyerville.

And most certain of all is the fact that Perkins has never again confronted him. He was released from the Portland hospital in October, 1982. He was rehired by the bank, but for shorter hours. Neither there, nor at the taverns, which he visits now only infrequently, will he discuss the night he met the watchman nor the watchman himself. Knowing that he went through a terrible year and a half after that meeting, no one ever talks about those things in his presence.

However, everyone believes that while Thomas Perkins, wearing his blue three-piece suit, sits on his chair on the porch of his huge, faded green house watching the arrival of dusk, he is thinking about one particular night in the spring of 1981—and about the watchman.

TONY LIBRA AND THE KILLER'S CALENDAR

by Richard Ciciarelli

King Arthur, also known as Tony Libra, English instructor at Halstrom College, opened his front door and bowed to Julius Caesar and Calpurnia as he ushered them in.

"Pretty good, Tony, though the beard could be a little longer." Bill Barkley, Ph.D. in mathematics, hauled his toga up on his shoulder. "Who's Guinevere?"

"Jeanne Unger, one of the department secretaries. George and Myra Wakes are here, too. He's Mahatma Gandhi and she's Indira."

The doorbell rang again. "Excuse me, please," Tony Libra told them. "Go on into the living room and get yourselves a drink."

On the front porch Libra found a nervous man dressed not in Halloween costume but in everyday street clothes. "Henry," Libra said, surprised. "What brings you here tonight?"

"A problem, Tony. I need some help."

"I haven't got much time, I'm afraid," Libra said. "I've got some people here for drinks before the dance."

"It won't take long," the visitor said. "Only a minute or two."

Libra led his latest guest down the hall and into the living room.

"Folks, look who's here," he announced. "You all know Henry Jameson, don't you?"

There was a chorus of greetings.

"Be right back," Libra told his guests. "This way, Henry."

In the den with the door closed behind them, Libra asked, "Now, what's up?"

"Have you read in the papers lately about the trafficking of hard drugs on campus?" Jameson said.

Libra nodded. Several students had been arrested for cocaine possession but had refused to say where they got it. The police had no clues.

Jameson glanced at the door. Reassured that it was still tightly closed, he leaned forward a little. "I think I know who's supplying the drugs. It's one of our own faculty members."

"What?" Libra exploded in disbelief.

"I have no real proof," Jameson went on, "but I happened to overhear two students discussing it. They mentioned a faculty member by name."

"Who?"

Jameson shook his head. "I don't want to tell that to anyone except the police—maybe."

"Maybe? Why maybe?"

"That's where you come in," Jameson said. "You've been connected with police work. You'll know how they'll react. I can't be sure what those boys said was true, and I'd hate to go around accusing an innocent person to the police. What should I do?"

"Ask for Chief Backus. Tell him you're a friend of mine and that I referred you to him. He'll handle things very discreetly, believe me."

"You're sure? I don't want this person to suffer if he's innocent."

"Don't worry, Henry," Libra said. "The police can't do a thing without real evidence. If there is none, they'll dismiss your story as idle talk."

"You won't say anything yourself, will you?" Jameson asked. "Not to anyone?"

Libra frowned. "Of course not. Now, how about a drink?"

Jameson shook his head. "Oh, no!" He paused awkwardly. "I don't think I could enjoy it." He rose.

"In case anything happens to me," he said with an odd expression, "just remember to check up on the calendar."

Six hours later Henry Jameson was dead.

"We've been tracing Professor Jameson's movements during the past twenty-four hours," Police Chief Wilbur Backus explained, "and we learned he visited you here last night, perfessor." Several times in the past Backus had called upon Libra for help; this time the visit was more official.

Libra nodded. "Henry did stop in last night, about eight thirty." He recounted Jameson's story.

"And he never mentioned the faculty member's name?"

"Never." Libra shrugged. "A matter of conscience for him, evidently."

"Well, we don't have much to go on. Apparently Jameson was walking along beside the park when he was attacked. His assailant struck from behind, stabbed him several times below the left shoulderblade. We found a large jackknife several feet away from the body; it appears to be the murder weapon. From the look of things, there wasn't much of a struggle, so Jameson must have been taken by surprise."

"He wasn't a very big man," Libra said. "Not much bigger than me, in fact."

Backus looked at his five foot six inch, one hundred twenty-five pound friend and nodded in agreement. "He looked a little soft, though."

"No doubt he was. Henry never was one for physical fitness. His whole life was his scholarly work. He was a philologist and loved it. He had written several books on the English language and any number of papers on word oddities and etymologies. That takes time. But go on. Who found him?"

"Two students coming home from the costume ball," Backus said. "About two o'clock in the morning. Jameson was dead and the streets were empty."

Libra spread his hands. "Well, for whatever it's worth, he did say something to me you should know. He said as he was leaving that if anything happened to him I should check up on the calendar."

"On the calendar?" Backus looked puzzled. "He had a small pocket calendar in his jacket but we didn't find anything significant in it. Maybe you can make some connection. Unless . . ." the chief snapped his fingers restlessly.

"What's on your mind?"

"It's a long shot, but who knows? You said you had company, faculty company, last night when Jameson came to your house?"

"Sure," Libra said, "but what . . . Now, wait a minute, chief. Are you implying that one of my guests is the cocaine supplier who killed Jameson to silence him?"

"Why not?" Backus asked. "Jameson told you a faculty member might be the supplier, and you said yourself he kept staring at the door as if he were afraid someone was listening. On top of that, he refused to have a drink with them." He flipped back several pages in his notebook. "Now, you said your guests were . . . ?"

Libra looked unhappy. "George Wakes and his wife, Myra, Bill and Anne Barkley, and Jeanne Unger."

"Do we concentrate on the men?"

"Not necessarily. Myra Wakes teaches math. Jeanne Unger is on the staff. I don't know whether that lets her out or not."

"Think hard," Backus urged. "Did Jameson give any hints? Did he ever say 'he,' specifically?"

"He may have," Libra said, "but even if he did, I'm not sure it would help. Jameson's grammar was impeccable, and formal. He'd automatically have used the masculine pronoun to refer to his suspect whether it was male or female."

"Well, we'll start with your party, anyhow. I'd like to get word to these people to meet at the police station later today. Can you be there about two?"

"If I must."

At two o'clock Libra presented himself at the door marked "Chief of Police." Backus was at his desk.

"The jackknife we found near the body was the murder weapon, all right," Backus said. "It's a fairly common type and several years old, almost impossible to trace. No fingerprints."

"How about our calendar clue?"

"Here's the pocket calendar we found on Jameson's body. See if you can make anything of it."

Backus tossed a small pocket memo pad across the desk. It was of the monthly type, each page labeled with the date and, where applicable, the holiday and the phase of the moon. The rest of the page was blank for personal reminders.

Libra turned slowly through it. Most of Jameson's notes referred to classroom assignments. Some dealt with research on his latest book, others were simply initials. Libra took them for birthday reminders since October 11th, his own birthday, was marked "TL." October 31st was blank.

"Is it possible Henry meant some other calendar? Maybe a desk calendar in his office or at home, or the next month's insert for this pocket pad?"

"We've looked. He had only a wall calendar at home; it had no markings on it at all. The desk calendar in his office is marked exactly the way this one is. We couldn't find a November version of the pocket date book."

The intercom on Backus's desk interrupted him. "The people from the college are all here now, chief. They're in Room 102."

"Good afternoon," the chief said, "and thank you for coming. I thought perhaps you could help us with our investigation. Earlier today Professor Libra told me you were all present when Henry Jameson visited his house. Maybe you saw something Professor Libra missed in Professor Jameson's actions. Or perhaps he mentioned something revelatory to you at some time or other."

Everyone around the conference table looked blank, but the chief went genially on. "Now," Backus said, "which of you is George Wakes?"

Wakes, a tall man in a corduroy suit, identified himself.

"Mr. Wakes, what is your connection with the college?"

"I'm chairman of the math department. I also teach math and act as advisor to one of our fraternities."

"Were you very close to the victim?"

"Not particularly, no," Wakes said. "We'd nod to one another now and then, but I really never saw him much. I'm in the math building a lot, and Jameson spent most of his time in the English building."

"You never socialized with him?" Backus asked.

"Jameson seldom attended social functions. Once in a while he'd go to something special like a president's dinner, but that's about all."

"Last night when you were at Professor Libra's cocktail party did Professor Jameson say anything to you?"

"No. He came in, said hello, and disappeared with Tony into the den. When they came out, Tony offered him a drink but Jameson turned him down and left. I don't remember his saying anything to anyone except to Tony."

Backus turned to the lady who sat at George Wakes's left. "May I assume you're Mrs. Wakes?"

"Yes."

"Mrs. Wakes, what is your connection with the college?"

"I'm a math instructor. I teach calculus and analytic geometry."

"A moment ago your husband spoke of his relationship with Professor Jameson. May I ask yours?"

"I don't think it will help. I saw Henry Jameson even less than my husband did. I was with George at most of those few social functions Jameson did attend, but I rarely get around the campus the way my husband does and so I hardly ever saw him there."

"I hate to repeat myself," Backus apologized, "but did you notice the dead man speaking to anyone at Professor Libra's party?"

"No. As my husband said, he glanced in when he came and again as he left but that's all."

The chief went on to Bill Barkley, who responded with a shrug. "I'm in the math department, too," he said. "I teach everything from freshman geometry to differential equations. I advise the chess club and the junior class."

"And your relationship with Professor Jameson was . . . ?"

"Practically nil. In fact, I knew him more by reputation than anything else."

"What sort of reputation?"

"Students' talk," Barkley explained. "The kids thought Jameson a bookworm and too fastidious. It seems he corrected them constantly and demanded precision in their language. They didn't like that."

"Sounds like he might have been a good teacher?"

"Oh, the kids didn't mind when he corrected their written work: they expected it. What they objected to was his insistence on oral exactness."

Backus turned to Libra. "Is that the way Jameson really was?"

"Yup. At least, in the classroom. Outside the classroom he was no different from any of the rest of us."

"Mrs. Barkley, have you any official connection with Halstrom College?"

"No. I'm a housewife; that's responsibility enough for me."

"Then I suppose your knowledge of Professor Jameson was even less than these other people's?"

"That's right. I think I was introduced to him once or twice before last night, but I never really spoke to him."

"That only leaves you, Miss Unger," Backus smiled.

"I work as a secretary in the English office.

What I do, basically, is type notes and tests and other materials the English teachers pass out to their students."

"That means you've been in touch with Professor Jameson quite often, then."

"Well, yes and no. Whenever Professor Jameson had work for me, he'd leave it in a manila envelope with a note explaining what he wanted done. I'd put the typed work on his desk when I had finished. We really didn't exchange many words."

"Since Jameson was quite a bit older than you, I assume your social paths seldom crossed."

"Never. In fact, last night at Tony's was the first time I'd ever seen him off campus."

Backus made some notes and leaned back in his chair. "Did any of you leave the living room last night while Tony and Professor Jameson were in the den?"

"What difference does it make?" Bill Barkley asked.

"Professor Jameson told Tony something in private—something potentially dangerous to him. Something that may have led to his death."

"And Tony thinks one of us killed him?" Barkley was outraged.

"No, he doesn't," Backus said. "It was all my idea. Tony refuses to believe one of you could be the murderer. All personal feelings aside, however, I must know if any of you were out of sight of the others while they were talking."

"We all were," Jeanne Unger confessed. "I went into the kitchen to get more ice."

"I went to the bathroom," George Wakes said grudgingly.

"I went to the bedroom to get my compact out of my purse," said Anne Barkley.

Bill Barkley sighed. "I stepped onto the patio for a breath of fresh air."

"And I went into the dining room to see the beautiful gloxinia Tony has growing next to his hutch," Myra Wakes said.

Backus shook his head. "This is ridiculous. There's either not enough information to check on or there's too much. If I asked where you all were at about one thirty in the morning, I suppose you'd all say you were home in bed."

Five heads nodded in unison.

"Husbands will corroborate wives and vice versa, no doubt. And Miss Unger, of course, is too young and sweet to be guilty of murder."

"You don't have to be sarcastic," Myra Wakes snapped.

Tony Libra leaned slightly forward in his chair. Something was bothering him—something someone had said—but he couldn't quite put his finger on it.

"What I want to know," Bill Barkley announced, "is why we're suspects and Tony isn't."

"That's right," said Anne. "After all, you said Jameson was killed because he knew something dangerous, and Tony was the only one he talked to."

"That's it!"

Libra's shout, coupled with his sudden leap to his feet, startled everyone.

"What's it?" Backus asked.

"Chief, I know who killed Henry Jameson."

"You've figured out the calendar clue?" the chief asked.

"No," Libra admitted. "It was something else, but I've been wondering . . . Is there a dictionary handy?"

Backus nodded to a uniformed policeman sitting unobtrusively in the corner. The man left the room.

"What is this calendar clue you're talking about?" Jeanne Unger asked.

"Before Professor Jameson left Tony's house," Backus explained, "he told Tony to check up on the calendar if anything happened to him. Up to now, we haven't had any idea what he meant by that." He turned to Libra. "Why the dictionary?"

"You remember that I mentioned Henry was an expert at word meanings, at their origins and oddities. Remember, too, he was a stickler for correctness of speech, yet he used the phrase 'check up on the calendar' when speaking to me."

"So?"

"So, what if Henry meant some other kind of calendar altogether?"

"Like what?"

"I don't know yet. But the man was a word expert. What if, somehow, he was actually naming his assailant; hence the term 'check *up* on.' Why not just 'check the calendar'?"

The uniformed policeman returned with a dictionary. Libra opened it.

"Here it is," he said slowly. The room was very quiet. "There's a 'calendar' here spelled c-a-l-e-n-d-*e*-r, not *a*-r like the twelve-month kind."

"Well?" Backus demanded impatiently. "What does it say?"

Libra read: " 'Mendicant dervish of Persia or Turkey.' "

"What the heck is that?"

"A dervish is a fakir," Libra explained. "One of those people who charm snakes and walk on hot coals and sleep on beds of nails."

"I don't see how that helps," said George Wakes.

"Chief," Tony said, "what picture do you get when you hear the word 'fakir'?"

"Someone in a loincloth, maybe wearing a turban."

"And at my party who was dressed like that?"

"The one who came dressed as Mahatma Gandhi." Backus rose.

Everyone turned toward George Wakes.

"You're crazy!" Wakes sneered. "Are you saying that Jameson was talking about me when he said 'check the calendar'?"

"Yes," Libra said flatly. "I am. I think when Henry saw you he assumed you were a fakir, or calender. He didn't think of Gandhi. Note the phrase 'check up on,' please. He was telling me to check up on you. He hoped I'd get evidence of your guilt."

"Well, if that's all you've got to go on, your evidence is pretty weak."

"But it's not," Libra said. "Something that was said in this room earlier bothered me. At first I couldn't pinpoint it, but it came to me when Anne Barkley reminded me that I was the only person Jameson talked to."

"So?" Wakes said.

"So you said I offered Jameson a drink and he turned me down."

"Isn't that true?"

"Yes," Libra replied, "but when I issued that particular invitation, Henry and I were in my den, not in the living room as you said. How could you have known what I said unless you were listening at the door?"

"I don't know. I must have heard you tell someone."

"No," Libra disagreed. "The only person I told about my conversation with Henry was Chief Backus."

Backus spoke to one of his officers. "Norris, escort Mr. Wakes to my office and inform him of his rights. I'll join you in a minute."

Myra Wakes, eyes filled with tears, watched her husband leave.

"Thanks, perfessor," Backus said. "I think we can close this one with a little routine footwork now. You've been a big help."

"Yeah," Libra said half-heartedly as he watched Jeanne Unger put her arm around Myra Wakes.

"You don't sound very happy."

"Happy? That was a Halloween party that cost me two friends. Not much fun, after all, chief."

IN THE MORGUE

by Dashiell Hammett

Walter Dowe took the last sheet of the manuscript from his typewriter with a satisfied sigh and leaned back in his chair, turning his face to the ceiling to ease the stiffened muscles of his neck. Then he looked at the clock: 3:15 A.M. He yawned, got to his feet, switched off the lights, and went down the hall to his bedroom.

In the doorway of the bedroom he halted abruptly. The moonlight came through the wide windows to illuminate an empty bed. He turned on the lights and looked around the room. None of the things his wife had worn that night were there. She had not undressed, then; perhaps she had heard the rattle of his typewriter and had decided to wait downstairs until he had finished. She never interrupted him when he was at work, and he was usually too engrossed by his labors to hear her footsteps when she passed his study door.

He went to the head of the stairs and called: "Althea!"

No answer.

He went downstairs, into all the rooms, turning on the lights; he returned to the second floor and did the same. His wife was not in the house. He was perplexed, and a little helpless. Then he remembered that she had gone to the theater with the Schuylers. His hands trembled as he picked up the telephone.

The Schuylers' maid answered his call ... There had been a fire at the Majestic Theater; neither Mr. nor Mrs. Schuyler had come home. Mr. Schuyler's father had gone out to look for them, but had not returned yet. The maid understood that the fire had been pretty bad ...

Dowe was waiting on the sidewalk when the taxicab for which he had telephoned arrived. Fifteen minutes later he was struggling to get through the fire lines, which were still drawn about the theater. A perspiring, red-faced policeman thrust him back.

"You'll find nothing here. The building's been cleared. Everybody's been taken to the hospitals."

Dowe found his cab again and was driven to the City Hospital. He forced his way through the clamoring group on the gray stone steps. A policeman blocked the door. Presently a pasty-faced man, in solid white, spoke over the policeman's shoulder:

"There's no use waiting. We're too busy treating them now to either take their names or let anybody in to see them. We'll try to have a list in the late morning edition; but we can't let anybody in until later in the day."

Dowe turned away. Then he thought: Murray Bornis, of course! He went back to the cab and gave the driver Bornis's address.

Bornis came to the door of his apartment in pajamas. Dowe clung to him.

"Althea went to the Majestic tonight and hasn't come home. They wouldn't let me in at the hospital. Told me to wait—but I can't! You're the police commissioner—you can get me in!"

While Bornis dressed, Dowe paced the floor, babbling. Then he caught a glimpse of himself in a mirror, and stood suddenly still. The sight of his distorted face and wild eyes shocked him back into sanity. He was on the verge of hysterics. He must take hold of himself. He must not collapse before he found Althea.

Deliberately, he made himself sit down, made himself stop visualizing Althea's soft, white body charred and crushed. He must think about something else: Bornis, for instance . . .

But that brought him back to his wife in the end. She had never liked Bornis. His frank sensuality, and his unsavory reputation for numerous affairs with numerous women, had offended her strict conception of morality. To be sure, she had always given him all the courtesy due her husband's friend; but it was generally a frigid giving. And Bornis, understanding her attitude, and perhaps a little contemptuous of her narrow views, had been as coolly polite as she. And now she was lying somewhere, moaning in agony, perhaps already cold . . .

Bornis finished dressing and they went quickly to the City Hospital, where the police commissioner and his companion were readily admitted. They walked down long rooms, between rows of groaning and writhing bodies, looking into bruised and burned faces, seeing no one they knew. Then to Mercy Hospital, where they found Sylvia Schuyler. She told them that the crush in the theater had separated her from her husband and Althea, and she had not seen them afterward. Then she lapsed into unconsciousness again.

When they got back to the cab, Bornis gave directions to the driver in an undertone, but Dowe did not have to hear them to know what they were: "To the morgue." There was no other place to go.

Now they walked between rows of bodies that were mangled horribly. Dowe had exhausted his feelings: he felt no pity, no loathing, now. He looked into a face; it was not Althea's; then it was nothing; he passed on to the next.

Bornis's fingers closed convulsively around Dowe's arm.

"There! Althea!"

Dowe turned. A face that stampeding leather heels had robbed of features; a torso that was battered and blackened and cut, and from which the clothing had been torn. All that was human of it were the legs; they had somehow escaped disfigurement.

"No, no!" Dowe cried.

He would not believe this begrimed, mangled thing was exquisite white Althea!

Through the horror that for the moment shut Dowe off from the world, Bornis's vibrant, anguished voice penetrated—it was almost a shriek:

"I tell you it is!" Flinging out a hand to point at one smooth knee. "See! The dimple!"

THE BLACK CAT

by Lee Somerville

She was an old cat, coal black, lean and ugly. Her right ear had been chewed and her old hide showed scars, but she had a regal look when she sat under the rosebushes in the plaza and surveyed us with yellow-green eyes.

If the witch cat had a name, we never knew it. Miss Tessie fed it, as she fed other strays. She even let the old cat sleep in her store in rainy weather. But mostly the cat slept under the rosebushes in our plaza in Caton City, Texas. We have a pretty little plaza, or square, here in the center of town. It has a fountain and a statue of a tired Confederate solder facing north, ready to defend us from Northern invaders, and a bit of grass and lots of rosebushes.

Nobody dared to pet the old cat. People gave the cat scraps of bread and meat from hamburgers and hot dogs. She accepted this placidly, as a queen accepts homage from peons. Now and then a stray dog came through our small dusty town, saw the cat, and made a lunge at it. The cat would retreat to the base of the fountain, turn, lash with a razor-sharp claw that sliced the poor dog's nose. The dog would run howling while townspeople laughed. Our dogs, having learned the hard way, left that cat alone.

When I was fourteen, my mother's jailbird distant relative, Cousin Rush, came to live with us. My little brother Pete and I had to give up our room to this scruffy relative, but that wasn't the only reason I disliked him. I despised his dumpy figure and his smelly cigars and his scaly bald head and his way of looking at me with beady small eyes and nodding and winking.

Mama told me to show Cousin Rush the town, and I had to do it. This was the day before Halloween, and half the town was in the theater across the street from the plaza, rehearsing for the Heritage Festival we have every Halloween night. Miss Tessie was at the front of the theater, selling plastic masks of Cajun Caton and Davy Crockett. We have this play about Cajun Caton and a Delaware Indian, Chief Cut Hand, saving the town from Comanches on a Halloween night in the early 1800's. It ends with Cajun Caton, town hero, leaving his eight children and one wife later on and going off with Davy Crockett and getting killed in the Alamo during the Texas Revolution against Mexico in 1836.

Cousin Rush bought a mask from Miss Tessie. He smiled and flirted and talked of the Importance of History. His face smiled, but his eyes remained cold and scornful, and I could tell he thought this heritage business was hillbilly country foolishness. He'd already told me Caton City was a hick town filled with stupid people. It didn't compare with real towns.

As we started walking across the plaza, the black cat jumped from the rosebushes and ran in front of us.

To keep walking in a straight direction would have meant bad luck. I sidestepped, made a little circle, and prevented bad luck. I'm not superstitious, not really, but no use taking chances.

Cousin Rush laughed at me. Then, to show his scorn of superstition and black cats, he did a fat-legged little hop and skip and kicked that cat in the stomach.

The old cat doubled up on Cousin Rush's sharp-toed shoe. She clawed at his sock, then bounced into a rosebush. She landed on her feet, stood there, weaving, hurt. Cousin Rush kicked again, and she dodged. She ran into the street, stopped, looked at Cousin Rush with yellow-green eyes. As he popped his hands together, making a threatening noise, she stood her ground for a moment, then ran into Miss Tessie's store.

"You didn't have to do that," I said.

Cousin Rush stood there, the October sun beating down on his bald head and his cigar sticking out of his fat face. "You country bumpkins don't have to act ignorant, but you do. The only way to deal with a black cat running across your path is to kick the manure out of the cat. It's a callous world, Brian, and the only way to deal with it is to skin your buddy before he skins you."

"We don't act that way here," I disagreed.

"You are fools," he stated. He blew cigar smoke and looked at people milling around in front of the theater, talking and being friendly. "Now, tell me about this Heritage Festival you'll have tomorrow night. As I understand it, half the town is in the play, including the sheriff and his deputy. The other half—and that includes a lot of people that make this a sort of homecoming—will buy tickets and make cash contributions to the historical society. I understand this crazy old maid, this Miss Tessie, has collected a neat bit of cash."

"She's raising money for a historical marker to honor her ancestor, Cajun Caton."

"Yes. That's the idiot the town is named for."

"He was not an idiot. Caton and Davy Crockett were both killed in the Alamo, and they were Texas heroes."

Cousin Rush blew more smoke. "And there are

at least a hundred people in this town descended from Caton. I understand that during the finale of this play, which Miss Tessie wrote, it has become a custom for every man in the audience to put on a mask to honor Cajun Caton or Davy Crockett? Hmmm."

I didn't like the sudden suspicion I had. I'd heard Mama and Dad talking in whispers, telling that Rush had served time in a Texas penitentiary for small-time robbery. I didn't like the cold, greedy look on my cousin's face.

I could have reported my suspicion to Sheriff Mitchell or to Deputy Haskins except for one thing—my mother was an Adams. Every Adams is intensely loyal to other Adamses, and don't you forget it. Cousin Rush was Rushid E. Sarosy, and his daddy had been a shoe salesman in Dallas, but his mama was Verney Adams to start with. Verney was a hot little blonde who was born with a female urge and grew up around it. She left Caton County fifty-six years ago for the big city, but she was still an Adams.

I had a suspicion, from the calculating look on his face, that Cousin Rush would burglarize some place tomorrow night when everybody was in the theater, or he'd rob the box office at the theater, wearing a mask like everybody else would wear.

I couldn't talk to Mama about my suspicions. If I was wrong and Cousin Rush didn't do anything bad, she'd say I was disloyal to the name of Adams.

As we left the plaza, the old black cat that Cousin Rush had kicked came out of Miss Tessie's store and looked at us as if she were casting a spell. I shivered.

I still wonder if what happened that night was just coincidence.

* * *

My little brother Pete had been unsuccessfully baiting that animal trap for a week. The trap was in the back yard. Here in Caton City, which is in northeast Texas, just south of Oklahoma and not far from Arkansas between the Red River and the Sulphur River, things were different. Coyotes and raccoons and possums and other animals came into town at night to raid garbage cans. Pete had been baiting that animal trap, actually a cage, for a week with cornbread, beans, cabbage, and such, hoping to catch a raccoon and make a pet of it. On this night, with a big moon beaming down, he had jerry-rigged a Rube Goldberg device that would turn on a light if the trap door was triggered.

Cousin Rush had our room now, so we slept in beds on our big screened-in back porch. About midnight the signal light came on to show the trap door had slammed down. Pete got out of bed in his underwear and ran barefoot to the trap, waving a flashlight.

He came back in a hurry. "Brian, we got trouble!"

I sat up, sniffed. "I smell it." The smell of skunk was not all that strong, showing the animal was fairly content, but it was definitely skunk.

"You got to shoot it."

"Hell, no! If you shoot that skunk, it'll make a smell that will wake up the town," I cautioned. "It has plenty of food and water and room to move around in that cage-trap. After it eats, it will probably go to sleep, won't it?"

Pete thought this over. "I guess so, unless it's disturbed."

"Okay. I'll make sure the yard gates are closed, so no dogs or other animals can disturb that skunk. We'll figure what to do after it gets daylight tomorrow. Let sleeping skunks sleep, that's my motto."

After Pete had gone back to bed, I lay awake, thinking. I could take a long fishing pole, hold the cage as far from me as possible, and move gently. I'd have to get that skunk out of our back yard somehow. . . .

I finally went to sleep and dreamed that Cousin Rush robbed Miss Tessie of all the Heritage Festival money. He got by with it because he was wearing a mask and all the men in the crowd he joined afterward wore masks. Nobody knew which masked man had the money. I woke up. Then I went to sleep again and this time I dreamed Cousin Rush didn't get away with it after all. He came out of the theater with the money still in his hands, and the old black cat cast a spell on him and made him throw the money in the air.

And I dreamed the old cat was really a witch in disguise.

When I woke up, it was Halloween Day and I still didn't know what to do about Cousin Rush. Maybe I was suspicious of him because I didn't like him.

But later in the day, as I listened to him talk with Miss Tessie, I became more alarmed. Oh, it was just general talk, discussion of the fact that Cajun Caton wasn't really a cajun. He was from Henry County, Tennessee, and he had picked up that nickname in Louisiana in what Miss Tessie described as an "indiscreet house."

I watched as Cousin Rush got his Oldsmobile filled with gas and the tires and oil checked. Looked like he was planning for a trip. He couldn't go to Houston, because police would arrest him if he went back there. He'd have trouble with his fourth wife in Dallas, and was wanted on charges there. But the way he was fussing around his car, it looked as if he would go somewhere in a hurry.

Long before the Heritage Play started that night, he parked his car on the north side of the plaza near the biggest rosebush. Then he went into the theater early, carrying a cape and a mask as some other men were doing.

I stood looking across the plaza, worried. The black cat came from the rosebushes, sat on the base of the fountain, and stared back at me. Darkness came, and a full moon rose. Stars shone.

Looking at that cat, I knew what I had to do. Maybe it wouldn't work, but maybe it would. I had to try.

After the play was well under way, with everyone except me in the theater, I got a long fishing pole and some cord. Cautiously, holding my breath at times, I carried that animal cage-trap the three blocks to the plaza. The skunk, his belly full of cornbread and cabbage and beans, slept most of the time.

I learned later that during the last two minutes of the play a man wearing a mask and a cape went inside the box office where Miss Tessie was counting money. He didn't speak a word, but he pushed a small pistol in Miss Tessie's face and motioned for her to sit down. He tied her to the chair. She opened her mouth to scream, and he jammed a handkerchief in it. Nobody would have heard if she had screamed because the audience and the cast were singing the finale.

The man put his pistol inside his cape, took handfuls of the paper money she'd been sorting. He stuffed money in his pockets and inside the cape pockets, and left with some money in his hands.

He walked out of the theater as the townspeople, wearing capes and masks, also walked out.

I knew which one was Cousin Rush. I could tell by the prissy walk and the dumpy figure.

A couple of kids ran ahead of him across the plaza, but I pulled the cord I had rigged to the trap door. With that door open, and with all the noise, the skunk would come out. He would not be disturbed or afraid, because skunks are not usually afraid. Even a grizzly bear would tippity-toe around a skunk.

The two kids apparently saw him, hollered, "Uh-oh," detoured slightly, and kept running. Cousin Rush paid them no attention.

Then Miss Tessie's old black cat ran out of the rosebushes, ran right in front of Cousin Rush, ran back into the bushes.

Cousin Rush slowed in his fast walk to the Oldsmobile. It was a beautiful night, bright as day with white moonlight and black shadows. Just as Cousin Rush got near his car, a small black animal came out of the rosebushes again, right in front of him.

If he had climbed in his car without noticing, he would have gotten away with robbery. Being Cousin Rush and being naturally mean, and probably thinking this was Miss Tessie's old black cat, he kicked the skunk.

Then he bent over, ready to kick again. He got that spray full in his face. He staggered back, threw both arms in the air, hands spread wide. Money fluttered high, caught the wind, and blew all over the plaza. Cousin Rush fought for breath, ran into the monument, bounced off, stumbled against the fountain, coughed, gasped, vomited, waved his hands again.

He tore off his mask and cape, and money came from the pockets inside the cape and swirled in the air. People stood watching, wondering.

Somebody found Miss Tessie bound and gagged and cut her loose. She ran into the street, screaming she'd been robbed.

With all those dollar bills and five dollar bills and ten dollar bills floating in the air around Cousin Rush, he became the Prime Suspect. Nobody went near him for a while, though. The smell was nauseating.

Finally Sheriff Mitchell spoke firm words to Deputy Haskins. Haskins looked reluctant, but Mitchell gave the orders. Don't take him to our clean jail, he said. Take him to the old county stables and lock him up for the night.

The skunk got away in all the excitement. Nobody would have touched him anyway. I knew I would pick up the cage-trap when everybody left, or I'd be incriminated. I didn't want Mama to know I'd had anything to do with trapping Cousin Rush.

Citizens picked up the money that was blowing around and put it in a well-ventilated place for the night. Then people left for the American Legion Barbecue and Dance. Some of those who had gotten close to skunk smell while picking up the money might have to stay outside the Legion Hall, but they'd eat barbecue and drink Blanton Creek bourbon and they'd survive.

As the crowd left the plaza, and as Deputy Haskins started Cousin Rush walking twenty feet ahead of him to the stables, I saw Miss Tessie's old black cat sitting on the base of the fountain. Her eyes glinted in the Halloween moonlight, and I'll swear that cat was laughing.

THIS IS DEATH

by Donald E. Westlake

It's hard not to believe in ghosts when you are one. I hanged myself in a fit of truculence—stronger than pique, but not so dignified as despair—and regretted it before the thing was well begun. The instant I kicked the chair away I wanted it back, but gravity was turning my former wish to its present command; the chair would not right itself from where it lay on the floor, and my 193 pounds would not cease to urge downward from the rope thick around my neck.

There was pain, of course, quite horrible pain centered in my throat, but the most astounding thing was the way my cheeks seemed to swell. I could barely see over their round red hills, my eyes staring in agony at the door, *willing* someone to come in and rescue me, though I knew there was no one in the house, and in any event the door was carefully locked. My kicking legs caused me to twist and turn, so that sometimes I faced the door and sometimes the window, and my shivering hands struggled with the rope so deep in my flesh I could barely find it and most certainly could not pull it loose.

I was frantic and terrified, yet at the same time my brain possessed a cold corner of aloof observation. I seemed now to be everywhere in the room at once, within my writhing body but also without, seeing my frenzied spasms, the thick rope, the heavy beam, the mismatched pair of lit bedside lamps throwing my convulsive double shadow on the walls, the closed locked door, the white-curtained window with its shade drawn all the way down. *This is death,* I thought, and I no longer wanted it, now that the choice was gone forever.

My name is—was—Edward Thornburn, and my dates are 1938–1977. I killed myself just a month before my fortieth birthday, though I don't believe the well-known pangs of that milestone had much if anything to do with my action. I blame it all (as I blamed most of the errors and failures of my life) on my sterility. Had I been able to father children my marriage would have remained strong, Emily would not have been unfaithful to me, and I would not have taken my own life in a final fit of truculence.

The setting was the guestroom in our house in Barnstaple, Connecticut, and the time was just after seven P.M.; deep twilight, at this time of year. I had come home from the office—I was a realtor, a fairly lucrative occupation in Connecticut, though my income had been falling off recently—shortly before six, to find the note on the kitchen table: "Antiquing with Greg. Afraid you'll have to make your own dinner. Sorry. Love, Emily."

Greg was the one; Emily's lover. He owned an antique shop out on the main road toward New York, and Emily filled a part of her days as his ill-paid assistant. I knew what they did together in the back of the shop on those long midweek afternoons when there were no tourists, no antique collectors to disturb them. I knew, and I'd known for more than three years, but I had never decided how to deal with my knowledge. The fact was, I blamed myself, and therefore I had no way to *behave* if the ugly subject were ever to come into the open.

So I remained silent, but not content. I was discontent, unhappy, angry resentful—truculent.

I'd tried to kill myself before. At first with the car, by steering it into an oncoming truck (I swerved at the last second, amid howling horns) and by driving it off a cliff into the Connecticut River (I slammed on the brakes at the very brink, and sat covered in perspiration for half an hour before backing away) and finally by stopping athwart one of the few level crossings left in this neighborhood. But no train came for twenty minutes, and my truculence wore off, and I drove home.

Later I tried to slit my wrists, but found it impossible to push sharp metal into my own skin. Impossible. The vision of my naked wrist and that shining steel so close together washed my truculence completely out of my mind. Until the next time.

With the rope; and then I succeeded. Oh, totally, oh, fully I succeeded. My legs kicked at air, my fingernails clawed at my throat, my bulging eyes stared out over my swollen purple cheeks, my tongue thickened and grew bulbous in my mouth, my body jigged and jangled like a toy at the end of a string, and the pain was excruciating, horrible, not to be endured. I can't endure it, I thought, it can't be endured. Much worse than knife slashings was the knotted strangled pain in my throat, and my head ballooned with pain, pressure outward, my face turning black, my eyes no longer human, the pressure in my head building and building as though I would explode. Endless horrible pain, not to be endured, but going on and on.

My legs kicked more feebly. My arms sagged, my hands dropped to my sides, my fingers twitched uselessly against my sopping trouser legs, my head hung at an angle from the rope,

I turned more slowly in the air, like a broken windchime on a breezeless day. The pains lessened, in my throat and head, but never entirely stopped.

And now I saw that my distended eyes had become lusterless, gray. The moisture had dried on the eyeballs, they were as dead as stones. And yet I could see them, my own eyes, and when I widened my vision I could see my entire body, turning, hanging, no longer twitching, and with horror I realized I was dead.

But *present*. Dead, but still present, with the scraping ache still in my throat and the bulging pressure still in my head. Present, but no longer in that used-up clay, that hanging meat; I was suffused through the room, like indirect lighting, everywhere present but without a source. What happens now? I wondered, dulled by fear and strangeness and the continuing pains, and I waited, like a hovering mist, for whatever would happen next.

But nothing happened. I waited; the body became utterly still; the double shadow on the wall showed no vibration; the bedside lamps continued to burn; the door remained shut and the window shade drawn; and nothing happened.

What *now*? I craved to scream the question aloud, but I could not. My throat ached, but I had no throat. My mouth burned, but I had no mouth. Every final strain and struggle of my body remained imprinted in my mind, but I had no body and no brain and no *self*, no substance. No power to speak, no power to move myself, no power to *re*move myself from this room and this suspended corpse. I could only wait here, and wonder, and go on waiting.

There was a digital clock on the dresser opposite the bed, and when it first occurred to me to look at it the numbers were 7:21—perhaps twenty minutes after I'd kicked the chair away, perhaps fifteen minutes since I'd died. Shouldn't something happen, shouldn't some *change* take place?

The clock read 9:11 when I heard Emily's Volkswagen drive around to the back of the house. I had left no note, having nothing I wanted to say to anyone and in any event believing my own dead body would be eloquent enough, but I hadn't thought I would be *present* when Emily found me. I was justified in my action, however much I now regretted having taken it, I was justified, I knew I was justified, but I didn't want to see her face when she came through that door. She had wronged me, she was the cause of it, she would have to know that as well as I, but I didn't want to see her face.

The pains increased, in what had been my throat, in what had been my head. I heard the back door slam, far away downstairs, and I stirred like air currents in the room, but I didn't leave. I couldn't leave.

"Ed? Ed? It's me, hon!"

I know it's you. I must go away now, I can't stay here, I must go away. Is there a God? Is this my soul, this hovering presence? *Hell* would be better than this, take me away to Hell or wherever I'm to go, don't leave me here!

She came up the stairs, calling again, walking past the closed guestroom door. I heard her go into our bedroom, heard her call my name, heard the beginnings of apprehension in her voice. She went by again, out there in the hall, went downstairs, became quiet.

What was she doing? Searching for a note perhaps, some message from me. Looking out the window, seeing again my Chevrolet, knowing I must be home. Moving through the rooms of this old house, the original structure a barn nearly

200 years old, converted by some previous owner just after the Second World War, bought by me twelve years ago, furnished by Emily—and Greg—from their interminable, damnable, awful antiques. Shaker furniture, Colonial furniture, hooked rugs and quilts, the old yellow pine tables, the faint sense always of being in some slightly shabby minor museum, this house that I had bought but never loved. I'd bought it for Emily, I did everything for Emily, because I knew I could never do the one thing for Emily that mattered. I could never give her a child.

She was good about it, of course. Emily *is* good, I never blamed her, never completely blamed *her* instead of myself. In the early days of our marriage she made a few wistful references, but I suppose she saw the effect they had on me, and for a long time she has said nothing. But I have known.

The beam from which I had hanged myself was a part of the original building, a thick hand-hewed length of aged timber eleven inches square, chevroned with the marks of the hatchet that had shaped it. A strong beam, it would support my weight forever. It would support my weight until I was found and cut down. Until I was found.

The clock read 9:23 and Emily had been in the house twelve minutes when she came upstairs again, her steps quick and light on the old wood, approaching, pausing, stopping. "Ed?"

The doorknob turned.

The door was locked, of course, with the key on the inside. She'd have to break it down, have to call someone else to break it down, perhaps she wouldn't be the one to find me after all. Hope rose in me, and the pains receded.

"Ed? Are you in there?" She knocked at the door, rattled the knob, called my name several times more, then abruptly turned and ran away downstairs again, and after a moment I heard her voice, murmuring and unclear. She had called someone, on the phone.

Greg, I thought, and the throat-rasp filled me, and I wanted this to be the end. I wanted to be taken away, dead body and living soul, taken away. I wanted everything to be finished.

She stayed downstairs, waiting for him, and I stayed upstairs, waiting for them both. Perhaps she already knew what she'd find up here, and that's why she waited below.

I didn't mind about Greg, about being present when he came in. I didn't mind about *him*. It was Emily I minded.

The clock read 9:44 when I heard tires on the gravel at the side of the house. He entered, I heard them talking down there, the deeper male voice slow and reassuring, the lighter female voice quick and frightened, and then they came up together, neither speaking. The doorknob turned, jiggled, rattled, and Greg's voice called, "Ed?"

After a little silence Emily said, "He wouldn't—he wouldn't *do* anything, would he?"

"Do anything?" Greg sounded almost annoyed at the question. "What do you mean, do anything?"

"He's been so depressed, he's—Ed!" And forcibly the door was rattled, the door was shaken in its frame.

"Emily, don't. Take it easy."

"I shouldn't have called you," she said. "Ed, *please!*"

"Why not? For heaven's sake, Emily—"

"Ed, *please* come out, don't scare me like this!"

"Why *shouldn't* you call me, Emily?"

"Ed isn't stupid, Greg. He's—"

There was then a brief silence, pregnant with

the hint of murmuring. They thought me still alive in here, they didn't want me to hear Emily say, "He *knows*, Greg, he knows about us."

The murmurings sifted and shifted, and then Greg spoke loudly, "That's ridiculous. Ed? Come out, Ed, let's talk this over." And the doorknob rattled and clattered, and he sounded annoyed when he said, "We must get in, that's all. Is there another key?"

"I think all the locks up here are the same. Just a minute."

They were. A simple skeleton key would open any interior door in the house. I waited, listening, knowing Emily had gone off to find another key, knowing they would soon come in together, and I felt such terror and revulsion for Emily's entrance that I could feel myself shimmer in the room, like a reflection in a warped mirror. Oh, can I at least stop seeing? In life I had eyes, but also eyelids, I could shut out the intolerable, but now I was only a presence, a total presence, I *could not* stop my awareness.

The rasp of key in lock was like rough metal edges in my throat; my memory of a throat. The pain flared in me, and through it I heard Emily asking what was wrong, and Greg answering, "The key's in it, on the other side."

"Oh, dear God! Oh, Greg, what has he done?"

"We'll have to take the door off its hinges," he told her. "Call Tony. Tell him to bring the toolbox."

"Can't you push the key through?"

Of course he could, but he said, quite determinedly, "Go *on*, Emily," and I realized then he had no intention of taking the door down. He simply wanted her away when the door was first opened. Oh, very good, *very* good!

"All right," she said doubtfully, and I heard her go away to phone Tony. A beetle-browed young man with great masses of black hair and an olive complexion, Tony lived in Greg's house and was a kind of handyman. He did work around the house and was also (according to Emily) very good at restoration of antique furniture; stripping paint, re-assembling broken parts, that sort of thing.

There was now a renewed scraping and rasping at the lock, as Greg struggled to get the door open before Emily's return. I found myself feeling unexpected warmth and liking toward Greg. He wasn't a bad person; an opportunist with my wife, but not in general a bad person. Would he marry her now? They could live in this house, he'd had more to do with its furnishing than I. Or would this room hold too grim a memory, would Emily have to sell the house, live elsewhere? She might have to sell at a low price; as a realtor, I knew the difficulty in selling a house where a suicide has taken place. No matter how much they may joke about it, people are still afraid of the supernatural. Many of them would believe this room was haunted.

It was then I finally realized the room *was* haunted. With me! *I'm a ghost,* I thought, thinking the word for the first time, in utter blank astonishment. I'm a ghost.

Oh, how dismal! To hover here, to be a boneless fleshless aching *presence* here, to be a kind of ectoplasmic mildew seeping through the days and nights, alone, unending, a stupid pain-racked misery-filled observer of the comings and goings of strangers—she *would* sell the house, she'd have to, I was sure of that. Was this my punishment? The punishment of the suicide, the solitary hell of him who takes his own life. To remain forever a sentient nothing, bound by a force greater than gravity itself to the place of one's finish.

I was distracted from this misery by a sudden agitation in the key on this side of the lock. I saw it quiver and jiggle like something alive, and then it popped out—it seemed to *leap* out, itself a suicide leaping from a cliff—and clattered to the floor, and an instant later the door was pushed open and Greg's ashen face stared at my own purple face, and after the astonishment and horror, his expression shifted to revulsion—and contempt?—and he backed out, slamming the door. Once more the key turned in the lock, and I heard him hurry away downstairs.

The clock read 9:58. *Now* he was telling her. *Now* he was giving her a drink to calm her. *Now* he was phoning the police. *Now* he was talking to her about whether or not to admit their affair to the police; what would they decide?

"Nooooooooo!"

The clock read 10:07. What had taken so long? Hadn't he even called the police yet?

She was coming up the stairs, stumbling and rushing, she was pounding on the door, screaming my name. I shrank into the corners of the room, I *felt* the thuds of her fists against the door, I cowered from her. She can't come in, dear God don't let her in! I don't care what she'd done, I don't care about anything, just don't let her see me! *Don't let me see her!*

Greg joined her. She screamed at him, he persuaded her, she raved, he argued, she demanded, he denied. "Give me the key! Give me the key!"

Surely he'll hold out, surely he'll take her away, surely he's stronger, more forceful.

He gave her the key.

No. *This* cannot be endured. *This* is the horror beyond all else. She came in, she walked into the room, and the sound she made will always live inside me. That cry wasn't human; it was the howl of every creature that has ever despaired.

Now I know what despair is, and why I called my own state mere truculence.

Now that it was too late, Greg tried to restrain her, tried to hold her shoulders and draw her from the room, but she pulled away and crossed the room toward . . . not toward *me.* I was everywhere in the room, driven by pain and remorse, and Emily walked toward the carcass. She looked at it almost tenderly, she even reached up and touched its swollen cheek.

"Oh, Ed," she murmured.

The pains were as violent now as in the moments before my death. The slashing torment in my throat, the awful distension in my head, they made me squirm in agony all over again; but I *could not* feel her hand on my cheek.

Greg followed her, touched her shoulder again, spoke her name, and immediately her face dissolved, she cried out once more and wrapped her arms around the corpse's legs and clung to it, weeping and gasping and uttering words too quick and broken to understand. Thank *God* they were too quick and broken to understand!

Greg, that fool, did finally force her away, though he had great trouble breaking her clasp on the body. But he succeeded, and pulled her out of the room, and slammed the door, and for a little while the body swayed and turned, until it became still once more.

That was the worst. Nothing could be worse than that. The long days and nights here—how long must a stupid creature like myself *haunt* his death-place before release?—would be horrible, I knew that, but not so bad as this. Emily would survive, would sell the house, would slowly forget. (Even I would slowly forget.) She and Greg could marry. She was only 36, she could still be mother.

For the rest of the night I heard her wailing,

elsewhere in the house. The police did come at last, and a pair of grim silent white-coated men from the morgue entered the room to cut me—it—down. They bundled it like a broken toy into a large oval wicker basket with long wooden handles, and they carried it away.

I had thought I might be forced to stay with the body, I had feared the possibility of being buried with it, of spending eternity as a thinking nothingness in the black dark of a casket, but the body left the room and I remained behind.

A doctor was called. When the body was carried away the room door was left open, and now I could plainly hear the voices from downstairs. Tony was among them now, his characteristic surly monosyllable occasionally rumbling, but the main thing for a while was the doctor. He was trying to give Emily a sedative, but she kept wailing, she kept speaking high hurried frantic sentences as though she had too little time to say it all. "I did it!" she cried, over and over. "I did it! I'm to blame!"

Yes. That was the reaction I'd wanted, and expected, and here it was, and it was horrible. Everything I had desired in the last moments of my life had been granted to me, and they were all ghastly beyond belief. I *didn't* want to die! I *didn't* want to give Emily such misery! And more than all the rest I didn't want to be here, seeing and hearing it all.

They did quiet her at last, and then a policeman in a rumpled blue suit came into the room with Greg, and listened while Greg described everything that had happened. While Greg talked, the policeman rather grumpily stared at the remaining length of rope still knotted around the beam, and when Greg had finished the policeman said, "You're a close friend of his?"

"More of his wife. She works for me. I own

The Bibelot, an antique shop out on the New York road."

"Mm. Why on earth did you let her in here?"

Greg smiled; a sheepish embarrassed expression. "She's stronger than I am," he said. "A more forceful personality. That's always been true."

It was with some surprise I realized it *was* true. Greg was something of a weakling, and Emily was very strong. (*I* had been something of a weakling, hadn't I? Emily was the strongest of us all.)

The policeman was saying, "Any idea why he'd do it?"

"I think he suspected his wife was having an affair with me." Clearly Greg had rehearsed this sentence, he'd much earlier come to the decision to say it and had braced himself for the moment. He blinked all the way through the statement, as though standing in a harsh glare.

The policeman gave him a quick shrewd look. "Were you?"

"Yes."

"She was getting a divorce?"

"No. She doesn't love me, she loved her husband."

"Then why sleep around?"

"Emily wasn't sleeping *around*," Greg said, showing offense only with the emphasized word. "From time to time, and not very often, she was sleeping with me."

"Why?"

"For comfort." Greg too looked at the rope around the beam, as though it had become me and he was awkward speaking in its presence. "Ed wasn't an easy man to get along with," he said carefully. "He was moody. It was getting worse."

"Cheerful people don't kill themselves," the policeman said.

"Exactly. Ed was depressed most of the time, obscurely angry now and then. It was affecting his business, costing him clients. He made Emily miserable but she wouldn't leave him, she loved him. I don't know what she'll do now."

"You two won't marry?"

"Oh, no." Greg smiled, a bit sadly. "Do you think we murdered him, made it look like suicide so we could marry?"

"Not at all," the policeman said. "But what's the problem? You already married?"

"I am homosexual."

The policeman was no more astonished than I. He said, "I don't get it."

"I live with my friend; that young man downstairs. I am—capable—of a wider range, but my preferences are set. I am very fond of Emily, I felt sorry for her, the life she had with Ed. I told you our physical relationship was infrequent. And often not very successful."

Oh, Emily. Oh, poor Emily.

The policeman said, "Did Thornburn know you were, uh, that way?"

"I have no idea. I don't make a public point of it."

"All right." The policeman gave one more half-angry look around the room, then said, "Let's go."

They left. The door remained open, and I heard them continue to talk as they went downstairs, first the policeman asking, "Is there somebody to stay the night? Mrs. Thornburn shouldn't be alone."

"She has relatives in Great Barrington. I phoned them earlier. Somebody should be arriving within the hour."

"You'll stay until then? The doctor says she'll probably sleep, but just in case—"

"Of course."

That was all I heard. Male voices murmured awhile longer from below, and then stopped. I heard cars drive away.

How complicated men and women are. How stupid are simple actions. I had never understood anyone, least of all myself.

The room was visited once more that night, by Greg, shortly after the police left. He entered, looking as offended and repelled as though the body were still here, stood the chair up on its legs, climbed on it, and with some difficulty untied the remnant of rope. This he stuffed partway into his pocket as he stepped down again to the floor, then returned the chair to its usual spot in the corner of the room, picked the key off the floor and put it in the lock, switched off both bedside lamps and left the room, shutting the door behind him.

Now I was in darkness, except for the faint line of light under the door, and the illuminated numerals of the clock. How long one minute is! That clock was my enemy, it dragged out every minute, it paused and waited and paused and waited till I could stand it no more, and then it waited longer, and *then* the next number dropped into place. Sixty times an hour, hour after hour, all night long. I couldn't stand one night of this, how could I stand eternity?

And how could I stand the torment and torture inside my brain? That was much worse now than the physical pain, which never entirely left me. I had been right about Emily and Greg, but at the same time I had been hopelessly brainlessly wrong. I had been right about my life, but wrong; right about my death, but wrong. How *much* I wanted to make amends, and how impossible it was to do anything anymore, anything at all. My actions had all tended to this, and ended with this: black remorse, the most dreadful pain of all.

I had all night to think, and to feel the pains, and to wait without knowing what I was waiting for or when—or if—my waiting would ever end. Faintly I heard the arrival of Emily's sister and brother-in-law, the murmured conversation, then the departure of Tony and Greg. Not long afterward the guestroom door opened, but almost immediately closed again, no one having entered, and a bit after that the hall hight went out, and now only the illuminated clock broke the darkness.

When next would I see Emily? Would she ever enter this room again? It wouldn't be as horrible as the first time, but it would surely be horror enough.

Dawn grayed the window shade, and gradually the room appeared out of the darkness, dim and silent and morose. Apparently it was a sunless day, which never got very bright. The day went on and on, featureless, each protracted minute marked by the clock. At times I dreaded someone's entering this room, at other times I prayed for something, anything—even the presence of Emily herself—to break this unending boring *absence.* But the day went on with no event, no sound, no activity anywhere—they must be keeping Emily sedated through this first day—and it wasn't until twilight, with the digital clock reading 6:52, that the door again opened and a person entered.

At first I didn't recognize him. An angry-looking man, blunt and determined, he came in with quick ragged steps, switched on both bedside lamps, then shut the door with rather more force than necessary, and turned the key in the lock.

Truculent, his manner was, and when he turned from the door I saw with incredulity that he was *me.* Me! I wasn't dead, I was alive! But how could that be?

And what was that he was carrying? He picked up the chair from the corner, carried it to the middle of the room, stood on it—

No! No!

He tied the rope around the beam. The noose was already in the other end, which he slipped over his head and tightened around his neck.

Good God, *don't!*

He kicked the chair away.

The instant I kicked the chair away I wanted it back, but gravity was turning my former wish to its present command; the chair would not right itself from where it lay on the floor, and my 193 pounds would not cease to urge downward from the rope thick around my neck.

There was pain, of course, quite horrible pain centered in my throat, but the most astounding thing was the way my cheeks seemed to swell. I could barely see over their round red hills, my eyes staring in agony at the door, *willing* someone to come in and rescue me, though I knew there was no one in the house, and in any event the door was carefully locked. My kicking legs caused me to twist and turn, so that sometimes I faced the door and sometimes the window, and my shivering hands struggled with the rope so deep in my flesh I could barely find it and most certainly could not pull it loose.

I was frantic and terrified, yet at the same time my brain possessed a cold corner of aloof observation. I seemed now to be everywhere in the room at once, within my writhing body but also without, seeing my frenzied spasms, the thick rope, the heavy beam, the mismatched pair of lit bedside lamps throwing my convulsive double shadow on the walls, the closed locked door, the white-curtained window with its shade drawn all the way down. *This is death*